ISLINGTON

Please return this item on or before the last date stamped below or you may be liable to overdue charges. To renew an item call the number below, or access the online catalogue at www.islington.gov.uk/libraries. You will need your library membership number and PIN number.

7-18

2 2 AUG 2018

Islington Libraries

020 7527 6900   **www.islington.gov.uk/libraries**

D1150778

Lou
out of
Luck

NAT LUURTSEMA

WALKER
BOOKS

First published 2018 by Walker Books Ltd
87 Vauxhall Walk, London SE11 5HJ

2 4 6 8 10 9 7 5 3 1

Text © 2018 Nat Luurtsema
Cover illustration © 2018 Agathe Sorlet

This book has been typeset in Sabon

Printed and bound by CPI Group (UK) Ltd, Croydon CR0 4YY

British Library Cataloguing in Publication Data:
a catalogue record for this book is available from the British Library

ISBN 978-1-4063-6656-3

www.walker.co.uk

MIX
Paper from
responsible sources
FSC® C020471

For Diarmuid

1

DOUBLE DATE!! Woo hoo!

Oh, me? I'm just off on my very first double date with my sister, Lavender; her boyfriend, Roman; and MY boyfriend, Gabriel. No big deal, don't freak out, but it would seem that *someone* has got cool lately. Hashtag blessed.

Gabe and I have been going out since November, when we had our first kiss. (In hospital. It was romantic but smelt antiseptic.) It's now January, so we're pretty long-term by my standards. (No previous boyfriend, no previous standards...) I wasn't in hospital because I was ill. We had been performing an underwater synchronized swimming routine in a fish tank that fell apart in a TV studio. I ended up falling off the stage in my swimsuit (*so* undignified and all over YouTube), which led to public shame and concussion. I was getting over my failure to make it as an Olympic swimmer by training Gabe's team of dancers in synchronized swimming. They would have all been way too cool to talk to me ordinarily but they needed me to coach them for a TV show.

They say you find love when you least expect it.

Not that I'm saying it's love, but sometimes, when we're bored or queuing for chips, we'll kick each other gently on the back of the leg and I'm pretty sure it's code for: *My darling, I adore you, join me on my horse and we'll fight dragons.*

My older sister, Lavender, met Gabriel's older brother, Roman, through our adventures in synchronized drowning, and now they're going out too! This isn't great for Pete – he was the third member of the swim team and I haven't got any sisters left.

Even my mum and dad are together again, after ten years of divorce, so it's an emotionally complicated house. But it's working all right. FOR NOW.

"Double date, double tra-la-la..." I sing tunelessly to myself.

I drag an eyeliner pencil over my left eyelid. I am not a visual treat. I'm broad, tall and strong and I dress like I'm about to wash a car. My hair is so big and bushy it's like an animal trying to flee my head. But I'm trying to make the best of myself. First steps include: slouching less, buying cleanser and learning about make-up.

I think it's going pretty well. My eyeliner follows the line of my eyelashes and sweeps up a little at the edge. Just like on the YouTube tutorials – except I'm not calling everything "super-kyewt".

Confident, I tackle the other eye and give it its own beautiful neat sweep of black eyeliner. I am so good at this! Such an adult. New year, new me. I step back from the mirror and stare at my face.

Aargh! No!!

This is not super-kyewt.

I have meddled with the unholy science of make-up.

GAZE UPON THE HORROR I HAVE BIRTHED, AND TREMBLE!!

I look like a flipping sloth. My eyes are drooping down towards my ears. I scrub it all off and start again. But now I've got to sharpen the pencil, and the last thing my sore eyes need is something sharp heading towards them. I give up. My eyes are streaming and my hands are black. Great. That's the look I was going for: Dirty Hands Snivelling Girl.

I head downstairs to the kitchen. A small snack should get me back in the mood for a double date. Crisps for the mouth, cucumbers for the eyes.

Mum and Dad seem to be Up to Something in the living room. They're talking in low voices, and I find them busily assembling a fort – four chairs placed back to back, a duvet draped over the top and cushions scattered inside. It's well built – they have honed their craft over many years – but I'm confused. The last time we needed a family fort was two years ago when Lavender had her wisdom teeth pulled out. To comfort her, we all sat in a duvet fort and she filled it with bloody tissues until it looked like a horror film and I begged to be let out.

Lavender appears behind me. "What are they doing?"

"We're going to have a lovely afternoon in as a family," Mum chirps, plumping up a cushion.

"Well, that *does* sound nice..." Lav puts on her diplomatic voice but I haven't got time for that.

"Noooo," I whine. "We're going on a double date! I've never been on a double date. I even put eyeliner on!"

"Where?" Dad says.

"It was wonky and my face looked like a melting sloth so I had to wash it off – please don't laugh at me, Mother, I can see you behind that cushion. The point is, I made an effort."

"Anyway." Lavender stands in front of me, blocking my babbling. "Gabe and Roman are expecting us, so we have to get going."

"I just called them to cancel," Mum says, smiling like she's not just SMASHED MY BRILLIANT SATURDAY PLANS TO DUST.

Lavender and I exchange a mystified look. Something

is really up. Is one of them ill? Are they divorcing AGAIN? Technically they're divorced, so I don't know how that would work. Dad's still out of work, so he couldn't afford to leave. I stop complaining and start fretting as I pull off my boots and crawl into the fort. Lav follows and we sit and look at each other, like, *Now what?*

"Are you going to join us then?" I ask. Mum and Dad aren't even in this "lovely" family fort! She's now clattering around in the kitchen and he's standing holding four or five remote controls and pointing them at the TV. I'm about to complain some more (I'm not whiney, I'm *annoyed* – I can't turn it off like a light switch) but I can smell cheese on toast and the Harry Potter music starts swirling around the room.

Humph. Well, this is quite nice actually. Not as nice as seeing Gabe, though… I tap out a quick text to him.

Sorry about today! Parents are weird. Xx

That's cool. Hope you're OK – what's
the family emergency? xx

I show Lav his message and she pulls a confused face to match mine. A moment later, she holds up her phone – Roman has sent her a similar message. Except … I notice they sign off with four kisses. Gabe and I only do two.

I see there are also quite a few unicorn and princess emojis.

Gabe and I mainly use the poo emoji – it best represents our cheery outlook on life. But perhaps I should up my game. There's a lot of flags I never use.

Mum and Dad shuffle into the fort on their knees, armed with toasted cheese sandwiches and cups of hot chocolate. But I'm still not pleased about my cancelled double date so I keep a snooty face on while I eat. Like the queen visiting a disappointing cheese factory.

"So," Dad says at a look from Mum. "How are my girls?"

"OK," we say.

"How's school?"

"OK."

"How are your friends?"

"OK."

He sighs, and I try to think of something interesting for him. Lav beats me to it.

"Lou's cool now." She nods at me, pulling stringy cheese out of her sandwich. I stroke an eyebrow and await parental congratulations.

"*Are* you?" Mum looks astonished. Bit rude.

"Yes."

"Why?"

"Because ... of the TV show. And boyfriend. And I got

a stub on Wikipedia, and even the mean girls at school don't bother making fun of me any more. They say things like, *Hey, girl! Cute top!*"

"*Hey, girl! Cute top?*" Mum repeats. "And you don't puke all over them?"

"No!" I say. "Because it's nice to be accepted, even by shallow people."

Mum purses her lips. "Lou, I raised you better than that."

"No, you didn't."

"I don't think we did," Dad reflects. "We were busy splitting up so we just stuck her in front of the TV."

Mum glares at us over her sandwich and the mood turns frosty. Dad dials back to my earlier point.

"Well, I'm pleased for you," he says. "If you actually *are* cool. The coolest person at MY school had a leather jacket and a motorbike and his mum had snogged Donny Osmond…"

"Who's Donny Osmond?"

"Bieber for the elderly."

"Oh."

"If you're cool then the criteria for being cool must have been lowered. You don't even have a tattoo."

"Not that you SHOULD," Mum says, quickly.

Lavender has a tiny tattoo that they don't know about. I'm not very good at lying so I stare at my legs.

Lavender breaks the silence.

"Can we open the side of the fort and watch TV?"

"Not yet." Mum puts down her sandwich and dusts her hands as if she's about to lift something. Not me, I hope – for her sake. Six foot and still growing. The basketball team try to recruit me at least once a month, despite my lack of interest.

"Your dad and I have something to tell you."

"You're splitting up *again*?" I blurt out. "You've just got back together! Make your minds up!"

"You're ill?" Lav says, eyeing Dad narrowly. "That's why Dad's lost weight."

"*Have* I?" He's thrilled.

"No! Look, you know your dad is still out of work," Mum ploughs on.

"I hate it when you call each other *your mum* and *your dad*," Lav tuts.

"Me too," I say. "You only do it when you're breaking up or that time when Dad found a lump on his—"

"YES, THANK YOU," Dad interrupts. "No need to bring that up. What your mu— Flora is trying to say is that she's losing her job too."

There's a long silence in the fort as Lav and I stop chewing and stare. My cheese feels greasy in my mouth and I don't want it any more.

What happens when neither of your parents are

earning any money? I wonder. And is there a polite way to ask this question?

"Like me!" Dad says, pointing between him and Mum and doing a little sit-down dance. "Twinsies!"

"Do you think that's helping, Mark?"

"No." He stops.

Mum strokes my hair. "The university has had its funding cut and a load of us have to go. But I'm not worried!"

"Why not? You should be," I say, and earn myself a hard nudge from Lav. "Lavender, PLEASE. I bruise like a peach."

"It's OK," says Mum, looking determinedly cheerful. "We'll tighten our belts—"

"They're already quite tight!" I blurt, thinking of Mum's recent embargo on brand-name sweets.

"And you girls have more than enough clothes. Lou, just PLEASE stop growing."

Hahahaha. OK, that's cool. I know she's joking, *très* LOL, but it is actually a genuine fear of mine that I will never stop growing.

"We have lots of things we don't need and can sell online," Dad says.

"Do we?" I ask. I'm not exactly drowning in frivolous possessions. Although ... I start mentally pricing up my school books – shame to lose them, but, oh well, it's for the family – bye-bye, physics! See ya, maths!

"And," Mum says brightly, "I'll go to the Jobcentre with your dad. That'll be something we can do together."

"But Dad said the Jobcentre is like a big shop that sells chairs and sadness."

Mum glares at Dad. "Thank you, Mark."

"I was feeling down when I said that! Anyway, tell them the worst bit."

"It's not the worst bit."

"Agree to disagree."

Mum takes a deep breath. "The mortgage payments on this house are quite high. If I don't find work soon, we'll fall behind. And we might ... MIGHT ... have to sell the house and move in with Grandma."

"Evil Grandma or Dead Grandma?" I ask.

"Which do you think?" she asks drily.

"Well, I know which I'd *prefer*."

Evil *is* a strong word to apply to an old lady with a dodgy hip, but she's worked hard to earn that name. She's a big fan of saying things like "your bald spot is getting bigger", or "the younger one doesn't have the looks of the first, does she?" when you're standing right in front of her. I usually give her a baffled shrug, like, *What do you expect me to do about it? This is my face.* Which is apparently "surly". Am I meant to laugh, as if she's made a lovely joke that we can both enjoy? "Well, I won't say

ANYTHING then! You're in a nasty mood," she'll say, with a sad sigh.

Dad pins back one side of the fort so we can watch Harry Potter.

"Where's the red-headed boy gone?" Mum asks.

"There," Dad says, baffled. "Right there. Literally on the screen under the red hair."

"He looks older."

"Older than what?"

"Than in the first film."

"Yes," I say, while Lavender ignores us and scrolls through her phone. "He got older."

"Ah. OK. I'm not really into wizards and goblins," she confides.

"It's not magic!" Dad says, exasperated. "It's a normal boy going from eight to eighteen!"

Perhaps I was a tad dramatic about missing my double date yesterday. I'm spending today with Gabe too.

Hannah says Gabe and I spend ALL our time together, so sometimes I lie about what I'm up to. Last week I told her my aunt was taking her guinea pigs to a guinea pig show out of town and would need me to help her bathe them when she arrived because they usually get car sick and puke all over themselves. "Once you've got vomit in a tiny guinea pig ear, that's twenty minutes dabbing at it with a moistened cotton bud."

I used to think the best lies are the elaborate ones, but it's possible that I'm wrong.

Hannah is my best friend, no question. But hypothetically, if there was a category for best friend whom I also like to kiss, Gabe would win that one. Especially since Hannah got a brace.

In my defence, Gabe and I have been going out since the end of November and it's January now... That's really not very long, and Hannah was away skiing for some of that time anyway. I didn't get jealous of snow, did I? Plus I spend all my school days with her. Gabe's in the year above, so I only really see him on the weekends.

Last term, when Hannah was at High Performance Training Camp, I was stuck at school with no friends, more likely to get a unicorn than a boyfriend. So it's brilliant to have people fighting for my company.

Obviously, I would never say that to Hannah. She came back from swimming camp with anxiety issues and eating problems, and now she has a therapist. He's called Hari and she can call him by his first name. He's very cool – she thinks he has a neck tattoo but can never get a close enough look.

Hannah sees Hari every Monday after school, and sometimes she sneaks in questions from me so I can get some free therapy. He must think she's extremely complicated as she has all the problems of two different people. Dad overheard us discussing this once and warned me to be careful; he used to copy his old neighbour doing yoga until he fell awkwardly and trod on his head.

Mum's brothers are throwing her a surprise birthday party today, but of course they told her about it *weeks* ago so that she could do all the work of organizing it. This is typical of my uncles. I was allowed to invite a friend but I begged for two, Gabe and Hannah. I was hoping that if they both came to this party they'd get on and I could hang out with my best friend and my boyfriend at the same time instead of having to choose between them.

Oh, foolish, optimistic Lou.

Hey Han, want to come to my mum's birthday party? There'll be loads of cute guys there!

Really?

Course not. Spotty cousins. Crisps in bowls. Terrible music. You in?!

I assume Gabe's going?

Gabe…? Oh, that guy! Yes, he is.

I don't want to be a gooseberry.

Autocorrect fail!

Gooseberry = third person in a romantic situation.

Is that a saying?

Cos gooseberries are sour?

Cos it's horrible to kiss sour things?

Han?

Hannah??

I DIDN'T MEAN YOU WERE SOUR AND

UNKISSABLE. I'M SORRY.

Haaaaaaaaaaannah?

I'm getting dressed for the party, wondering if I should attempt make-up again. I want to try contouring. I've been watching YouTube videos but Lavender says it gives you a face like a stripy egg. Apparently, Amelia from her form does it so badly that she looks like she's been to a five-year-old's birthday party and had her face painted like a tiger.

Of course, it's all very well for Lav to criticize. She *has* cheekbones. Amelia and I have to doodle ours on.

Dad pops his head around my bedroom door. "Is your sister in the shower?"

"Shower?" I lie smoothly. "Sis-ter?"

He cocks his head like a cat hearing a firework. "How long has she been in there?"

The cost-cutting begins. He's always treated hot water like a precious substance, but I can see he's about to step it up a gear. He starts banging on the bathroom door.

"Laven-DER! Out now or I'll turn the hot water off."

"I'm halfway through washing my hair!"

"I'll pick the lock!"

"And what?" she shouts back. "Drag me out naked? You really want to try that?"

Twenty minutes later, we're all sitting at the kitchen table and Lav isn't talking to Dad. He didn't fancy wrestling her out of the shower, so instead he turned the kitchen taps on and off until she marched out, tired of the boiling → freezing → boiling routine.

Dad's made a special birthday lunch for Mum and we've bought her presents – mostly stationery, which always goes down well. She is currently unwrapping her fourth highlighter pen. Although she only uses them at work, so I guess they're not as useful now. Awkward.

I sneakily scoop a few tactless presents off the table before she has a chance to open them. There are only so many red pens you need if you're not marking papers.

Lav's phone vibrates and Dad picks it up.

"Dad! That could be personal!"

"I know!" he says. "That's why I do random checks, to make sure there's nothing *too* personal. Why is Roman texting you *Toot toot*? Is that a bosoms thing?"

"Ew."

"*Daaad.*"

"Mark, don't say *bosoms*, you're not a nineteenth-century governess," Mum says, admiring a glittery notebook from me.

Lav explains. "Roman's outside, but he's too polite to hoot his horn, so ... toot toot."

"But not polite enough to get out of the car and come in... *Hello, Mark. Hello, Flora. You're looking well today, Mark, have you lost weight? No, Roman, thank you, though. It's a new thing I'm trying – vertical stripes to flatter my curves. Plus I have started drinking green tea and I think it's a diuretic, or maybe I'm not very well, but either way I think my over-active bowels are slimming me out...*"

We leave Dad talking to himself and head outside. Roman looks irritable, and when he and Gabriel get out of the car, I see why. They are dressed identically.

"Aaaaahhh," Mum says from the doorway. "Our girls are dating the same boy in small and large."

"Mother!" Gabe is the "small" version. I *am* much taller than him, I have to dip when we kiss. Sometimes when I do, he points a dainty toe behind him like a woman in a film. I wish he wouldn't.

"I told him to change but he wouldn't," Ro complains.

"They're my nicest clothes!" Gabe protests.

"Mate. It looks like our mum dressed us."

"Come on. She still buys *some* of our clothes."

"If we get drunk..." Dad begins, changing the subject.

"We won't," Mum interrupts him.

"No, no, no, certainly not," he agrees demurely. "But

IF we do, we'll get a cab home. Come on, Flo, birthday treat!"

Mum slings on a trench coat over her silky dress and drapes a vintage scarf around her neck. She always just chucks layers of clothes on as she's leaving the house and somehow they all sit right and make her look like a French spy.

"Am I OK in what I'm wearing?" I say to Lav, suddenly feeling scruffy.

"You look great," Gabe says, pushing me into the car.

Hannah says it's amazing I've become cool without improving my dress sense. Which would be mean if said in front of others, but as there were only the two of us there, it was just good BFF straight-talking. Plus it's so true. I'm wearing a T-shirt they gave away free at the bank when Dad took out a loan. It has a pig on it. The pig is wearing a top hat and is therefore more smartly dressed than me.

We follow Mum and Dad's car. It's going very slowly and coughing out some ominous dark fumes.

"Your parents need to get their car seen to," Ro points out. "That'll cost a packet if they leave it and end up needing their whole exhaust replaced."

Since Roman passed his driving test and got a car, he's started making remarks about car maintenance. All the time. I nod politely. Gabe slumps on my shoulder and starts fake-snoring.

We pull into the pub car park next to Mum and Dad, who both look concerned at the rattling noises coming from underneath their car.

"Birthday girls don't worry about fan belts," Dad announces. (I've never heard that saying before.)

"Exhaust pipes," Ro corrects him.

"Potayto potarto."

Dad takes Mum's hand and leads her towards the pub like a queen. She has been ordered to act surprised when everyone jumps up and shouts, "Surprise!"

This doesn't work for any other emotions, I've realized. You can't yell "Jealous!" or "Hungry!" at people and expect them to feel it.

I'm at the back of the line, so all I hear is "SUR—", then loud crashing and splintering noises and a very convincing scream from Mum. I don't think she was acting. Her big and boisterous family decided it would be a good idea to climb on tables and jump down *onto* her. I have a few cousins who are around eighteen – years *and* stone – and by the time I push my way into the pub, I can see them staggering to their feet and apologizing to squashed relatives on the floor.

The barman is already telling Mum there's zero chance of her getting her deposit back – and Happy Birthday, by the way. I can see Evil Grandma laughing herself hoarse in the corner.

Dad presses a glass of Prosecco into Mum's hand, steers her away from Grandma and tells her to enjoy herself because Louise and Lavender are in charge of making sure there are no further damages. "Right, girls?" he says, giving us a bossy look and a big glass of Coke each. Oh great. PAR-TAY.

I can see this isn't going to be a fun-packed afternoon for Lav and me, though it's amusing watching Mum introduce her "new" boyfriend to her family, saying, "Yes, he does look familiar. You were at our wedding about twenty years ago and then we got divorced?" Poor Dad's getting a chilly reception. The problem with going out with your ex-husband is that when you divorced him everyone agreed that he was a waste of space, you could do MUCH better and he wouldn't age well.

"You got out at the right time," they said. "He'll develop man hips."

Basically, everyone in this room has bad-mouthed our dad at some point. But I've got no time to feel sorry for him, I'm on Crowd Control.

"Lou!" Lav points behind me at three young cousins trying to get into the top of the jukebox to see how it works. We rush towards them, while Gabe and Roman melt away mysteriously into the crowd. *Thanks, guys!*

"It's good you're curious about, um, science –" I grab the smallest cousin and prise a heavy ashtray out of his hand – "but we're trying to have one family party where the police aren't called."

"Who invited Buzz Killington?" he says, cockily, and they all laugh at me.

"Ha ha," I retort and resist the urge to grab all three of them and suspend them by their belts from a high coat hook.

I look around for Gabe but all I see is Uncle Vinnie's girlfriend, Nicky, lecturing the barman over his "stingy" spirit measures. Lavender rolls her eyes at me – this is our department.

"Hey, Nicky!"

The distraction works. She squeaks and throws her arms in the air when she sees us. Relieved, the barman sneaks off.

"Look at you two, like a pair of models!" she crows.

I stifle a sugary burp. So not cool.

"Hey, have you seen your *dad's* here? Isn't that weird? Do you think he'll fight Flora's new fella?"

"I'd like to see that," says Lav, honestly.

"And Eddie's back from travelling," Nicky says.

"Travelling? He's forty-eight." Lavender is baffled.

"How long did he go for?" I ask.

"Eighteen months, twelve with good behaviour,"

Mum says, appearing behind Lav. *Prison*, she mouths at us as she kisses Nicky hello.

"Have you seen your uncle Don?" Mum asks me.

"No, why?" I say warily, sensing he's about to become my responsibility.

"He's playing Pin the Tail on the Donkey in the beer garden. On the donkey. In the beer garden."

3

"Good girl? … Please?"

I hold out a carrot. The donkey, puffing heavily, gives it a suspicious look. I leave it on the ground for when she's more in the mood.

Uncle Vinnie and Uncle Don are sitting on a bench, panting with laughter.

"Did you see it, Louly?"

"Yes," I say, taking their drinks off them. "It was very funny, and I think you should never do it again. How are you drunk *already*?"

"Little tip –" Uncle Don holds up a finger with a wise air – "skip lunch."

The barman pokes his head out of the door. "Have they been bothering my Angelina?"

"We're all just having a laugh!" I say, avoiding the question.

"Your dad wants to see you anyway. And you two –" he

points at my uncles – "she's an old lady, treat her with respect."

I leave Angelina to her carrot and Vinnie and Don to each other. Lavender grabs me as soon as I'm back inside.

"No," I say, pre-empting her. "You deal with the next thing. I did the donkey."

"Dad says we can have a drink!"

"I've got a drink," I say.

"No, a *drink* drink."

"Oh, a *drink* drink?"

We squeeze past an impromptu dance floor and head for the bar. Am I going to get drunk today? Am I finally going to find out what it feels like? BIG DAY. I have lied at school, airily *implied* I've had some drunken nights at family weddings, and that time we went abroad: *No, no one saw me – we were in France. No one from school can back up my story but it definitely absolutely happened. I was SEEHHR DER-RUNK. But no witnesses.*

Sometimes I tell such a good story I forget I'm lying, but Hannah's face reminds me. She'd never tell on me, but she won't back me up either.

Everyone else I know has got drunk at some point, but if you have swimming training six times a week, drinking isn't appealing. Old habits die hard, I guess. Who wants to be sick in a changing room toilet at seven the next morning?

Hannah's still training, so if there's to be drunkenness, it's a good thing she didn't come to the party, I tell myself. Yes, that makes me feel less guilty about the whole gooseberry misunderstanding. I check my phone. Still no reply; she can really hang on to a moody silence.

Lav corners Dad by the bar with, "You said we could have a *drink* drink, so…?"

"That doesn't sound like something I'd say."

"You probably said it in a deeper voice," I chip in.

"Champagne, please," Lav says airily. Dad raises his eyebrows and she backtracks. "Well, I don't *mind* Prosecco…"

"Yes," I say. "I also don't mind Prosecco. I'm not fussy!"

"Al?" Dad turns to the barman. "Two half-pints, please. Bitter and a stout. Pop 'em on my tab. And … the party discount, right?"

Al is a large man with a small face. He looks thoughtful.

"Mark, I've got a very robust craft ale just in, if you're interested?"

"Lovely. Swap it out for the stout." Dad turns back to us with a little half-pint of mud in each hand, Al smirking behind him.

"What?" Lav is disgusted. "What is this?"

"Is it a cocktail?" I pipe up. "It's very brown. I don't want to say *too* brown, but…"

"It's this or nothing."

I'd rather have nothing but I don't want Lavender to think I'm a wimp.

"Fine."

He hands them over as if they're precious. I take the darkest brown one and give it a sip. It tastes like sweat. Lav and I swap and taste each other's. They are equally rancid.

We go and mingle, sipping our drinks and occasionally retching uncontrollably. The music has got louder now, and I can see Nicky dancing with her elbows out, sharp and at eye-level, carving out dance floor space for herself.

A slow song comes on, and I see Lav look for Roman. Obviously she's too cool to slow-dance with her boyfriend at a family party, but hey, it would have been nice to be *asked*. I haven't seen Gabe or Roman since we got here. I've been too busy averting disasters. I glance around and spot Roman easily as he's so tall. A semicircle of young girls are standing around him, looking up adoringly. One of them is handing him another drink so now he has a bottle of beer in each hand. He is loving the attention.

"Oh, thanks, Fenella. No, I didn't actually *meet* the *Britain's Hidden Talent* judges..." – he pauses for comic timing – "just nearly drowned them!"

We nearly drowned them, but whatever.

Lavender makes an exasperated noise. I don't blame her, Roman has been milking his brief TV fame for all it's worth and it is annoying. Lav says she can't even look at his Instagram – it's turned into a never-ending stream of brooding selfies in flattering light. He has about a hundred girls who "like" every shot and make comments like, omg u look gr8 hunny.

I feel quietly proud that Gabriel didn't hog the lime-light in the same way. Well, tbf he had a big relapse of his ME straight afterwards and spent three weeks in bed, so he didn't have much choice. But STILL. I win the boy-friends. No one calls him "hunny".

Speaking of which, Lavender points Gabe out to me, next to the jukebox. He's actually bending over it, floppy with giggles. I push my way through the crowd towards him, Lavender following.

"Gabe?" He spins round, looking guilty. Up close I see he's sweaty and his eyes are bleary. Two or three empty pint glasses sit precariously on top of the jukebox. Someone's had more luck getting drunk than we have. Gabe flings his arm around me, with some difficulty given the height difference. I kindly bend at the knees. I don't have much choice as he's hanging quite a lot of weight on my neck.

His breath is sour – it's as bad as the bitter. I've never

thought this before but I hope he doesn't try to kiss me.

"You know I think you're very special, Lou Brown," he says, firmly, waggling a finger in my face. Lav is watching. It's not my most romantic moment.

"Yes," I say, uncertainly.

"You just know who you *are*, you know? You gotta really strong sense of YOU, OK? And I like that you dress like that and I just think you're great. And sorry I don't say it more and I get a bit caught up with my *things*."

He flaps his hand around to loosely indicate "things" and slaps me gently round the head in the process. He doesn't notice.

"Uh-huh," I say, because drunk praise is worth less than normal praise, so I don't feel too flattered.

"And also, may I try your drink, please?" He gives me big puppy-dog eyes and I'm happy to hand it over. He downs it in a couple of gulps.

I hope Mum doesn't mind that Gabe has been drinking. I look around for her just as everyone else does likewise, because Dad, Nicky and Uncle Vinnie have started singing a loud, tuneless "Happy Birthday to You..."

So, Uncle Vinnie and Uncle Don actually did *two* things for Mum's party. They booked a pub and bought her a massive cake in the shape of a pile of books. Uncle Don is carrying it towards her. We cheer while she tries to blow out the candles. It's not easy. Don's swaying and the cake is wobbling. All around them, people are putting their drinks down, getting ready to catch a cake and a man.

In the silence while Mum blows out the candles, I can hear Grandma say, "How old is Flora now...? I thought she was older than that." Mum gives her a determined smile over the cake. I glance at Lavender and she shakes her head. We can't be in charge of Grandma too. We'd need a lion tamer for that.

When the candles are finally blown out, Cousin-June-twice-removed grabs the cake off Don and takes it somewhere safer. Mum makes a lovely speech, thanking everyone for coming and saying how surprised she is! And how happy she is to share it with Mark again. Most people say, *Aaaah,* though a couple roll their eyes and Grandma gives a disgusted snort.

Ten minutes later I'm handing slices of cake around the room.

"You're definitely going to eat it," I say firmly to a small relative. Rob. Bob? Something like that.

He nods, solemnly. Is it Toby?

"Not going to throw it?" I press him for a promise before I hand it over.

"Why would I throw it?"

I shrug. "For fun, to get someone in the face, you know, high jinks."

At least Mum's having a nice time. She and Dad are now slow-dancing, cheek to cheek. Perhaps, *maybe*, if they weren't my parents, it would be sweet. But they are my parents. People take photos of them then get tapping on their phones, presumably writing things like, *OMG – you'll never guess* and *I give it six months*. Mum and Dad nuzzle noses and that is my absolute limit.

Lav and I head outside. I feel a soft thud on the back of my head. I pause and look behind me. Rob or Bob or Toby gives me a shy, angelic smile. I put a hand to my hair and it comes back covered in icing, jam and sponge.

4

"Bye, Uncle Vinnie!" We wave at him while Uncle Don tries to drag him into a waiting cab. The cab driver eyes them suspiciously.

"Les go fru McDonald's, mate." Uncle Vinnie squashes his face against the driver's window. "My treat, anything you like. We'll go supersize. They can't stop us."

From the pub, we hear "Happy" by Pharrell Williams for the fifteen-thousandth time and there are howls of rage, then Dad appears, dragging a giggling Gabriel out. That's what he was doing with the jukebox.

Dad has some trouble getting the boys in our mini-cab. "Bend. No ... lads, bend at the waist, not the knees. WHY ARE YOU SQUATTING?"

"Mark, just shove them in," says Mum.

"I can't bring them home drunk *and* injured."

Mum leans across. "Roman, take my hand."

"I'm sorry, Flora, I gotta girlfriend." Mum grabs him by the wrist. "I am flattered, though," he tells her, as she yanks him into the car.

"Don't worry, Mum's not one of your fan club," Lav tells him acidly as she and I get in after him, but she's wasting good sarcasm.

"Right." The taxi driver is bored now. "Can we go?"

"Radio on, please!" the boys shout from the back, and they sing along to everything that comes out of the speakers, including the adverts. I'm glad Hannah didn't come. She'd have been one angry, sour gooseberry by now.

Dad puts his hand on Mum's knee. Lavender moves it to his own knee, but it finds its way back to Mum. Lav's not impressed.

"Do you think you'll get the deposit back?" she asks, successfully squashing the romantic mood.

"No," Mum sighs. "There was a fight in the toilet, Nicky stole a bottle of whiskey, the jukebox is broken and the landlord said his donkey was traumatized. Although I have no idea what that means."

I pause in my quest to rid my hair of icing and glance back at the sudden silence behind me. Roman and Gabe are fast asleep on each other. It takes a while to wake them when we get back to their house, and their mum, Janet, comes out to say hi. She watches us shaking her sons and doesn't look thrilled at the state of them, which is fair.

She gives them both a beady look. "I don't want either of you oversleeping tomorrow."

They wrinkle their noses at the thought of school.

"Might go to bed now," Roman mumbles. Lav and I get tired waves from them both as they slope off. I hope Gabe's all right. He hasn't had an ME relapse since Christmas, but I can't imagine his doctor recommends loud parties, alcohol and donkeys.

Janet turns back to Mum, but Dad holds up a hand.

"We cannot afford to chat," he tells her. "Taxi's on a meter! Byebyebye."

We drive off, Lav and I waving goodbye to Janet out of the window to make up for our hasty exit. Dad leans towards the driver and starts trying to haggle money off because neither of the boys were sick in the back. "And you thought they would when you quoted for the journey, right? Factored in a little sick charge?"

"Fine," the driver admits grudgingly. "I thought the little one would blow."

I feel proud of "the little one".

We get home exhausted, though Dad's jubilant at saving five pounds. He goes into the kitchen and carefully puts the change into a teapot on the window sill. This is his cunning hiding place for cash. It used to be a secret until Mum's work friend Aggy came round one time and filled it with tea without checking inside. I came home to find Dad furiously hair-drying fivers on the kitchen counter.

I go to my room and scroll through Twitter. Hannah's retweeted my tweet of a photo of a plug that looks like a screaming face. What does this mean: *I'm annoyed but it's not terminal? I like you enough to RT something* but not enough to text you back a friendly emoji?*

*(Something HI–larious)

There's a knock on the wall from Lav's room and I pop in to see her. She's emptied her wardrobe out onto her bed, which I'm surprised doesn't collapse under the weight. "Is there anything you want?" she asks. "I was going to put a load of stuff online to sell."

"Are you not tired?" I ask her.

"I had four Cokes and a lemonade," she tells me. "I'm so full of sugar I could fly."

I pick through the piles but Lav has the sort of elegance that means she looks great in weird clothes. If I wore her lace and denim jumpsuit to school, I'd be sent to the nurse. So I say no, sell it all.

I watch Lav carefully spread a shirt on the floor then stand on a chair to get a photo of it. She looks at her phone and makes an unimpressed face before showing me. Yeah, it doesn't look enticing, crumpled on the floor like the Invisible Man just fainted.

"You should *wear* it," I suggest. "If you look pretty in it, people will want to buy it."

"You think?"

"Yes. That's how advertising works."

Lav touches up her make-up and I roam the house looking for a nice wall. I'm tempted by the green tiles in the bathroom and stare at them, stroking my chin. I make a little square with my fingers to imagine how it would look in a photo. Bit gloomy.

"Oi, Lou – this isn't for the National Portrait Gallery!" Lav calls from her room.

Portrait? I scoff to myself. Only fools take photos in portrait. I'm going landscape.

I decide, after much thought, that Mum and Dad's room has the most stylish wallpaper, so I get Lav to stand on their bed.

"Lav, stop wobbling."

"I can't help it. When did they get a water bed?"

I check under the covers. "You're standing on a hot water bottle."

I take some excellent photos, even if I say so myself. It helps that Lav is so pretty, but I take credit for turning her the right way and pointing three reading lamps at her.

I only realize how late it's got when Mum and Dad are standing next to the bed in their pyjamas asking if they're going to have to sleep around Lavender's feet?

"So unreasonable," I tell them. "We are working to improve the family finances, actually, thank you." I leave Lav to upload the photos and pad to bed, happy with my day's work until I realize that *I* have nothing to sell. I look around my room: everything I own is scuffed, chipped or broken, and no one will buy my clothes. Maybe I could sell my hair? I examine it in the mirror and run my fingers through it. They immediately get stuck.

I can't think who'd want my hair unless their dog had bald patches.

I lie in bed, feeling quite sugar-buzzed myself. I should go to sleep but Hannah's annoying me. She still hasn't replied to my messages, so I write something that no self-respecting best friend can ignore.

Han? Mum's lost her job. Now both parents are out of work. (Poo emoji, scared face emoji, more poo.)

Immediately dots appear. Thank you. This is major news and deserves a reply.

Oh no! But you'll be OK, right?

I don't know.

Of course you will. They can sell something.
Don't they have a flat somewhere?

A flat somewhere. I. Can't. Even.

Hannah, though an otherwise wonderful friend –
understanding, hilarious and only-moody-when-her-brace-
is-tightened – is also rich. Sometimes she forgets that
other people aren't.

No, I reply, trying not to sound exasperated. Of course
we don't have "a flat somewhere".

But they've got savings, right?

No!

Why not?

I massage my head and delete my first response as it's
quite rude.

Because there's no money to save. They
fritter it away on things like food and bills.

That still looks snappy, so I add some emojis to soften
the blow. Any old things – vegetables and a mouse.

Oh. That's awful. What are you going to do?

Lav's selling clothes. I'm trying to think
how I can make money too.

I'll think.

Thanks, pal.

Hannah's good at thinking up ideas, I'll give her that. If she comes up with a money-making plan, all is forgiven. And if not, I'll ask Hari for tips on staying calm when life gets a bit "much". I decide to listen to a podcast about UFOs – I like this one, it makes my problems seem small as no one is trying to abduct me or probe my brain via my bum. (Surely it would be quicker to go via the ear?)

While I'm listening, I give my bedroom a quick tidy (by which I mean Hiding Mess in Drawers). I find an old notebook wedged under my desk and pull it out, vaguely recognizing it. About two years ago we were reading Anne Frank's Diary in class (5/5, would recommend), and Mr Peters suggested we all started keeping diaries to record our thoughts and feelings. This was mine – for a bit.

I flick through it, wondering at Past Me's thoughts and feelings. They weren't extensive – I only filled eight pages.

MONDAY – Muffins and Nutella for breakfast.
Felt stodgy all day. Spaghetti for lunch – it
was OK. I hate Lavender by the way.

By the way is scrawled really heavily. Then there's three long columns of numbers and I realize they're a record of my old swimming times. Past Me is booooooring.

The front cover of the diary has a picture of a cake on it and beneath that the word WORRY. Food worries? Bit negative. Who bought me that? Good job Past Me didn't develop an eating disorder.

Tuesday – how many times a week should you
poo? Or is it daily? Need fibre.

Admittedly, Anne Frank had World War II to write about, but I have a nasty feeling World War III could have erupted around Past Me and I would've written Crispy Puffs for breakfast. Skimmed milk – ugh.

I chuck the Worry Diary in my bag and get into bed, keeping the UFO podcast on because I'm sure I won't be able to fall asleep. I lie there, pondering how even something like this would be dull by the time it reached my diary. Abducted by aliens last night. They don't have the crisps I like – boo.

5

I wake up with my headphones tangled around my neck and Mum telling me off. "I told you!" she says loudly in my sleepy face. "About that BOY who DIED when his headphones STRANGLED him. Did you think it was a joke? It HAPPENS. Exactly like this!" She brandishes my headphones at me, chucks them on my desk and stomps off. She pauses at the door. "There's orange juice on your bedside table," she adds grudgingly, like I don't deserve it.

I feel more cheery than I did last night. There's something about the morning that announces, "Everything is going to be FINE!" and you believe it. At night-time this optimism is followed by a whisper: "Unless it *isn't*...?"

I put on clothes that look like they were ironed before I bundled them in a drawer, to make today feel GOOD. My hair isn't terrible, Mum and Dad might find jobs soon and I haven't attempted eyeliner. I stroll downstairs with an upbeat feeling.

A feeling which is soon squashed.

"Listen," Mum says to the table in a curiously shy tone.

"What have you done, Mother?"

"Remember my friend Aggy – she used to work at the uni?"

"Filled my money pot with tea!" Dad says immediately.

"No," Mum says, "she filled your teapot with tea, like a normal person. YOU filled a teapot with money."

"She's not a normal person." Dad's not ready to let this go. "She quit that job saying that if she had to listen to one more mopey sex-obsessed student poem, she'd tear her clothes off and run screaming from the campus."

Lav and I look at Mum for her take on this. Mum holds her hands up. "OK. She's unusual. But she's lovely. And –" she turns to me – "she practically lives round the corner!"

"Riiiiight," I say, warily. I don't know why she's telling me.

"So she's offered to drive you to school while we're having trouble with our car."

"But, but, no!" I say. "Roman drives me to school. Roman driving me to school has been the number one thing that has made me cool! Gabe helped, obviously – added

47

to the package – and my personality might've contributed a little ... but not much if I'm honest."

"Lou, he only drives you half the time. The rest of the time he has free periods and goes in late or leaves early. If Aggy drives you, you have a guaranteed lift."

"He goes back to pick up Lav even when he leaves early!"

Dad looks up. "I give your mum lifts. I wouldn't ferry *her* relatives around."

Fine. Good point. But... "Why didn't you say 'That's a lovely offer, but how about some money instead?' Ask for the cash equivalent of the petrol. Or a new exhaust or whatever it is the car needs."

"Lou." Mum is stern. "Don't be bratty."

"Yeah," Dad adds. "You'll have no lifts when Lav and Roman break up... What?"

Lav has finally looked up from her phone and is giving him a stony-faced stare.

"Ninety-nine point three per cent of all relationships between the under-nineteens end within five months," he defends himself. "I read that on the internet. But hey, prove me wrong, Ms Zero Point Seven Per Cent."

It's like they've each chosen a daughter to annoy this morning. I seethe gently.

"So, does Aggy's daughter go to my school?" I ask.

"Son," Mum says.

"Oh, yeah? What's his name?" Lavender joins the conversation.

"Dermot."

"Oh … my…" Lavender exits the conversation again.

Dermot.

He's in my class – not that you'd notice. He's the most spacey person I've ever met in my life. He's like a ghost that drifts in and out of school, with no friends, rarely speaking in class. Our mums have been friends for years and I had no idea he was her kid. He dresses in old-fashioned clothes that smell musty and make his bum flat like an old man. The other day he started using a wicker basket as a school bag. By lunchtime I saw him crouched in the corridor picking chewing gum out of the wicker.

I get a sinking feeling in my stomach. The feeling of my social standing at school plummeting downwards, fast.

I go upstairs to clean my teeth and I'm surprised to get a phone call from Gabe.

"Hey!"

"Sssshhhh…" he croaks.

"Oh dear. How's your head?"

"It hurts. I was sick. My mouth is drier than it's ever been."

"You did drink a lot of—"

"Lou, please don't list drinks I drank or I will be sick right now down the phone to you."

"OK."

Let's hang on to some of the mystery, keep it romantic. I decide to distract him with my terrible news. I won't see him in the car this morning or any morning ever. He isn't as devastated as I'd like. He says, "You're not great in the mornings anyway…"

"That's a funny way to say 'I'll miss you'."

I hear him give a small hiccup and decide not to bully him when he's hungover.

"I don't understand why your year are so nasty to Dermot. He's nice. He gave me a stuffed otter once."

"I think it's his clothes and odd sense of humour and his wicker school bag— Hang on. A stuffed otter?"

"Torquil. He's got little shoes and a monocle."

"Can I have him?"

"No."

"Please?"

"It's still a no from me."

"But I love bad taxidermy! You've seen my Instagram."

"Well, then you won't want Torquil – the detailing is exquisite."

I sigh. Gabriel and Dermot aren't that different. It's just luck that Gabe is cool while Dermot is bullied. I'm going to be nice to Dermot, I promise myself.

"I'll see you at breaktime?" I say.

"I've got to talk to my politics teacher."

"Lunch?"

"Advanced maths. The weekend?"

"Fiiine."

Gabriel puts a lot more effort into school than I do. I never thought I'd need an education – I was going to be an Olympic swimmer. I just needed to read enough to find my way to the pool. But now I'm not going to be a swimmer, I have to actually study, especially if my parents keep falling in and out of employment. I'll probably end up being the breadwinner.

My throat suddenly feels tight with anxiety and I try to ignore it as I swish mouthwash around my gums.

"Lou, they're here!" Mum yells up the stairs and my good resolutions go down the plughole. Fantastic, they're mad for punctuality. This couldn't be worse if the car was made of wicker and full of spiders. I drag myself miserably downstairs, where Mum pops my hat, scarf and rucksack on me and pushes me firmly out of the door.

"Bye, then," I say hollowly as Mum waves at Aggy over my head. Aggy drives a big, rusting van. Like a serial killer. I approach the passenger door. Dermot gives me a shy wave, which I return because I'm in a bad mood but I'm not a monster.

I can see Aggy beside him. It's impossible to miss her – she has a shock of bright pink hair. "The door sticks!" she calls down to me and I pause mid-wave.

"What—? WHOAH!"

The passenger door swings open under a violent kick from Dermot and stops, with a gentle *boop*, on the end of my nose.

"I'm sorry!" He gives me a stricken face as I climb into the van, checking my face is intact. "The door *usually* sticks."

We head off to school. The van has a bouncy sort of swing to it. It's fun to be so high up. Although, when we speed up as we turn onto the main road there are some worrying rattling noises. Aggy has an injured thumb as well, so every time she wants to change gear, she shouts "GEAR!" and Dermot does it for her. He doesn't get it right every time and there are a lot of lurching motions and grinding noises.

Plus, that musty smell I always notice around Dermot? I know where it comes from now, the van stinks like a damp shed. I make a note to put body spray in my bag in the future in case I absorb the smell. Mum and Dad had better get a job soon, I tell myself, hanging on tightly to the door handle.

"HOW DID YOU HURT YOUR THUMB?" I shout over the roar of the engine.

"WHAT? OH, MOVING FURNITURE. I DO HOUSE CLEARANCES. YOU'D BE AMAZED AT THE WEIRD STUFF YOU FIND."

I look at Dermot, who's wearing a three-piece mustard-coloured corduroy suit and holding a violin case as a lunchbox and think, *Nah – I wouldn't.*

"SO I WAS MOVING SOME GEAR!"

...

"GEAR, DERMOT! CHANGE GEAR!"

Dermot fumbles with the gear stick – "I thought you said you were moving some gear!" he defends himself.

"NO, NO, NO, DOWN!" Aggy shouts, as we approach a sharp corner in fifth gear, which even I know is not The Done Thing. Dermot hurriedly wrenches the gear stick into second gear and we whizz around the corner so fast I'm not sure all the wheels stay on the road.

"SO –" Aggy continues the conversation as if we're not tweaking the nose of Death – "I WAS MOVING SOME FURNITURE. I HAD A CHAISE LONGUE – YOU KNOW THOSE SOFAS WITH ONLY ONE ARM?"

"OK!" I shout back, because no, I don't, but I can imagine.

"AND IT FELL DOWN THE STAIRS TOWARDS ME. MY COLLEAGUE RAHUL GRABBED MY HAND TO PULL ME OUT OF ITS PATH, BUT HE ONLY GRABBED MY THUMB AND..." She makes a horribly graphic cracking noise and I nod, queasily. I won't risk telling Gabe this story today.

★　　★　　★

By the time we reach school, I'm clammy and nauseous. I decide to skip breakfast for as long as Aggy is driving me. I have a sneaky peek around the school car park for any witnesses. The only people I see staring at us are little kids in the lower years, who are, of course, nothing to me. Mere plankton.

I can't wait to get out of the van, although ... it's not that easy. I flap the handle a few times, uselessly, and look back at Dermot.

"THROUGH THE WINDOW THEN?" Aggy suggests, and I would rather not but there's a blaring of car horns behind us.

"Why are there maintenance men in the car park?" yells a snooty voice. I lower my rucksack out of the window and lean my body out after it.

"LOU, DON'T YOU WANT TO GO FEET FIRST?" I hear Aggy yell, helpfully.

Yeah, feet first. That would've been a better idea. I'm dangling face first out of an actually-quite-high van window, walking my hands down the door to reach the ground. There's a jolting feeling beneath my hips.

"THE DOOR'S UNSTUCK!" Aggy bellows happily.

I can't share her joy as the door swings open slowly, with me draped over it, arse in the air.

I can hear sniggering. Dermot helps me out of the window as best he can. I am long and gangly, he is spindly and I can only imagine how ridiculous we look. My feet finally hit the ground and I straighten up, a bit dizzy.

"ARE YOU OK, LOU?" Aggy shouts, just in case there's anyone in the car park who isn't already looking at me.

"Yes, thank you, Aggy," I say quietly, before she shouts out my surname or year group, too.

"SEE YOU TONIGHT!" She gives me a thumbs-up and speeds off, tyres squealing.

Dermot hands me my rucksack and says, "You know, many of the world's greatest artists and musicians were bullied at school."

"Why are you telling me that?"

"I thought it might bring you comfort in the next twenty seconds," he says drily and we turn to see that a sizeable audience has gathered to laugh at us, including the three nastiest (and also the prettiest and best-dressed, it PAINS ME to admit) girls in our class – Cammie, Melia and Nicole. They haven't bothered to be mean to me in months, and twice now, Melia has said, "Hey, girl! Cute top!"

(Fact check: the top is never cute. My clothes come in packs of three from the supermarket and cost less than onions.)

I knew this friendliness wouldn't last for ever and

55

I walk towards the school entrance, feeling wary. I see Gabe, Roman and Lavender across the car park, thankfully not near enough to share my shame. Lav and Roman let go of each other once they reach the steps. There's a rule in this school where boys and girls aren't allowed to be within twelve inches of each other. It's not practical. Some of the corridors are so narrow that you'd have to edge along the wall like spies to pass someone of the opposite sex. Plus there *is* a creepy way to point a ruler at someone – the Year 7 boys have got it down to a fine art. And there's a kid in Sixth Form who declared themself gender fluid and walks wherever they want.

As I pass Cammie, she's openly laughing at me and ... I don't know, maybe it's hormones, temper or the blood that rushed to my head while I was folded over the van door ... but I roll my eyes right in her face, and push past her. It's not rough, but our shoulders definitely brush.

If I'm telling this story later, I'll say I shoulder-barged her. If I live long enough to tell anyone.

6

As Dermot and I walk to class, I'm trying to identify his smell. It's like curtains in an old house that recently had a flood. It's not too bad – you just have to breathe through your mouth. We chat and I ask him leading questions about stuffed semi-aquatic mammals but he doesn't offer me one. I may have to be less subtle.

Hannah runs up behind us and grabs me. We exchange a look of *Eek!* I'm glad she's not still cross at me. I've shoulder-boofed Cammie – I need all the allies I can muster.

"Hi, Dermot," she says. "Snazzy suit."

"Thanks." He shows her the paisley lining and she makes impressed noises.

Are Dermot and I friends now? I feel like if we arrive together every morning, it'll seem weird to suddenly ditch him and sit separately – and I do want to be nice to him – but I don't know if I can take the social humiliation that he brings with him. I'm shallow for thinking this, but it's all happening privately in my head so no one will ever know.

We reach our form room. Hannah and I always sit together, but ... should I sit with Dermot cos his mum gave me a lift?

"I'll sit over there," Dermot says hastily, and heads to a desk as far from ours as possible. I feel relieved, then mean.

Hannah sits down and turns to me urgently. We always have to talk quickly in the morning before Mr Peters starts the register. She smells of chlorine and her hairline is wet; she's been swimming and the smell makes me feel nostalgic. I used to love coming to class with my blood pumping from fifty laps in the pool.

"So, your parents..." she says and my heart leaps.

YES! We will make a list and tackle the problem of my parents together and I will stop feeling so queasy and anxious. And who cares about swimming anyway?

"I haven't come up with any ideas *yet*," she says. "I'm sorry! Debs kept me late at training. You know what she's like. And it's actually really difficult to be fifteen and earn money."

"Well, duh, Han! My parents are old and *still* can't earn money."

"But I'll think of something," she promises me. "I just need time to think about it."

Mr Peters claps to get our attention and I nod and face forward. I don't know why I thought Hannah would have the answers, but a list is a good thing to cling to in bumpy times. My eyes prickle. What is wrong with me? I am a bag of feels at the moment. I wipe my nose firmly. I am not upset, I'm *fine*. Possibly hormonal or low on sugar.

"Now, there's something I want to talk to you about."

Mr Peters doesn't seem enthusiastic. I wonder if it's another Sex Education talk. I found the last one interesting, although Cammie and Melia hijacked it – but they knew a LOT. I'd give anything to know if it was from the internet or real life.

"At the end of term we're going to have a small prom." Mr Peters pats his hands downwards to shush the excited hum of chat that springs up from the class. Even I get a bit giddy and say *ooh* to Hannah. Oh my goodness, I might get to take my BOYFRIEND to PROM. When did my life get so amazing?

"Yes, yes, it's truly magical," says Mr Peters. "Oh to be alive and witness such times."

"Isn't prom supposed to be after our exams, in the summer, Mr Peters?" Melia looks embarrassed for him – not knowing such basic rules of Life.

"Yes," he acknowledges. "But between you and me,

last year got so swept up in their prom duties that we had a record number of resits. Call me boring, but I'd rather they passed their exams. So prom will be smaller and earlier this year."

He has to shout over another excited thrum. "And your exams are still VERY, VERY important. If it looks like you're in danger of forgetting that, there will be NO prom."

Nicole says, as if it's a foregone conclusion, "Mr Peters? So my uncle is a DJ and he has contacts in the industry so I can get us a great deal on the sound system and VJs."

What's a VJ? I mouth at Hannah, who shrugs.

"And Melia's family runs a caterers. They'll do the catering!" butts in Cammie. Melia looks a little over-whelmed by this.

"Hang on a minute," says Mr Peters. "I've been put in charge of this. I need to assign –" he checks something scribbled on his hand – "four people to the Prom Committee. So..."

Three hands shoot up – Cammie, Melia and Nicole. A couple of others follow, but Cammie shoots them a glare and they style it out as scratching their heads, or pointing out a ceiling feature. Cammie eyeballs the whole class-room, to check no one else dares muscle in on her turf.

I get a sudden rebellious urge to put my hand up too,

but Hannah, good friend that she is, senses this and grabs both of mine tightly under the table. She doesn't even look at me.

"One more volunteer?" Mr Peters says.

Cammie has a calculating look on her face, as if she's assessing who will be most useful to her – someone who's easygoing and won't cause trouble. She whispers something to Nicole.

You know sometimes you think you understand your life? And then it throws a big surprise hard at your face.

"What about Hannah?" Nicole says.

Hannah? My Hannah!? NO!! They only want her because she was off school for months and is still all lost and readjusting!

"Great, and Hannah makes four!" says Mr Peters, happy to be done. "Oh, if that's OK by you, Hannah?"

Han looks a bit shellshocked. "Uh..." is all she manages.

"I think she'd be great," says Cammie warmly.

"So great," Melia agrees.

THIS IS HOW THEY GET YOU.

Compliments. No fool can resist compliments. But don't trust them – these are mean girls who do not have your best interests at heart. They're liars and our tops are not cute! This is nothing but revenge for a shoulder-boof.

I am squeezing Hannah's arm to communicate this but

clearly she doesn't speak Arm. "Yeah, sure." She smiles. "I'd love to. And my cousin's in a band, so…?"

"That's awesome, I never knew!" Melia practically sparkles at her.

Theft. Outright friend theft from beneath my nose. This school is the pits. Hannah looks strangely pleased. She clearly doesn't realize she's being used. She's an innocent prawn!

Actually, I think I mean pawn. Like in chess? This is why I don't say everything that lands in my head.

7

"It might be fun!" Hannah whispers. I shake my head firmly.

"Well, not with that attitude," she tells me, her voice barely a decibel above breathing. "Lou, don't be so—"

"Girls, stop talking or I will split you up!" our chemistry teacher yells at us from the front. Everyone wants to split us up today.

And don't be so *what*, Hannah?

Melodramatic, jealous, pessimistic?

I clamp a piece of magnesium in pincers and hold it above the Bunsen burner flame. It sparkles purple, as does everyone else's and the room fills with delighted *oohs*.

I do not *ooh*. I will not be charmed by purple fire, I have bigger problems.

"Ooh," says Hannah.

I put the pincers down and try to be mature. It's just a

prom – a couple of meetings a week, maybe on the night they'll be all "You GUYS! We did it! Group hug!" And that will be annoying, so I'll go and stand in the toilet for five minutes. But if that's the worst of it, fine. These girls can never compete with my friendship with Hannah. We've been to Accident and Emergency together seven times. That sort of stuff bonds you, and no one can get in between that—

My thoughts are interrupted by a piece of paper nudging my elbow. It's a note. I take it off the boy next to me and start to open it.

"No," he hisses, making me jump. "For *her*."

Sourly, I hand the note to Hannah. She opens it and nods as she reads it. Even before she gives a little wave across the room, I know who it's from. I busy myself tidying up the magnesium dust on the desk. There's barely enough to fill a mouse's bellybutton so I take my time sweeping it carefully. I'm not jealous, I am sweeping.

When the lesson ends, Hannah leans across the desk to say, "Lou, listen."

"You have to meet the Prom Committee at lunch," I say dully.

"Yes, and can you take my rucksack? We're going to dash to the art and design workshop on the other side of school and see if we can use it as our base for designing decorations. Thaaaanks."

I nod as she runs off with frankly impolite excitement and I'm left eyeing up two massive rucksacks.

In the end, I have to hook one on the front of my body and one on the back and waddle slowly to the cafeteria like a hippo. I'm glad we're not allowed phones in school or I bet someone would film this and add some *bom-bom-bom* tuba tune to it.

As I sway down the corridor, I spot Gabe in a classroom having an animated discussion with his politics teacher. I loiter in the doorway, feet planted wide to spread the weight, but he doesn't spot me, so I wander off. I admire how keen Gabe is on his schoolwork but I wonder if a more dim boyfriend might think *I* was the most interesting thing in his life and shower me in single-minded devotion? That would be nice.

I sit down at an empty table and dig my lunchbox out of my bag. I open the Tupperware and stare inside.

You know what no one ever said EVER? "Cheer up and eat couscous!"

Can't believe Mum packed me off to school with couscous. I dig through the grains and find some vegetables lurking in there that I definitely recognize from yesterday's buffet. Hello again. I look discreetly around the room for someone to talk to but there's no one I feel confident in joining. The worst thing is when you sit down next to someone and they ignore you. You feel like a lingering bad smell. I can see Ro and Lav but they're eating together, just the two of them, and I don't want to feel like a gooseberry.

A day ago, Hannah was *my* gooseberry! Life comes at you fast, eh?

I shovel my couscous down, bored and lonely. If this is going to be how I spend lunch every school day till prom, I'm not looking forward to it.

Half an hour later, I wobble into the next lesson and give Hannah back her bag. I am such a good friend, I think to myself as I rub my aching shoulders and ignore her boring prattling. About bunting or something. I do not care.

It's almost a relief to climb into Aggy's van at the end of the day – thankfully, she parks right at the bottom of the car park so not many people see me hop in. Aggy clearly doesn't care about school, popularity or proms. She regales us with a disgusting but hilarious story about a rats' nest she found inside a sofa in an old house. The rats were poking their heads out of the upholstery and appearing in the guts of cushions apparently. It was like Whack a Mole – except she and Rahul didn't have the heart to hurt them, so they were shooing them out of the house with socks on their hands. Shoo a Mole.

"No!" Dermot is squirming at this story. "Stop it!

I can feel their little feet all over me!"

"Such a sensitive child," Aggy says, messing up his cravat to annoy him.

I laugh till my eyes water. "When was this?" I ask, wiping at my wet cheeks.

"Today!" she says brightly. "The furniture's in the back! Don't worry, I got all the rats out, I reckon. Probably."

I stop laughing.

"STOP. THE. CAR!" Dermot says.

Seconds later, we're out of the car, shivering by the side of the road and slapping ourselves all over.

"You're a mile from home," Aggy warns us.

"And you're driving a van of vermin, so..." Dermot spreads his hands like he's won the argument, and I'm on his side.

"Thanks, though, Aggy," I say politely around him.

"I'll see you later." She waves at us and clanks off in a cloud of exhaust.

Dermot and I walk the rest of the way. We don't chat much but it's a comfortable silence, broken up every now and then by one of us shuddering. Aggy's a great storyteller, but he's right, I can feel little feet all over my body.

As soon as we get to my house, I race in.

"Go shower!" Dermot instructs me.

"I will. You too!" I say.

Ten minutes later: "You can't shower twice a day!" Dad is knocking on the bathroom door.

"I can when I travel in a van full of rats!" I shout back. "Blame Mum!"

8

Lunch the next day is as bad as I feared. As soon as the bell rang, Hannah raced off to another prom meeting and Dermot was nowhere to be seen. I'm so bored I actually rummage through my school bag to find some homework – anything to make the time pass.

I accidentally pull out my old Worry Diary, and laugh again at the front cover – the picture of the cake above the word WORRY. So weird.

As is laughing alone. I stop immediately.

I flick through and find a blank page where I left off, aged thirteen. Without really thinking, I grab a pen to see if I can do any better. It turns out to be as moany as me-two-years-ago, but at least I don't hate Lavender any more.

WORRY DIARY

* Hannah KEEPS calling them Cams, Mell and Nic. Like they're all too busy for syllables.
* Mum and Dad are out of work and money's tight. We've had lentils for dinner two days running and I have to keep running outside to fart.
* I think Dermot is my new best friend.
* I'm running out of that oil that makes my hair calm. If we can't afford to replace it, I'll have to shave my head.

Finally, it's Friday afternoon, and I am so glad to see the back of that week! It was rubbish, beginning to end. I ate alone every day – without my diary I would've felt a right loner. At least I look busy scribbling in that. What Prom Committee needs to meet four times a week? It's a small prom, Mr Peters definitely said *so*. A bowl of Wotsits, a box of party poppers and Spotify, surely that's all you need!

I'm not sure if it's as a result of the loneliness or just that I'd never bothered to spend time with him before, but Dermot is starting to grow on me. I like our journeys to and from school, and we even sit together in a couple of classes. Other boys are constantly trying to trip him up or flick gum at him, and I want to stand up for him but

I can't think quickly enough on my feet so end up saying lame things like, "Heeyyy ... GUYS" or "Come *on*."

Yes, that is I, Lou Brown, Defender of the Unpopular, Hero to the Shy and Mocked. Someone make me a cape! Oh, thank you, Dermot, a musty moth-eaten paisley cape with a stain. You're too kind.

Anyway, all week I've been looking forward to Friday, when Lav and I are going to Roman and Gabe's after school to watch films with them and Pete. I hardly ever see Gabe at school, so this is nice. And I never see Pete these days. I text him sometimes.

Hi Pete! How are you? How's college? Anything new with you? I cut myself a fringe. It looks quite bad!

He never replies.

So by five o'clock on Friday, I'm watching a zombie film (2/5, it's no Anne Frank's Diary) and stuffing my face with sweets. Thank goodness for boyfriends whose parents still buy snacks. Roman and Lav are wrapped around each other on a big armchair, Pete is sitting between Gabe and me on the sofa so he doesn't feel left out. Gabe offered to snuggle him but he declined.

Since Ro and Lavender have been going out, I've had plenty of opportunities to observe their kissing technique and have now decided which one I hate the most. You'd think the full-on snogging where they bend each other's noses would be the worst, and yes, it's definitely a low point in my day. But the kissing they're doing now is my number one least favourite. They're giving each other little pecking kisses, like they're teeny tiny birds nibbling at bread.

I'm delighted when Pete takes a wet sweet out of his mouth and chucks it in Ro's hair.

I'd much rather listen to Pete and Roman argue – it's a familiar, almost soothing sound. They settle down after a few minutes.

"You should do your hair like that," Ro says to Lav, nodding at a girl on the screen. She has long dark hair with bright rainbow-coloured streaks at the bottom.

"I dunno," Pete says. "I don't think it'll flatter my cheekbones."

"Ha ha." Ro nudges Lavender with his shoulder as she's not answering him. "Don't you think that'd look great on you?"

"Um. Not really," she says. "It's a bit – you know – LOOK AT MY HEAD."

"That's what I mean. It's cool."

"I like it how it is," she says mildly. "Brown."

"Fiiiine," he says. "But it would look amazing on you."

Roman loves people noticing him. To be fair, when

you're that tall and handsome, if you didn't like being stared at, life would be hell. Lavender is just as beautiful, but it's not the sort of beauty that people gawp at across the street.

Gabe interrupts my thoughts. "I saved you all the black ones," he says, tipping a load of wine gums into my hand. Which is worth a hundred gross nibbly kisses because those are my favourite. Pete leans over and steals half of them before I can stop him.

"How's college?" I ask and he shrugs.

"It's OK. It's just… I don't know."

"Just…?"

"You know."

No, Pete, I really don't. Getting in his head is like trying to prise apart Lego with wet hands.

"Don't like the course?" I ask.

"The people?" Lav guesses.

"All the girls are … hairy?" Roman suggests and the conversation turns to arm hair.

We carry on watching the film – there's a lot of axes thudding into heads and brains falling out. Whenever there's a particularly gory scene, I look down and sort carefully through my identical black wine gums – but subtly so no one realizes I'm such a wimp.

"Want to go to the cinema tomorrow?" Roman asks the room.

"Can't afford it," Lav tells him, honestly.

"I'll pay!" he says, but she squirms and makes uncomfortable noises.

"Let's just go for a walk," she says.

"A walk? That sounds horrible. Are you mad?"

"His hair goes frizzy in the rain," I pipe up. Which is mean but we all know it's true. Pete laughs till he chokes on a sweet and I feel proud of myself.

"I've joined this new debating team," Gabe tells me. "So I'm going to be busy at the weekends. You could sign up too if you want? You need to audition but—"

"If I wanted to spend my weekends discussing big issues with people cleverer than me, I'd come round here," I say. His parents are very clever and like debating ideas, whereas my family only argue if they need to, like when someone ate the last packet of crisps. Back when we had crisps.

We all have our eyes fixed on the screen as we talk. The film is terrible and yet we're somehow compelled to keep watching. Just as the teenage hero is creeping down the stairs to the basement to investigate the zombie-ish noises ("IT'S CLEARLY A ZOMBIE, THERE'S NO NEED TO CHECK!" Gabe is pleading with the screen) Lav makes me jump by yelping.

"*What?*" I snap.

"Check your phone. It's Dad."

Will you be horny later? X

Eh?

"It's…" says Lavender.

"Don't even say it!" I interrupt her. "It would warp my mind and I would become strange and have to go and live in the woods."

"It must be for Mum," she says, ignoring my fragile mental health. "A sexy text for Mum."

I'll start packing for the woods now. Lots of thick socks.

Pete takes my phone off me and reads the message. He starts laughing.

"That's awful!" he crows.

"Shut up!" I tell him.

The film is now completely forgotten.

Another text.

HORNY!!!

"STOP. IT!" The five of us shout at my phone.

Gabe looks traumatized. "I can never look your dad in the eye again."

"Trust me," Lav says. "It's worse for us."

One more text.

H. U. N. G. R. Y!

Stupid autocorrect.

I'm roasting cauliflower.

Dad's had a rubbish phone for years but his Jobcentre advisor told him he needed to get to grips with new tech and he's started using an old smartphone. It's not going well – as you can see. But he is trying.

9

"Are you OK?" Lav finds me in Gabe's hallway, half into my coat and doing deep breathing exercises.

I nod, too dizzy to talk. I started compiling a list in my head of ways to help Mum and Dad, which made me feel overwhelmed and panicky, so I started doing what I could remember of Hari's breathing exercises. The ringing in my ears says I've remembered wrong. I think I did the one that's for childbirth.

Roman drops us home, and there's an awkward moment where two people are kissing two other people goodbye. Lav and Roman kiss for longer than me and Gabe. Ours *is* a proper kiss, but obviously I'm not going mad with tongues in someone else's car on my parents' driveway.

I'm not.

Lav clearly isn't so worried.

Judgey face

Lav and I bundle into the house, start taking our coats off and then, on second thoughts, put them back on. The house is freezing – I can see my own breath in the hallway.

"Mum?" Lav calls and we exchange a concerned look. "Dad?"

"Boo!" Dad leaps out at us from the living room and we both scream. I blame the film – my nerves are wrecked. Lav slaps him and he laughs at us.

"What's going on, Dad?" I ask.

"Well," he says, dropping his voice but keeping a cheery smile on his face – it's not reassuring. "Your mum is having a bit of a … wobble, shall we say. So I've turned all the heating and lights off to cheer her up."

"Does she like being cold and sitting in the dark?"

"No! She was just worried about bills and—"

"Hi, girls, it's all right," Mum calls from the living room. Her voice sounds hoarse and snotty as if she's been crying.

"Why don't you grab your mum a glass of water?" Dad suggests and I head to the kitchen, determined to make her a glass of water that will cheer her right up.

I use my favourite glass, blue and owl-shaped. But it's still not special enough and water is très bland. So I rummage in the fridge for a lemon, a lime at a push. I find nothing but a banana. Can you put banana in water? I mean, I know you *can*, but should you?

I prepare a refreshing delicious banana water and bring it into the living room, where Mum is sitting on the sofa, pretending she hasn't been crying. She's all puffy with a broad fake grin on her face. She looks like a clown balloon.

I sit close to her and put my head on her shoulder. I'm not used to seeing her like this. She's usually busy and confident and perfume-smelling, dashing in and out of the house with a sense of purpose and a big shoulder bag full of essays.

"Did you drop a banana in her water?" Lavender asks. "I can fish it out with a fork."

"There wasn't any lemon," I say.

"Right, obviously."

Dad nudges Lav.

"Good job, champ," she says. "Banana water."

"Um," Dad begins hesitantly. "Did you get my texts?"

We turn and look at him. That's all the answer he needs.

"Did you show the boys?"

"Of course," Lav says.

"We were traumatized!" I inform him.

"Oh, girls, don't embarrass your dad," says Mum, with a proper grin now.

We scoff at that. Dad has embarrassed us so many times, from giving us lifts in his pyjamas, to saying to a boy's parents, "Is your son the handsome one that Lavender always goes on about?" And once he pulled a muscle in his groin on Sports Day and spent the afternoon clutching his privates. Finally some payback!

"I'll dish up dinner," he says. "You all relax and watch TV."

"Before we have to pawn it," Mum mutters.

"No!" It bursts out of me before I realize. "Sorry," I say. But I do love the TV. It's been around my whole childhood, like a family dog that has loads of films in it.

Dinner is a challenge. Even though I am – of course – hard as nails, I have watched a lot of pale zombie brains splatter this evening. So when Dad lifts the lid to reveal a *whole roast cauliflower*, I flinch.

"What?" Dad demands. "It's nutritious, cheap ... and big."

"Yes," I say, trying not to look at it. "Yum, yum, yum. Big. Pale."

Dad spears the cauliflower with his fork and dumps it on the plate in the middle of the table. Mum, Lavender and I grab at the side dishes, hastily spooning potatoes and beans onto our plates to leave as little space as we can for the main dish.

"Hey," Dad protests. "Stop it."

"Sorry," I say, grabbing one last potato.

"Right, so shall I carve it or slice it like a pie?"

We all think about this, considering the cauliflower from various angles.

"Mash it and spoon it out?"

"We could pass it around and take bites out like an apple?"

"Spear it and lick it like a lolly?"

"Slice?" Mum says, and we all agree, because she's got enough problems without an argument over cauliflower.

Dad delicately slides a couple of slices onto my plate, where they steam, white and shiny.

"Do you think I should've put seasoning on it?" he asks, with a flicker of self-doubt.

"No, no," Lav reassures him. "Let the natural cauli-flower ... ah ... flavour come out."

I reach for the salt.

Mum and Dad want to hear about school – it's honestly worrying that I have nothing interesting to tell them. I can see Lavender struggling too.

"Oh, wait!" I remember and tell them about prom.

"Would they like me to help?" Dad asks, his eyes lighting up.

"Because you're a prom expert with a degree in Party Animalism from the College of YOLO?" Lav asks.

"Because," he protests over our giggles, "I'm a project manager, and a prom is a project to be *managed*?"

"That sounds so boring," I tell him. Mum dings my knuckles with her fork.

"Fine," he says loftily. "Don't come crying to me when your prom is an unmanaged mess that can't meet its targets."

"It's not MY prom. And it doesn't have any targets."

"No targets? Well..." He shakes his head at his plate. "Oh wow. Good luck with that."

"Anyway," I tell them, moodily, "I'm not on the Prom Committee, only Hannah."

"Good!" says Mum brightly. "It'll be good for you girls to do things separately. Maybe you'll make new friends. Like Dermot."

"You're only saying that cos you don't like Hannah's parents and you want to hang out with nicer ones," I say.

"Eat your cauliflower," she says.

I'm on my second slice of pale, flabby vegetable matter when Dad's phone rings and he answers it, swivelling in his chair away from us. Lavender turns to Mum with a slice of cauliflower on her fork and nods at Mum's handbag. Mum shakes her head – no, she will not let Lav hide it in there.

Terrible parenting.

We keep eating in utter silence. The cauliflower is so

soft that I can't hear anyone chewing.

"No, I've not found any work yet," Dad is telling the person on the other end. He sounds defeated. I pat his shoulder as the closest thing to me.

"Yeah." Dad forces a laugh. "That's not exactly my... No. You're right. Take what I can get, till I'm back on my feet. Thanks, Vinnie."

"Vinnie?" Mum says when he's off the phone. "My brother?"

"Yeah," Dad says. "He might have work for me, just part-time sort of – but still, work!"

"Legal?" Lav asks. "Not something dodgy?"

"Yes! I mean no, not, you know." Dad is being vague. We all give him stern looks. "Part-time."

Part-time criminal work? Brilliant, maybe he'll only get part-time prison. That's one for the newly unearthed Worry Diary.

Dad changes the subject. "He offered me his season tickets for tomorrow."

"Football?" Mum is bemused.

"I know. I don't know anything about it," Dad says. "Lou, will you come with me and explain? You're so good with sport."

I glow a little, because no one is immune to compliments. And hey, he'd probably get nicer food in prison.

"This is horrible," Dad says, looking glumly at his

plate, and we all nod but keep going. Cos we should take what we can get. Until we're back on our feet.

Mum has some good news, though: "People are bidding on the items we put on eBay, we should have a bundle to post out next week. Although…" She pauses. "People are creepy."

So apparently, the photos of Lav got attention, not from good-hearted potential jumper-buyers but from creeps wanting to know how old she is and where she lives. Oh, sure, internet creeps – here's all her information. Stranger Danger's just a rhyme! Duh.

Mum had a satisfying afternoon telling them all to get stuffed. She has a huge vocabulary, and is an experienced creative writer. I bet she kicked arse. It's a shame Being Scathing Online isn't a job.

10

This house is so cold I may lose fingers.

I put my hands back under the duvet. I think I'll just dress under here this morning. I'll be standing outside with hundreds of football fans, probably next to a hot dog stand. If ever there was a day to skip a shower and get away with it, it's today! "Pee-yoo," I'll whisper, discreetly holding my nose. "Don't think the guy next to me showered thoroughly today – if at all!"

The perfect crime.

I go back to sleep for a couple of hours before I have to get ready. Dad's monitoring the hot water so closely he definitely knows I haven't washed, but it saves money, so he's not going to snitch on me. We're both bundled up in about eight thick layers. And there's a football scarf poking through the letterbox – Uncle Vinnie must have dropped it off as he passed this morning. I'm swaying slightly from the weight of clothing and decline this extra layer, so Dad winds the scarf delicately around his head like a cherry on a cake.

He opens the door and we step out, braced to freeze.

Huh. We turn and look back.

"It's actually," Dad marvels, "colder in the house than out here."

"We might as well live in the park."

"Never say never," he says grimly.

"Oh, great."

"*Joking.* Just wait for your mum to get her first Jobseeker's payment and she'll let us put the heating back on."

Lav opens her window and waves us goodbye as we stumble down the drive. "So glad I'm not going with you," she calls after us.

"She's jealous really," Dad assures me.

It's only a twenty-minute walk along the main road to the football stadium, and people in football scarfs keep joining us en route until we feel like a big gang. This is quite fun.

I link arms with Dad. "Why have we never done this before?" I ask.

Twenty-five minutes later, we're in a massive unmoving wodge of people. I guess it's a queue but it's as wide as it is long. Someone near me has bad breath, so I tuck my face into my scarf to filter out the cabbage smell.

It starts to rain.

"I know why we've never done this before, it's rubbish," Dad grumbles and I have to agree. The crowd moves forward so, so slowly. A delicious smell of onions wafts over and I perk up a bit. We're passing a fast food stand.

"Want something?" Dad asks, casually, and I so nearly say yes then I glance at him and realize he just asked out of habit.

"No, I'm fine thanks," I say, glad he can't hear my rumbling stomach over hundreds of people saying "Wet, isn't it?" and "Sorry, that's my foot you're on?"

"Sure?" He looks relieved.

"Yeah yeah."

"I packed some sandwiches," he says in a stage whisper and I give him a wink.

Having no money pinches all over and you don't realize how many times a day you give yourself a little treat until they stop.

My phone vibrates with a text that immediately pushes money from my mind. I show it to Dad and he starts laughing. Lav and Mum have got to go and see Evil Grandma today.

So even though it's raining, even though I'm crushed

in between Bad Breath Dude and Man Who Thinks Lou's Ribs Are a Nice Place to Rest His Elbow, I am determined to have a lovely time.

It's a pretty good game although the home team gets "annihilated" according to the melodramatic fans behind me.

"Good effort! Lovely running!" Dad yells. I don't think the people around us find him as funny as he finds himself. But I force myself to not shush him. He's going through a stressful time, and if he enjoys embarrassing me, then let him have his fun!

(Also, quick scan of crowd. No one from school is here.)

I have to keep pointing out what's going on in the game because Dad doesn't seem to be watching the players; his attention is elsewhere. I'm watching him suspiciously. What work has Uncle Vinnie offered him? I know Dad is a good person: he has morals – even if whenever we stay in a hotel he steals everything in the room. But that's an ethical grey area, we all agree as he drags his bulging suitcase through the lobby.

I don't trust Uncle Vinnie, though. He's always up to something and I'm scared about what he's going to drag Dad into. Dad's so desperate to bring home money that he might do something illegal. I know if I voice any worries, Dad will say, "It's fine, don't worry, everything's fine!" Which will just make me worry more because he's said that about everything from arguments between him and Mum (divorce when I was six) to my Key Stage 3 exams (RUBBISH results) and our ill dog, Mr Hughes (died two days later).

I'm glad when the game is finally over and Dad turns to me, his little bald spot shiny with excitement, and says, "Wasn't that great?" He starts singing, "Three–nil, three–nil, three–niiii-iiiiil," oblivious to the death stares from everyone around us.

I tug on his sleeve. "Dad. We LOST three–nil."

"What?"

I point at the dejected fans around us and, across the pitch, our mascot, the big-bottomed bee, dancing valiantly to lift the mood. Someone lobs some chips at him.

We hustle out of the stadium before anyone decides to take their feelings out on Dad's face.

We head off home. My legs are frozen numb and I inform Dad that if Mum doesn't let me turn the heating on, I'm putting myself in an orphanage. He agrees and cheers me up by showing me a series of angry texts from Mum about Grandma. We laugh, but...

"If one of us doesn't get a job soon, we might be seeing a lot more of her," Dad says, looking stricken. "We've got a big loan payment due in a month."

"Still," I say. "No need to do anything drastic. Or criminal." But he's not listening, he's popping into the newsagent's. I follow and give him a look when I find him loitering next to the Lottery tickets.

"What?" he protests. "I've never won it before – my odds are good."

I saunter down the aisle towards the magazines.

"Young lady?" The man behind the till points at me with a pen. "I'm not a library, you got that?"

"I know," I tell him.

I run my eyes over the shelf. There's no way I'm buying a magazine, I can get all this online, but no harm in killing time. I reach my hand towards a shiny women's mag. The newsagent's eyes follow my every move.

"I need to look inside," I protest. "So I know if the articles are relevant to my interests."

"Read the contents then. Page one," he says shrewdly.

"Uh-huh," I say, turning my shoulder slightly so he can't see what page I'm looking at.

He's not letting it go. "The library is a national institution," he informs the back of my head. "You can get a nice book from the shelf, sit and read, pay for nothing, and don't have to feel like you're annoying your local newsagent. It's a good system."

He's really bringing out my stubborn side. Now I'm

determined to read an article. I reckon I've got thirty seconds before he shames me into buying or putting it back. So I open the magazine at random and hope for a good piece. The other day, I read one about eyebrows – "They're Sisters Not Twins" – which made me feel better about the dodgy tweezing job I did on mine. Sisters can be very different.

I turn a page and find myself looking at a photo of Lavender.

11

Dad and I have NO idea why Lavender's photo is in the magazine. We spent about five minutes pulling it back and forth between us, arguing about it. The newsagent watched us creasing his magazine for as long as he could stand, then threatened to kick us out. So now we're scraping together two pound fifty to buy it.

Finally, we shove a pile of change and a button across the counter and leg it.

I read the article as we hurry home, and Dad steers me by the collar of my coat whenever I'm about to walk into a bin. The magazine is running a modelling competition called Sidewalk to Catwalk. There are photos of twenty-five finalists and one of them is Lavender. It's one of the photos I took of her standing on Mum and Dad's bed, wearing the clothes we were selling on eBay. She looks gorgeous but I'm surprised she didn't tell me she was entering the competition. I'm hurt. I *took* the photo!

Looking at Lav in the magazine, I feel like I don't know this gorgeous woman who may or may not be laughing at me. When I took the photo, there was a hint of a smile playing on her lips (she'd just stood on Mum's hot-water bottle) but now that half-smile looks haughty. I don't think I'd like this magazine-Lavender, we wouldn't be pals.

Dad's worried. "Is it a bit sleazy, though?" he babbles as we hurry home. "Is it a competition for *modelling* modelling or glamour modelling? Isn't she a bit young for that sort of attention? Did she mention it to you? It seems very unlike her – woah, wait!"

I stop and wait for him as he bends double and wheezes. His apology is muffled through his scarf. "If I talk and walk, I get breathless. I'm such a fat old man."

I pat his back supportively as a couple of football fans walk past. Bent double, with the club scarf on, Dad looks like he's taking the loss very badly.

"'S'all right, mate," one of them says. "We've been unlucky with injuries but we'll get back up there."

Dad pops his head up and I can see him scrabbling through his brain for something appropriate to say. His eyes dart about, as if his brain cells are tipping over dusty chests marked "SPORTSING" that he hasn't peeked in since school.

93

"Up the Bumbles?" he says finally and they give him a thumbs-up. He looks proud of himself.

We carry on walking home.

"So. Am I going to tell her off or what?" Dad asks.

"Are you asking *me* how to parent my older sister?" I exclaim. "Wow! I have so many ideas. Let's brainstorm! I think her curfew should be the same as mine. And I think we should have a conversation about sharing make-up—"

"I'll try your mother," he says, getting out his phone.

We arrive home to find the house cold and deserted. Dad lets me blast the heating briefly until Mum gets back, but I'm only allowed it in two rooms. Decisions decisions. I go for living room and bathroom as a cold toilet seat puts a downer on your whole day. Dad and I lean on the radiator in the living room and discuss the Offside Rule without coming to any conclusions except that we prefer netball.

"I don't miss the swimming. Am I allowed to say that now?" he confides. "It smelt mildewy, and I never recognized you once you had goggles and one of those snappy hats on so I was always cheering on the wrong girl. Boy, sometimes! At least with netball I could park my car near the court, eat a sandwich and rock out to Smooth FM. Oh, there's your mother!"

Mum and Lav open the front door just as I leap into the kitchen and turn the boiler off.

"It's very warm in here," Mum says suspiciously.

"We've been running around," Dad lies smoothly. "How's the Thing of Evil?"

Mum leans into one hip and holds up her hands to start listing. "Lavender looks too old for her age and she doesn't approve. My new haircut draws attention to my chin, which isn't my best feature."

"I love your chin," Dad tells her, and I nod though I've never thought about it before.

"And apparently you've dragged me down into unemployment with you."

"It's not contagious!" he objects and she throws her hands up.

"We can't live with her," Mum says firmly. "I can't believe I even thought about it. I'm not subjecting two teenage girls and their self-esteem to that … emotional sandblasting."

See? What a lovely vocabulary. She's so employable!

Mum goes on. "If it comes to it, I think we should look at moving somewhere cheaper."

Dad is nodding, but Lav and I are instantly wary. "Wha—? Hello, *moving*? You mean to a cheaper house but in this area?"

"No, a cheaper area altogether," Mum says.

"It's an option." Dad shrugs. They're doing that thing where they've discussed something before but pretend they're coming up with it in front of us. I'm wise to their tricks.

"But what about Gabe, Roman and all my friends?" ALL is a strong word – I know I don't have loads of friends. But it took me ages to make a handful. "I can't begin again from scratch – I'll be lonely till I'm twenty!"

"Well, don't panic until we have to," says Mum, in a reasonable tone.

Fine. Let me know when it's time to panic and I will Pee Ay En Eye See. There'll be shrieking, people will stare, you'll have to throw a bucket of water over me.

"Anyway," says Dad, following Mum into the kitchen with a significant look at me. He's going to talk to her about Lavender being in the magazine. I'm left with the aspiring model herself as she stomps downstairs in a tiger onesie and flicks on the TV.

"So …" I say, sliding casually up and down the radiator, "anything new with you?"

"Not really," she says. "That –" jerking her head at our parents in the kitchen – "is a bit worrying, but…"

We both shrug, like, *Whatchu gonna do?*

"Um." I'm trying to bring up the subject in a subtle way but all I can think of is fake-sneezing a noise like *shwodelling!* and saying, "Hey, you know what rhymes with that?"

"I saw you in the magazine. *Stylie* magazine?"

"What?"

"The competition! Well done."

She stares at me. "I've no idea what you're talking about."

Not a promising start.

"Laa-aav..."

Lav frowns at me as Mum and Dad bundle into the living room. Mum looks annoyed.

"Lavender, I'm not happy about this." Mum holds up a finger.

Lav holds up one back. "Me neither. What are you talking about?"

To cut a long story short, Lav swears she has no idea about any modelling competition. She reckons we've all gone mad. So Dad pulls *Stylie* magazine out and holds it up. Her photo face gurns at her, bobbly from the rain. She looks genuinely shocked to see herself. She's always been a good liar – she's stained a LOT of towels with hair dye over the years and wriggled out of blame. ("The radiator must be leaking purple water!") But on this, I believe her.

Dad says he's going to call the magazine first thing on Monday and ask some questions.

"Is there prize money?" I ask.

"It doesn't matter," Mum says firmly.

Fine. Cauliflower dinners for ever, then.

Bloop, Gabe texts.

Bloop, I reply.

It's a friendly thing to say when you've got nothing much to say.

Prepping for debating team tomorrow.

DWEEB.

… and proud! This team is amazing – they
got through to the finals of a worldwide
debating competition in Harvard last year!

Wow! I say, buying time while I google Harvard. Oh yes, American university, not a type of bread. That's Hovis. I don't know what I'd do without the internet. Thank you, Mr … Internet?

Who invented the internet? I need to google that too. There's always something I don't know.

You'll be amazing! You stay calm when you
argue – it's years of practice with P   And
you have a brilliant memory fo

I add a string of emojis – the unicorn, a snowflake. Sometimes I surprise myself by how good I am at being a girlfriend, especially as I've never done it before. But then I was very good at ice skating the first time I tried that.

Plus, apart from the kissing, it's exactly like having a best friend, so I've been practising on Hannah for years. Right down to pretending I'm not jealous sometimes when I am. Which happens a lot. That reminds me. I check in with Hannah, just a little text to see how she's doing and if she's around tomorrow. I wait a bit but no reply. FINE. Probably doing prom stuff. Examining VJs, sourcing chairs … whatever.

I can feel I'm being looked at. I raise my eyes from my phone to find my parents staring at Lav and me, both on our phones.

"Just saying I'm really enjoying spending quality time with the tops of your heads," says Mum, sweetly.

"I don't think I've seen your noses in days," adds Dad.

Lav lifts her face, keeps her eyes down and carries on texting Ro. Presumably updating him on a surprising day.

"You've spent all day with my nose!" I protest to Dad. "You, me and my nose went to the football, remember? I'm going to be taller than you soon so I'd enjoy the top of my head while you can still see it."

Mum and Lav laugh and I feel sassy. I may not know ALL the American universities off the top of my head or who invented the internet but I can be quite funny on a good day. I must remember that next time I'm getting down on my fluffy hair and distant-cousin eyebrows.

"Mum, can I go and see Ro tonight?" Lav asks. I bet she wants to talk to him about this *Stylie* thing. She could talk to me, but I can't think of a way to say it that won't sound sappy.

"If he comes and gets you," Mum says. "What? I'm sorry, petrol is expensive! Lou is getting lifts to school with her friend Dermot..."

My friend Dermot. She's making it sound like an absolute treat for me, not like I'm falling out of a van with my bum in the air.

I say nothing, though. A look at Mum's tired face tells me this would be bratty.

We watch the news together. It seems to be a particularly bad day for the world. There's floods, stabbings, fires. Every time a new tragedy crops up, Lav and I say, "See? That's what you get in *other places*." We're relentless, and by the time we point out that we even have better weather than anywhere else, Mum and Dad are laughing at our persistence and I feel close to my sister again.

The next morning, I poke my nose out of my duvet. *Argh, freezing!* I quickly reach out a hand, delve into my school bag and grab my Worry Diary. I retreat with it under the covers.

Better that I whinge in this than do it out loud. My parents are stressed, Gabe's always studying or debating and I bet Hannah's too busy with prom to pass my problems on to Hari this week. I want to thank whichever gloomy, fortune-telling relative bought me this two years ago as it's becoming very useful now.

WORRY DIARY

* We might have to move away from the only place I've ever lived!
* I'll be separated from Gabe and Hannah! (And Roman and Dermot. I'd miss Pete a bit too.)

* Model sister.
* Gabe thinks I'm less interesting than schoolwork.
* Cauliflower experiment may be repeated this week.
* Stupid prom has now completely stolen my best friend.
* I'll have to buy a prom dress. Ugh. With money we don't have.
* So very, very cold.

I can hear my family waking up and groaning at the temperature.

"Daaaaad! Turn the heating on!" Lav calls.

"Tweeting?" He feigns deafness. "I can't hear you. My ears are too cold."

"Mark, get up and do it!" Mum's awake now.

"Your mother's offering to get up, Lavender."

"No, I'm not. YOU get up!"

"ONE OF YOU GET UP! This is your parental responsibility!"

Dad's phone starts ringing and I hear him answer it.

"Lavender! Don't call me when we're both in the house. It's wasteful!"

"I'm on an all-inclusive—"

"I don't know what that means!" Dad bellows.

"I was just about to tell you! You interrupted me when I was just about to tell you. Why don't you stop shouting and *listen*?"

I can't take any more of this. "Why don't you all stop shouting and someone get up and make me a cup of tea and turn the heating on?"

Everyone makes rude noises back at me from their bedrooms.

"I'm the baby child of the family…" I whine.

"Good! So shift your young limbs and get the kettle on!" Mum is unsympathetic. "I gave birth to half of the people in this house and it really HURT."

"We know. You tell us every birthday." Lav is scathing.

"Well, some things shouldn't be forgotten."

"Daaaa-aaaad, you do it!"

"Oh yeah, sure, of course I should do it. I trap and release the spiders, I eat the crisp flavours no one likes, I buy the tampons, I take out the bins…"

"See, you're used to this sort of thing!" Lav is triumphant.

"With Lav it was too late for an epidural," Mum says, beginning a birth story we've all heard a hundred times. "And the pain, oh my god, the PAIN…"

I can hear Dad grumbling and getting up. No one wants to hear Mum's childbirth stories – they're like *Saving Private Ryan* with extra drama.

I get dressed on top of my pyjamas. Which may be a bit gross but it keeps the bed-warmth next to my skin. I spray deodorant in my hair to give me the illusion of a clean person. I stumble downstairs and into the kitchen. Mum looks me up and down but lets it pass. It's her idea to go without heating. I'm just adapting.

We've got new budget cereal now. Which is fine, but I do miss the friendly koala relaxing in a bath of chocolate milk. He always looked so happy about me eating his puffs of wheat. This cereal has an emu glaring at me from the front of the box as if I'm stealing off him.

I turn the box away from me. I don't need that attitude first thing in the morning.

"Right, today we're going to wrap and post all the things we've sold on eBay," Mum says.

Lavender and I shrug. I don't mind. Gabe's debating, Hannah's gone quiet again and that's the end of my extensive social options. Unless Pete EVER replies to my texts.

Dad's popping out to see Uncle Vinnie about this job. I want to ask him about it but Mum gives me a *shush* look so I go back to my breakfast. I have *seconds* to eat it before it becomes beige mush. I really don't like this emu.

"Right," says Mum. "Lavender's on clothes, Lou is on homeware."

Homeware?

"Mum!"

"What?"

"She gets easy squashy packages. I get lamps and egg cups?"

"I don't know what you're complaining about."

She and the emu are determined to ruin my morning. I go into the living room and kneel next to an anglepoise lamp. I try to encase it in bubble wrap, fighting its swivelling pointy bits. It's like trying to get a onesie on a giraffe.

Soon I'm sweating and cross. It doesn't get better.

"Lou?"

"*Mother*," I say through gritted teeth.

"Did you not think to write the buyer's address on the paper *before* you wrapped it?"

"Obviously not."

Mum hands me her notepad and points to the world's longest address, which ends in *Cambridgeshire and the Isle of Ely*. If I ever go there, I'm going to have a firm word with them. Why don't they call it CATIOE? I grip the lamp between my knees and start writing, super-delicately so my pen doesn't stab through the paper.

Lavender sticks her headphones in and starts listening to a podcast. Mum and I exchange a look. Lavender has started doing this always like it's normal and not RUDE. She may just as well be saying, "Bored of you now kthanxbye."

At least one of us is spending time with Mum, listening to her problems. I'm so the best daughter.

"So … how's things?" I offer.

"Aggy got offered a day's teaching at the uni yesterday," Mum says.

"I thought she quit and threatened to rip her clothes off?"

"She says no way is *she* going back, but she suggested me instead."

"Why didn't they ask you first? They know she hates it. You don't."

"Right?" Mum agrees. "I feel a bit hurt."

Stupid people making my mum feel bad, I think irritably, still spelling out *Isle of Ely.* Ugh, people are the worst.

We wrap for a couple of hours in a comfortable silence. Mum pops the TV on and plays films with good soundtracks so we can listen as we work.

Oooh! Gaaaabriel's calling! I don't want to be a massive hypocrite, but Mum waves at me wearily and plugs her own headphones in her ears. Sometimes I do understand Hannah's irritation at sharing me with a boyfriend.

"Hey hey!" I chirp happily down the phone at him.

"Lou P. Brown," he says gravely. He finds my full name very funny. Every bit of it is toilety.

"How was Fight Club?"

"*Debating* was brilliant, thank you. That is a seriously smart bunch of people. I felt quite outclassed."

"Shut up, you're the smartest person I know!"

There's a silence.

"Oi! I know smart people!" I tell him. "My mum teaches – taught – at a university. Creative writing, but still..." I add, lowering my voice so she can't hear me.

"I didn't mean that. I mean, I wasn't thinking anything, I was just eating a biscuit," he says but I don't believe him. I don't hear crunching.

"Anyway..."

Moving on, because I don't want to argue and it really annoys me that he thinks my friends are thick. OK, Hannah's grades aren't great but she is still in the running to be an Olympic swimmer, so he can stick that in his PowerPoint presentation. And I don't know about Dermot's grades but I think he's pretty smart.

"Tell me about the team, the guys, the clever duuudes. What are their names?" I ask, trying to hide the fact I feel a bit nettled.

"Lisa, Lara and Hazel."

All girls. All girl names there, I say. Luckily just in my head not out loud. Because there's no way that wouldn't sound petty.

"They're so smart."

"Good for them!" I say brightly. Remembering that I thought Harvard was a type of bread.

"Hazel's dad has a plaque dedicated to him at Cambridge."

"Wow-wee!" I say. I consider a joke about how MY dad has plaque on his teeth. But it sounds snarky, so I keep it to myself.

"Funnily enough," he bores on. "D'you know, Hazel was one of the first people to see our YouTube video and she sent it to all her friends. She was instrumental to our success."

"Yes! Arguably!" I say.

And arguably not! Cos, you know, *I* did a few things. Like:

* ✱ Choreographed it
* ✱ Trained you all, despite a lot of bad attitude
* ✱ Filmed it WITH CONCUSSION FROM ACCIDENTALLY HEADBUTTING A FISH TANK
* ✱ Put it on YouTube

Hazel:

* ✱ Viewed it
* ✱ Mentioned it to a couple of people
* ✱ Think that's it...
* ✱ Nope, nothing else

I look up and Mum is watching me. She can't hear what I'm saying but I can feel my cheeks have gone a bit hot and red. I scratch my chin, which itches in a lurking-spot sort of way. I feel irritable at Gabe and want to end the call but I don't want to hang up angry at him, I want to go back to when he said "Lou P. Brown" and my stomach went funny with fondness.

I take a breath and steer him onto less annoying ground. "What are you up to today?"

"I've got *loads* of schoolwork," he says, sounding like Hannah. Everyone's in a competition to be busy these days. "I have to do a big presentation tomorrow on *A Tale of Two Cities*."

"Pick small cities and it's less work," I suggest helpfully.

"*A Tale of Two Cities* is a novel by Charles Dickens," he says.

"Oh, yes, yes," I say airily. "Great novel. Very … um … geographical."

I give a weary chuckle, like, *Charlie D, what is he like?*

"But that's OK. You're clever!" I realize he's not feeling too sure about his cleverness right now. "I mean, not as smart as Lisa, Lara and Whatsit," I tease.

"Hazel."

"Right, right…"

"No. They were studying last term while I was floating in a fish tank."

I feel stung. It sounds like he's calling Lou Brown and the Aquarium Boys a waste of time. When it was the best thing that ever happened to me.

"OK," I say, in a small voice. "I'll leave you to it."

"Thanks!" He sounds genuinely grateful that I'm getting off the phone. Charming.

We hang up. I google *A Tale of Two Cities*.

Argh. "Geographical." Whoops!

I go back to wrapping. Now it's ten ugly egg cups. I wrap them so tightly I form a long, dense package you could use as a weapon. Which is what I feel like doing.

Dad clatters through the front door, full of gossip.

"Guess what!" he shouts from the hallway. "Vinnie had already seen your photo in *Stylie*, a girl at work recognized Lavender and showed him. And Nicky gets *Stylie* anyway so she'd seen it too! I told them you were pulling out of the competition. Still – bit exciting!"

I glance at Lavender, who's pulled out her headphones and looks uncomfortable. Dad hurries through the kitchen and out the back door, carrying a big bag. Seconds later he returns without the bag, still chattering away excitedly. "They've pinned your photo on the fridge!"

Dad's smile fades when he comes into the living room and sees Lav's face. She's not shy, Lavender, but all her friends are louder and more boisterous than she is. She doesn't like to be the centre of attention, especially not on our uncle's fridge.

"But ... you're still going to pull out!" Dad adds, hastily.

"Of course," Mum says.

"I just thought it was exciting. That's all. You might have won!" he says. "I bet Ro would LOVE it. He likes a bit of fame, doesn't he? Bit of ritz and glitz. Is that a saying?" Dad's very talkative today.

"Did you have a good day?" I ask. "How's Uncle Vinnie? What's in the bag?" But he's not talkative on that subject. He just carries on chattering to Lav.

Fine, ignore me cos I'm not the interesting model daughter.

"Ignore me, love, it's not very *you*, is it, that sort of thing?" he says to Lav, who looks relieved. "Although Nicky was disappointed—" he adds, but shuts up at a look from Mum. "Fine." He gives in. "The article does say one of your Pet Peeves is being put under pressure to conform. That and jealous girls."

"My Pet *what*?"

"Peeves. In your About Me section."

"I DIDN'T WRITE IT!" she yelps.

"Oh yeah yeah. I forgot."

"Probably just someone snooping on her Facebook page," I say spitefully, to bring him back down to earth.

"Who would do that?" Finally he gives me his attention. I make full use of it.

"Perverts and criminals."

The smile falls off his face. "Right, that's it. I'm calling *Stylie* on Monday and getting you out of this thing so fast it'll make your head spin!"

I text Hannah later to see if she fancies meeting up. I even offer to go to her house. (Which I usually try to avoid cos her parents are SO patronizing now I've flunked out of swimming. Whenever I tell them what else I'm up to, they say, "Good for you!" with their heads sympathetically on one side.) But Hannah says she's got behind on schoolwork and has to spend all weekend catching up.

So I stay home with my family, watching TV. Or trying to. Everything I want to watch, Mum and Dad say they've seen recently. I think I know how they're spending their days while we're at school.

13

WORRY DIARY

* Hazel and that lot.
* Charles Dickens. Charlie D. Must read more.
* Does Lav have a horrible creepy stalker?
* Hannah missing, believed dead. Well, not dead, but friends with "Cams, Mell and Nic". Which is worse.
* Mum and Dad. Constant worry.

I hesitate, pen hovering over the page. Maybe I'm being mean to Hannah. I'm allowed Gabe, so of course she's allowed to make new friends and have a hobby without me. HORRIBLE friends and a POINTLESS STUPID hobby but I don't want to be bitchy. I doodle a little flower over Hannah's name to soften my complaint.

"Lou!!" Mum marches out of the kitchen and shouts my name in my face.

I blink. "Hello."

"Oh, what are you doing?"

I shrug. I'm fully dressed and sitting on the stairs waiting for Dermot and Aggy because I've been up since 5 a.m. I find I can't sleep at the moment. I lie awake and imagine moving away, starting again in a new school, making new friends... And Mum and Dad still not being themselves.

I texted Hannah last night that we might have to move away.

Oh no! That sounds really sad.

That's actually what she said. She wrote that, looked at it and thought, *Yep, happy with that. Good Best Friend work. Na-night!!* Probably slept like a baby. Or a log. A baby log. A twig.

I am so tired.

I wanted something like, *Nooooo!! That's awful! I would DIE without you! Let's run away!* If she can't do that, I might as well swap her for a dog or a plant – something that will give me its undivided attention.

THEN – oh, this is the kicker – then I got a text about some band she saw (at a gig, I PRESUME) on Saturday night. (She's going to gigs without me? We've never even gone to a gig together!) Just as I was puzzling over it, she texted again.

Sorry, that was meant for someone else.

No prizes for guessing who.

Before I went to bed, I composed a couple of texts to Gabe but I knew he'd be working late into the night on his presentation – and I was too proud to pop up as his mopey girlfy, so I left it. I thought about texting Dermot, but we're not that close, and whingeing at him after ten at night felt strange. Maybe I'll *shout* it at him one day over the sound of crunching gears.

"Are you OK?" Mum says, looking concerned. She isn't wearing any make-up and her usually bouncy hair looks a bit limp, scraped back in a ponytail.

"You have a lovely chin, Mother," I tell her and gently pull her ponytail out. She smiles and fluffs up her hair and looks a bit more like herself again.

"Do you mind going to school with Aggy?" she asks, and like an idiot I shake my head.

"She's been good to me," Mum says. "I think she forced uni to give me that day's work."

"I wouldn't argue with her," I say, honestly.

"Oh, by the way, she said Dermot's going to ask you to a thing."

"What thing?"

Mum shrugs.

Great. It could be anything! With Dermot it could literally be anything. Line dancing, pottery, goat-shaving...

There's a frantic hooting from outside, the sort of rusty-sounding noise that can only come from one vehicle. We open the door to see Aggy's van crawling slowly past our house, door open with Dermot trotting alongside.

A fifteen-year-old boy in jodhpurs and a sparkly jumper is always going to look odd, but the trotting really makes it special.

"If I stop, it'll stall!" Aggy yells out of the window. "Got to jump in while it's moving. HI, FLORA!"

Mum waves back, looking a bit anxious.

"Be careful!" she says, giving me a hard kiss. "Don't go under the wheels."

"I'll try not to."

I run out, narrowly avoiding Roman's car as he pulls into the driveway. He folds his arms over his steering wheel and openly stares at my misfortune. It's so annoying to get a lift with Aggy with Ro still picking Lav up most mornings.

I ignore Ro's smirking and run alongside Dermot, who grabs me by the hand and tugs on it. I look at him.

"Are you trying to ...?"

"... fling you up there? Yes."

"I'll just jump."

I hop into the van, reach back and haul Dermot onto the seat next to me. He's so light it's like tossing a sequinned pancake.

"WOO!" Aggy seems to be enjoying this. "Go go go! Second gear."

Dermot's not in his usual position next to the gear stick so I yank the lever out of first gear and into second.

"HARDER!" Aggy and Dermot both shout at me. All right, guys, I think the term you're looking for is THANK YOU. I don't need this much drama on a couple of hours' sleep. I brace my foot on the floor and throw my full weight on the gear stick, relieved to feel it slot into place.

"I've got a new co-pilot!" Aggy grins around me at Dermot.

I roll my sleeves up.

An upside to the engine trouble is a quick dismount at the school gates. Aggy slows the van to a walking pace and Dermot and I slide off the seats and out the door, landing with a soft jump in the car park. I slam the door after us and Dermot bangs on it twice in a goodbye. We sling our rucksacks over our shoulders with a rueful look at each other.

Of course, the one time we look cool, there's no one to witness it.

I walk slowly towards school, looking around for Hannah. I'm dragging my feet as I want to see her before class, check we're OK. This may sccm clingy but I'm used to talking to Hannah near constantly now she's back in school and I don't like this distance that's cropping up between us. I'm still a bit cross about it but I'd rather fix it than fight.

Talking of clingy, Dermot is keeping slow pace with me.

"All right?"

"Just waiting for Hannah, so…"

Dermot doesn't get it. So … we stand and wait together.

"Nice jodhpurs," I say. They flare out at the thighs, which is not something I've ever seen before.

"Really?" he asks drily. "Or are you taking the mick?"

"Well –" I gesture at the empty yard around us – "I'm not an experienced bully but I think when you make fun of someone, you need an audience."

He laughs and I decide to show him my Cammie impression. It's excellent but obviously I don't dare bring it out too often.

"Yeah, great jodhpurs, Dermot," I say in her breathy, girly voice. She does this thing where her words are nice and her mouth smiles, but above it her eyes glitter with pure malice. "Did your mum find them in a dead person's house clearance?"

"Yep," he admits, cheerfully.

"Yah, and did she say, 'Darling, these will totes suit

your wicker handbag, you must have them'?"

"Nope. She said, 'Bin these, they stink.'"

That makes me laugh and I can't keep my impression up any longer.

"How about you?" Dermot drawls back.

"Me?"

"Yah, do you run through Oxfam waving your arms around and hoping for the best? Or does your mum buy your clothes at the supermarket with the vegetables?"

"With the vegetables," I say, honestly.

"It's a great look, rilly cute," he says, insincerely. "Can I take your photo? I have a Pinterest page."

"Shut up."

"It's called Street Style. But it's ironic—"

"Shut. Up."

"Because the people have no style. And I laugh at them later. And it's cruel so I love it."

I do like Dermot, he makes me laugh at unexpected moments.

He checks his watch. It's a yellow one in the shape of a flower that he pins to his jumper, like a nurse. "Maybe Hannah's ill today or at the dentist?" he suggests. "She's pretty late."

We finally give up and head towards form room, then notice that the corridors are completely empty. With a look at each other, we start running. I enjoy making fun of Cammie behind her back so much, time flies!

As we run we hear someone behind us. I glance back and see that it's Mr Peters. Obviously having punctuality problems today too.

"Excuse me!" he gasps, trying to get around us, but we speed up. "Argh!" He's really out of breath and we're running faster. "I would tell you off for being late," he pants, "but I appreciate that's hypocritical. Just let me get in the classroom first?"

"Will you tell us off for being late, though?" Dermot shoots over his shoulder.

"Of course not!"

We let him pass, and enter the classroom a nano-second behind him.

He reaches his desk, slaps his bag down and turns back to us, gasping, "What time do you call this?"

Traitor.

I edge towards the back of the classroom, breathing hard. Hannah's seat is empty – maybe she *is* ill? Dermot sits by himself at his usual desk so I join him. While Mr Peters calls out the register, I glance around the room and there's Hannah! With Cammie, Melia and Nicole. They always sit in a bank of four desks with their bags on the fourth chair so no one DARES sit with them. But now Hannah is in that seat. Hannah got a social promotion. She's their new pile of bags.

Did they have a sleepover? Giggling, secrets, sweets at 2 a.m., queasiness at 3 a.m.? I sneak a look at Hannah's hair. If it shows signs of being plaited, I'll know she's sleepover-cheated on me.

I can't cope with that betrayal, not today. While I'm staring at her hair for clues, Hannah turns her head and makes a little *Eek!* face at me. This face says:

Sorry. (Damn straight you are, Missy.)

Isn't this wild? Me, sitting with them? (Yeah, well done. So proud.)

I'm soooo busy. (Sigh.)

Don't be mad at me, OK? (Hmm… We'll see.)

The honest little voice at the back of my head says, *Maybe she got tired of taking second place to Gabe and decided she wanted more than the spare time you give her when you aren't seeing him?*

Shut up, little voice.

I'm lost in a fug of gloom, but out of the corner of my eye I spot Dermot staring across the room. I follow his gaze and see Karl and his mate Ash looking at a magazine and laughing silently. I recognize that cover and my stomach gives a squeeze. Karl and Ash look over at me, smirking.

"Karl? Bring that here, please?" Mr Peters' voice is calm and quiet but it's his dangerous voice. That's the sign that detentions are about to be flung about like confetti. Karl shoves his chair back, wearily, and slouches up to Mr Peters like this is all SUCH an effort.

As I feared, Mr Peters looks at the magazine and then straight at me. I dip my eyes down and at the desk. Interesting desk, very woody, some gum residue. Is that a rude word scratched into it? Of course it is.

I know they're looking at Lavender's photo and I bet Karl has drawn a penis somewhere on her face. Are there loads of this *Stylie* magazine going around school? The thought makes me want to punch someone, ideally Karl. I glance up and meet Mr Peters' eye. He looks embarrassed. I bet I'm right about the penis. He puts the magazine in the bin, then on second thoughts, pulls it out and sticks it in his bag so no one can grab it at the end of class.

As Mr Peters sends Karl back to his desk and continues with the register, Dermot whispers to me, "Want to come to a performance class thing with me?"

"Yeah, sure," I whisper back, paying zero attention to the question cos I'm so distracted wondering how many *Stylie* magazines are circulating around school.

"Cool!" Dermot gives me a little thumbs-up. "It's on Saturday morning. You can come to mine and Aggy can drive us there?"

I can hear Dermot is thrilled, and this worries me a bit. Because I just know we'll have very different ideas of what's thrilling.

"Sorry," I hiss under my breath, "what's this class?"

"Performance!" Dermot does a quick jazz-hands at me and I am now very concerned. At that moment, the bell goes and everyone jumps to their feet.

"The bell is for me not for— Oh, never mind." Mr Peters gives up.

As always, the class stampedes out into the corridor as if we've been held captive for years. I look for Hannah through the crowd but Melia's already pulling her away from me, saying, "Han, come on! If we run, we can get there before maths!" Before I can say, "Hannah, remember me? BFF here – not feeling that second F right now," she's been whisked away and I lose her.

I head to maths and suddenly see Lav, head down, making her way towards the exit. Where's she going? I turn back to Dermot. "Derm, can you ... make some excuse for me? I might be late."

"Shall I save you a seat?"

"Yeah, all right. Please!" I try not to notice how happy that makes him.

I chase Lavender. She's marching at top speed past people giving her looks. One guy is even pointing her out to his friends as if she's famous. I have a nasty feeling that this term is not going to be good for Lav.

I don't want to shout and call more attention to her, but I can't quite catch up. I lunge forward a couple of times, ploughing through the mass of bodies filling the school corridor, and finally grab her by her jumper. Lav turns around with such a hostile look on her face, I think she's about to slap me. But her face softens when she sees it's me and, without a word, she pulls me by my hoodie into a nearby staff toilet.

"Lav!" I squeak. "We're not allowed in here!"

"No one ever uses it," she says, covering her nose with her jumper sleeve.

"Why n—? Oh." I gag and cover my nose too.

She shrugs. "Drains."

"Are you OK, Lav? Are people being…?"

"Complete dicks? Yes, they are. There are SO many copies of that *Stylie* magazine going around school."

"Your friends will make sure no one dares—"

"My friends are loving the attention and manhandling me down the corridor. Earlier, Jess kept shouting, 'Don't be jelly cos she fay-fay.'"

"She did NOT."

"She did. She literally did that."

We stand in silence in the smell, appreciating the basic stupidity of her friends. I try a new approach.

"Well, don't worry, Dad's calling that magazine and they'll pull you out of the competition today."

She shakes her head and shows me her phone. A text conversation between her and Dad. I'm surprised to see how many emojis they use – Dad and I just text variations on Can I have a lift? and I'M HERE. WHERE ARE YOU?

"Dad rang them. And they asked if he knew how much the prize money was."

I open my eyes wide and raise my wonky eyebrows in a question.

"First prize is twenty-five thousand pounds," Lav says.

I catch sight of myself in the mirror. My eyebrows climb a little higher.

"Yeah," she says. "Exactly."

"So you're staying in the competition?" I ask. "Even though people are drawing penises on yo—"

"People are drawing *what*?"

"What? Nothing. Nowhere."

Lavender sighs and pinches the bridge of her nose. I try to cheer her up. "Hey, Lav, maybe lots of people are really pleased for you?"

"Yerthink?"

I can't maintain the lie. "Yeah, but ... no, they probably aren't."

"I've already been called vain, insecure and unfeminist for entering a modelling competition."

"You didn't enter!" I point out. "And hey, maybe some of them are being narky because they DID?"

"I didn't even think about that," she says, and it's nice to see her smile. "I just need to try and style it out.

Because if I won ... can you *imagine*?"

"It would be amazing! Mum and Dad would be so happy."

"Relieved, too."

"Yeah."

"Are you worried about them?"

"Yeah. Mum more than Dad?"

"Uh-huh."

The mood in the toilet sinks again so I say, "But twenty-five thousand pounds, Lav! Twenty. Five. Thousand!" and we do a little excited dance in the stinky fug. Then we can't take any more of the smell and bolt back out into the corridor. Lav douses me in body spray, then we have a quick hug and run off to our classes.

14

I rush to maths, thinking up a brilliant excuse involving a fox tangled in a discarded multi-pack Coke can plastic thing and me having to rescue it. I think the more elaborate the lie, the more truthful it sounds – though I have been proved wrong on occasion.

Anyway, I never get to use it, because when I poke my head apologetically around the door of the maths classroom, braced for a telling-off from Mr Uppan, I get a much more unnerving response. As soon as he sees me, he looks sympathetic. I have NEVER seen Mr Uppan look sympathetic. Annoyed, yes; disappointed; exasperated – but never sympathetic. It's eerie, like if a pencil started singing.

"OK, Louise?" he says, quietly. But not quietly enough. Heads are popping up around the room and people are starting to snigger. I've been an object of public ridicule a few times in my young life and I know the signs. Mr Uppan points me to my seat in an almost caring way and I stare VERY HARD at Dermot, who's absorbed in his algebra but blushing red to the hairline.

I sit down next to him. He doesn't look up, so I pinch his arm.

"I'm sorry." He shakes his head. "I'm not a natural liar."

"*Lou's bag broke. Lou had to speak to the head. Lou had a call from home. Lou needed to nip to the medical centre* – bit dramatic but OK. Any of these excuses would've been fine."

"I panicked! Mr Uppan asked if anyone knew where you were and everyone stared at me and usually I don't mind embarrassing myself but I was worried about embarrassing *you* and I thought if it had a grain of truth that might make the lie better and you *did* go off with your sister so I was trying to say that but kind of in a vague way..."

"What. Did. You. Say. Derm. Ot?" I hiss, quietly but forcefully.

He wipes spit off his ear. "I said you had a girl emergency. But I didn't mean it ... the way everyone took it."

I sneak a look around the classroom. About half of the class are whispering to each other and fighting giggles.

Cool. Just glad to be bringing joy, guys.

★　　★　　★

I spend the rest of maths focusing on the twenty-five thousand lovely pounds that would remove the dark circles from under my parents' eyes. It's a pleasant daydream and doesn't leave much headspace for maths – soz, Mr Uppan. When he sees my blank workbook, he looks less sympathetic and more irritable. That's the face I'm used to.

As soon as maths is over, Hannah dashes over, looking concerned. "Lou, are you OK?"

"Yes, I'm fine," I say in super dignified tones while Dermot pretends to be very interested in packing his wicker basket. "I was just talking to Lav."

"Oh, I thought—"

"No, just talking to Lav."

"Is something up with her?" Hannah looks concerned and I swear, I am just about to tell her, but then Nicole appears and there's no way I'm telling my sister's private business in front of that gossipmonger.

"Yeah," I say. "Yep. All good."

I take it back, Dermot. Neither of us think well on our feet.

There's an awkward silence, only broken by squeaky wicker noises as Dermot continues to pack his school bag.

Hannah looks hurt. "Sorry, wasn't being nosy. I was just worried."

"Yeah! Of course! Definitely. I know," I say and she looks expectant. But now Cammie and Melia are clustering behind her, bags on their backs, waiting for their precious Prom Committee to be a four again.

"All right. I'll see you later, maybe," Hannah says in a small voice.

"Lunch?" I say.

"I have to do …"

"Prom Committee stuff," I chorus with her and she looks wary as if I'm making fun of her – and I am a bit. I feel bad, so I say, "Hey, can I do anything to help?"

Three lessons later and it's lunchtime. Hannah's raced off to the art department to have a conversation about budget. I'm tempted to ask how much the prom is costing per student and could I just have my cash if I promise not to come? I bet what they're spending on one party would sort my family out for a month.

Feeling very sorry for myself, I'm waddling down the empty corridor, buckling under the weight of Hannah's bag, my bag AND Melia's bag. Cos when I said "Can I do anything to help?" they took me literally.

I stop for a moment and lean against the radiator, which is roasting hot and doesn't help. There's a little nudge on my back.

"Sorry," says Dermot. I turn around and he's bent

almost double under Cammie's bag, Nicole's bag and his own.

"You're forgiven for *girl emergency*," I tell him, most graciously.

"I'd better be," he grouches, dabbing his sweaty face with a silky handkerchief.

We stay there for a while, panting.

"Glad I wore sports casualwear today," he says, peeling himself off the wall to continue our trek to the canteen.

"Is that what those are?"

"Yes."

"Sports casualwear," I echo, doubtfully.

"Well, not in this century. But they were in the last one."

As we approach the big white swing doors that lead into the canteen, we can hear strange noises coming from the other side. We hang back. These doors should always be approached carefully, as some of the older boys find it funny to barge into them, sending unwary Year 7s flying on the other side.

They call it flicking. School calls it Anti-Social Behaviour.

But this sounds like something more sinister. I can hear cheering from a large group of kids, and not happy cheering, more aggressive. I swear I hear someone yelp

"Get him!". There's a crash, like a table going over. I look at Dermot, who hoists up the bags to get a firmer grip and tenses his legs, poised to run away if anyone comes charging through those doors.

I hear a scream and I jump. I know that voice.

"That's my sister!" I gasp at Dermot.

Dermot and I push against the swing doors, but they don't move – there must be people leaning against them. So we dump the bags, tripping over the straps, and stumble outside towards the other entrance. There are big windows in the canteen so I can see the mayhem inside as we get closer.

A table has been turned over. There's food everywhere. A large crowd is trying to look like it wasn't cheering on a fight, five seconds ago. I can see Karl from our class sitting on the floor, dazed and covered in food. Dermot nudges me and points out Lavender at the front of the crowd.

I see Mr Peters, his cardigan half off, glasses askew, holding Roman back. He begins ordering everyone out of the canteen, and the dinner ladies are emerging from the kitchen looking grim at all the cleaning up to be done. Even from a distance, Karl doesn't look OK. He was never the brightest penny in the jar as Dead Grandma would say, but right now he looks like he'd struggle to find his bum with both hands.

Mr Peters tells Lavender to go and she does, with some reluctant backwards looks. Dermot and I rush back to the corridor to intercept her.

Lav sees me, gives the tiniest shake of her head and hurries away. "Lav!" I shout after her but I know she's not going to look back.

"Bloody hell," says Dermot.

"Yeah," I say. "She's my sister. I just wanted to know—"

"No," says Dermot and pivots me by the shoulder, pointing at the floor.

Everyone went streaming through this corridor a minute ago and we had left all the rucksacks on the floor. They're lying tattered and crushed, their contents strewn all over the place. They look like bloodless roadkill.

Well, bloodless until we tell Cammie.

15

"Of course we didn't do it on purpose!" I hiss. "Look, mine is ruined too. Dermot's bag is ..."

"... cat litter," he says, examining a handful of crumbled wicker.

"I don't care," Cammie whispers back, icy calm. "Mine actually cost MONEY, can you imagine? Mine wasn't some nasty little budget supermarket tat, mine was designer."

"So was mine," adds Melia.

"And mine," says Nicole.

Hannah stays silent. THANKS, PAL. Feel free to jump in here at any point.

"So you have to buy us new bags," Cammie says, like that's sorted.

Melia and Nicole nod.

"Mine was from Miami? I got it on holiday? So you'll

need to look online for it," adds Nicole.

Finally, Hannah finds her voice. "Guys. Lou can't afford that."

"Fine, her parents can pay."

"No, her parents can't afford it either. They're—"

"Thank you, Hannah," I say, my voice as cold as Cammie's.

"I'm trying to say," Hannah hisses, exasperated, "that we shouldn't have made you carry all our stuff. I'll pay for the new bags."

Instantly, the mood changes.

"Honeeey…" says Melia, scandalized. "Don't do that!"

"We couldn't let you do that," says Nicole.

Cammie is shaking her head graciously, like how could Han possibly think they'd be so demanding?

They all turn inwards on their table of four. I can't even see Hannah now so I turn back to my little table of two with Dermot, feeling dismissed and covered in spit from all the hissing. He shrugs at me and we get on with our work. I do actually get a lot done when I sit with Dermot – he concentrates and listens, so I do too. I guess he got into good habits because he never had friends to distract him. That sounds mean; I don't mean it meanly.

Talking of mean, I sneakily texted Lav at the beginning of class to see what was going on and she's finally got back to me. Apparently, Karl was waving around a copy of *Stylie* magazine and he'd scribbled all over her face. I don't bother asking *what* he scribbled. I've known him a long time and he's never been an enigmatic soul, full of hidden depths and corners.

Roman told him to stop. He wouldn't. Then Ro threw himself across the table at him, and they had a fight. Not a fight like in a film but lots of pushing and grabbing at each other's jumpers.

I sympathize. I wouldn't know how to fight either.

But now Ro's in the Head's office – sispnsiion??

She must be texting sneakily under her desk too. I assume this means *suspension*. I send her a string of dismayed emojis, culminating in a line of poos. I really need a non-smiling poo emoji for moments like this. This guy looks far too breezy for this kind of situation.

Dermot kicks me under the table. I look up and stare at the interactive whiteboard, furrowing my brow in deep concentration.

"Lou, any ideas?" the teacher calls over to me.

"Acceleration!"

"No." Ms Peel looks weary.

"Energy?" I guess again. "*Iiiis* it a type of energy?"

Ms Peel is quite severe. She only wears black dresses, and they're cut so rigidly they could probably stand up by themselves.

"Louise, it's always a type of energy."

"I *see*. Hmm. So arguably, we could say I'm not wrong?"

There's an unfamiliar noise – Dermot is laughing. This sets a few other people off too. To my surprise, Ms Peel finally cracks a grin and says, "Half a point for being broadly correct."

I guess if I was a teacher I'd have a soft spot for weird Dermot too. I feel bad for always breathing through my mouth when I'm around him. I take a deep inhalation through my nose and instantly feel like a better human being.

"Lou?"

Ms Peel is staring at me as I take in lungfuls of Dermot.

"Um. Itchy nose, Ms Peel. Scratching it with air."

My phone vibrates with another text from Lav. I risk the wrath of Ms Peel and peek at it again.

Ro's loving it. Pretending he's not.

Fighting over his model girlfriend.

Right. Leather jacket and motorbike next.

She adds an unimpressed face. I send one back. How come Roman is cool for having a girlfriend in a modelling compctition but Lav is a trashy show-off for *being* the girl in the competition?

If Mum was here, she'd shout, "The Patriarchy!"

Well, old Mum would. New sad Mum might mumble it through a mouthful of biscuits with her eyes fixed on the TV.

I feel a sharp poke in my back where Melia has jabbed me with a long fingernail. I turn around warily to see all four of them looking at me. They're wearing friendlier expressions than they were half an hour ago.

(Hate that I now think of them as a four.)

"I just heard about Roman and your sister," whispers Melia.

"What happened?" Cammie demands.

I take great pleasure in giving them a wide-eyed shrug. I savour the annoyed looks on their faces and return to Dermot, who, after some whispered discussion, is letting me copy his answers. We agree that I am learning *as* I'm copying. It's all good.

I don't hear from Gabe all afternoon. I thought I would after our terse phone call last night but I guess he's distracted with his presentation. I decide to send him a mature, sensible text. Nothing gossipy about his brother's lunchtime antics, just Good luck with the cities! and then lots and lots of flags, peppered with sensible vegetables and civic buildings. I am so adult. I am MADE of adult.

As I'm heading to my final lesson of the day, my phone starts to vibrate, a long buzz that announces a phone call. I sneakily check it. Gabe! Happy-happy-joy-joy fireworks! I duck into a toilet to take a hushed phone call. I am breaking mobile phone rules quite heavily today.

"Hey!" I say. "What are you—?"

"Lou, what are you playing at?"

"I … sorry, what now?"

"I told you I was giving a big presentation today. I TOLD you."

"Yes!" I say defensively. "Dickens. Two cities. I *listen*."

"I gave it on my laptop."

"Y'and?"

"And you iMessaged me a HUNDRED vegetables!"

"And civic buildings."

"What?"

"Nothing."

"IMessages go to my laptop! Why are you sending me a corn on the cob? I've been working on this for days and a corn on the cob pops up right in the middle of the French Revolution!"

"I'm sorry. Did it look like a French baguette?"

"No, it did not look like a French baguette. Me and Hazel worked really hard on this and—"

"Why was Hazel working on it?"

"She was being helpful. Unlike you."

Hot sicky jealousy heaves inside me. *Me and Hazel, me and Hazel.* I GET IT. She's sooooo clever. And he's sooooo annoyed at me.

I take a deep breath and try to do the right thing. Which is not to yell "WHAT DOES SHE LOOK LIKE? PLEASE TELL ME SHE'S GOT A FACE LIKE AN OLD POTATO!"

"I'm sorry," I say.

He's not ready to let it go. "I'm tired, I worked really hard."

A REALLY OLD POTATO THAT YOU FORGOT ABOUT AT THE BACK OF THE CUPBOARD, COVERED IN ROOTS THAT LOOK LIKE TINY FINGERS?

"Did it go well, though – vegetables notwithstanding?"

I'm proud of *notwithstanding*. I picked it up off his mum.

But it doesn't help. He makes a non-committal noise and says he has to go.

I duck back into the corridor, feeling small. I don't think I'll tell Hannah about this. I suspect she'd be happy to hear that Gabe and I are fighting. Dermot is waiting for me and I head into English with him, sniffing hard and determined not to cry. If he notices, he doesn't say anything. We struggle into the classroom with our broken bags; books and pens keep falling through the rips and holes. I'm pretty sure I hear a tampon drop out but I don't look back. We're a dishevelled mess.

Finally, it's the end of school and I can't wait to get out. I don't want to bump into Gabe, I'm scared Cammie's mum will see her ruined bag and demand I pay for it and I'm sick of people asking me about Ro. So I stride out of school at top speed to skulk at the end of the car park.

"Wait!" Dermot is panting behind me. "Lou, these trousers don't really bend." I look behind and he is running stiff-legged like a gingerbread man. I slow down a little so he can catch up.

"I thought they were sports casualwear."

"Like I said, *last* century."

Lav appears behind him. "Can I catch a lift? Ro got sent home after lunch, and it's too wet to walk."

But Aggy's not here yet, so we're stuck waiting in the rain. Dermot's bag and mine are threatening to fall apart completely and I stuff my books up my jumper to protect them. Dermot phones his mum to "encourage" her to hurry up.

I take advantage of this to check in with my sister. "Hey," I say. "You all right?"

She shrugs. It's like, *No, but I don't want to talk about it*.

"It'll be all right, though, won't it?"

Another shrug.

I decide to be extremely annoying and goad her into some honesty. "It could be worse," I tell her. "I read about a woman in Kent? Who bought a micropig? But it wasn't a micropig, it was just a pig, only she didn't realize that for ages because of course it was small when it was young but it just kept growing and now she can't rehome it because she loves it and pigs are as intelligent as toddlers, and her house is ruined now. So, there's that..."

"Louise. I will shove you in that bush."

Charming!

With a loud clanking noise, Aggy approaches – well, her van. (If she was clanking like that, I'd be worried.)

She drives around the car park in very slow circles so I guess she still can't stop. We walk alongside, open the door and slide in. Dermot and I have mastered the knack of this now. Lavender's new to it and needs hauling onto the seat, arms and legs everywhere.

"I'm sorry," Dermot says, a little pink in the face. "I think I grabbed your thigh."

"Don't stress," she tells him. "It's not the worst thing that's happened to me today."

16

WORRY DIARY

* Gabe hates me and my corn on the cob emojis.
* I can't afford to replace three designer school bags.
* Hang on, I can't even replace mine.
* Is Lavender a social outcast?
* Is Roman a thug or just a drama queen?

The house smells cold and musty when we get in. If Mum and Dad get any more stingy with the heating, we're all going to smell like Dermot.

"Lavender, can we talk to you?" Mum calls from the living room and Lav makes an *Eek!* face at me. I take advantage of this to hurry my broken school bag upstairs and hide it.

I nip back downstairs to make everyone a delicious glass of water to be totes helpful/nosy. We're all out of bananas, so I put a cucumber slice in each glass. Classic recipe.

The glasses tinkle against each other on the tray as I head carefully into the living room.

Mum is saying, "We're not blaming you but Janet is very concerned..." She breaks off and waits for me to leave.

"Don't mind me," I chat mildly. "Carry on. Just bringing you all some water for this ... telling-off? If that's what's going on here."

Mum and Dad stare at me silently.

"Fine, I'll leave you to it. Drink your cucumber before it goes soft."

It would be so unreasonable if Roman's mum blamed Lav for disrupting Roman's schoolwork when I'd bet the Teapot of Money she never asked him to fight Karl. This is classic melodramatic Roman. I want to text Gabe and defend Lav, but I don't feel we're on the friendliest of footings yet. In fact, what if even now Gabriel is complaining about me to his new friends?

I don't want to think about that, so I decide to start my homework. I'm sitting in my bedroom, wearing three jumpers, with a sleeping bag swathed around my lower half. I never realized how draughty this house was until heating and hot water became luxuries.

Usually Hannah and I chat away on iMessage while we're doing our homework, but she's been quiet the last week or so, caught up in prom stuff. I miss her. I write a message and look at it. It's a bit manipulative. It might as well say BE NICE TO ME, I AM SAD.

But I press send anyway.

Hey Han, do you have those anxiety
exercises that Hari gave you?

She pings back immediately. Ah, see! I know it's not cool to be manipulative but it works.

Poor you! Are you stressed about stuff?

Yeah, Mum and Dad, etc.

And Lav?

I consider telling her about Lav.

Are you alone?

I'm at Nicole's.

I see.

Just for a bit.

I'll tell you later.

She doesn't reply but she does send over the Word doc of breathing exercises. So, she's annoyed but still cares.

XXX, I sign off, just as Dad is yelling up the stairs that it's time for dinner.

Dinner is the same as yesterday's as Mum and Dad have started cooking huge cheap meals and making them last a few days. Yesterday it was called Bean Surprise. It was a bean casserole and apparently the surprise was that there was no surprise. Mum said it was meta, and I spent the meal googling what that meant, trying to ignore her lecture about my data allowance. Tonight there's cheese melted on top and it's called Beany McBeanface. Lav and I make noises of approval mixed with ones of surprise. "Is this bean-shaped thing a BEAN? And ... onions? Oh my word, the surprises keep on coming!"

"So, Dad," I say, chasing a butterbean around my plate, "are you going to start that job for Vinnie soon?"

Dad looks shifty. "Um, yeah, well, it's complicated. I might be working Saturday."

"Might?" Mum asks.

"Yeah, it's a bit messy. The guy currently doing the job has a bit of a drink problem. Sometimes he shows up, sometimes he doesn't. No one wants to say anything to him, but if he doesn't turn up on Saturday, I'll step in."

"And, what? If he does show up you've just wasted a day?" Mum asks, sharply, and Dad shrugs.

"Charming," she tuts. "I'll have a word with Vinnie about this. Just because you're out of work doesn't mean your time isn't worth as much as anyone else's."

"Well, it kind of isn't," Dad says.

"How do you reckon?"

"Because today we spent six hours watching TV and eating bread."

"Mum!" She's always so *get off the sofa, you're missing the best part of the day.* What a hypocrite.

"Shut up and eat your Bean Surprise."

"Beany McBeanface," we all correct her.

"It's not fun doing nothing all day," Dad says.

"I wouldn't mind finding out," Lav retorts.

"I think Lav should have a day off school, until people stop being horrible to her," I say, being lovely and thoughtful.

"What?" Dad and Mum look surprised. "Who's being horrible to her?" Behind them Lav is shaking her head, looking daggers at me.

"I. Um." I look from Mum to Dad to Lav and I'm not sure what to say. "Girl Emergency!" I fork the last bean into my mouth and scoot upstairs.

Ten minutes later, there's a knock at my door.

"Enter!"

Lavender comes in, shaking her head at me.

"May I just say," I pre-empt her, "that if you TOLD me what was going on, then I wouldn't say the wrong thing over beans. So it's your fault. But also, sorry."

Lav sits on the end of my bed and wraps her feet in my duvet. "I'm freezing. OK, so Mum and Dad don't know that people are being bitchy over the modelling competition. Because if they did, they'd tell me to just pull out, and then..."

"No twenty-five thousand pounds."

"Right. So they think Roman is fighting over me in more of a vague romantic way."

"Which is why Janet is annoyed."

"Yeah. Because it sounds like I'm flirting with Karl and causing unnecessary drama and she wants her boys to be super successful and the stupid Brown sisters seem to do nothing but drag them into trouble."

I hadn't thought about it that way before. Gabe's mum's always been really nice to me, but then I guess that since I've been around he has been in hospital twice and a police station once and had a couple of ME relapses. I pick the skin on my lips.

"Does she think we're stupid?"

Lav isn't the queen of tact. "We're not geniuses."

"Is it geniuses? Or genii?"

"I don't know. This kinda proves my point."

I slump over my desk and she goes to leave. "Oh, Lav?"

"Yeah?"

"Can I borrow a dress or something for prom?"

"We sold them all on eBay. You wrapped them."

Ugh, brilliant. I'll have to beg something off Hannah. At least Lav has style. Hannah's as bad as me.

My phone vibrates and I grab it. I'll take any distraction right now. Hannah.

Are you in?

Uh ... yes.

Cool!

A minute later there's a knock at our front door and I get there first. It's Hannah, holding a fancy Herschel school bag. I've never had one, but I've always liked the look of them. On richer kids' backs, of course.

"Hey!" I say and give her a hug. "Oof – you're cold."

"I just thought I'd drop this round –" she holds out the bag – "cos yours is broken."

"Han, that's so nice of you!"

"It's nothing." She shrugs. "Just an old one I had lying around."

"It's still got the price tag on." I show her and she quickly rips it off, embarrassed.

"Hi, Hannah!" Dad calls, poking his head out of the living room.

"Hi, Mark." She gives him a little wave. "You look well."

"I'm drinking green tea," he tells her. "Is it a diuretic?"

"I … don't know."

"Well, either that or I'm not well. I'm spending a lot of time on the toilet and it's really slimming me out."

"That's nice!" she lies.

"Listen, Hannah. I had a bit of time on my hands – I'm between jobs at the mo," Dad says, holding up a rolled-up tube of paper. "I was just messing about and I made a project timeline for the prom. You might find it helpful." He shimmies off the elastic band.

"Dad, have you laminated it?" I ask.

"It's not a big deal. We were always laminating things at work. So, what I've done is take you through your workflow week by week. How big is your team?"

"Four, but—"

"Uh-huh." He's unrolling his poster – it's gigantic. "That'll work."

"Mark? It's really meant to be a thing by students…" Hannah's tone is firm.

Dad stops unrolling his laminated plan and starts rolling it back up, all in one swift movement. "Yeah, yeah, of *course*."

"It's just by students *for* students, so, you know…" Hannah is trying to be nice but he's clearly hurt.

"No, no, no," he says brightly. He snaps the elastic band back on and holds the tube up like a baseball bat.

"Thank you, though," she says.

"Cool, cool, that's cool," Dad says and swings his little tube towards an imaginary baseball, giving a little *pop!* when it makes contact.

We stare at him.

"OK then." He nips back into the living room, shutting the door behind him.

"Is he OK?" Hannah says quietly.

I gesture at where he was standing – *clearly not*.

There's a toot at the end of the drive from a car I don't recognize.

"Want to come say hi to Mum?" she says.

"Yeah!" I say, faking enthusiasm I don't feel. I grab a coat and follow her out.

"Hello, Barbra!" I say, leaning down to the driver's window. "New car?"

"It's not *new* new," says Barbra. "Six months old. I mean, very good value," she adds hastily. "I hate to be flashy when other people are, ah – struggling financially."

Next to me, I see Hannah giving her a look.

"It's very nice," I say politely.

"Of course, with BMWs you pay a lot up front but they're no trouble further down the line. I know some people buy them as a status symbol, but not me. I think it's just a good investment of five figures— Ow! Hannah!"

"Sorry," says Hannah, who seems to have accidentally slapped her mum's hand. "There was a fly."

"Anyway, how are your parents?" Barbra asks, in sympathetic tones.

"Um," I say, trying desperately to think of something better than, *I'm worried about them. They seem really sad and watch TV all day. We have no money and I think my uncle is dragging my dad into a life of part-time crime.* "OK-ish, you know?"

"Good for them," she says, with her head on one side.

I've run out of things to say. I get that a lot with Barbra.

"Anyway, we'd best be off," Barbra goes on. "Got to pick up a takeaway. I mean –" she catches herself – "we don't *usually* get takeaway midweek! Just so busy at work right now..." She remembers something. "You should come round when it gets warmer. Try out the new pool!"

"Mother," Hannah says, firmly, getting in the car.

"We got it because Hannah is still training all the time. I bet you're glad to be out of that!" Barbra laughs.

"Mother."

"I was just saying, Hannah! Or Louise will think we're profligate."

I won't think they're profligate. I have no idea what the word means. It sounds medical.

"Right, right, yes, bye!" Barbra says, as Hannah waves goodbye to me. And they drive off.

I go back in to find Dad sitting at the kitchen table, reading some Jobcentre forms. The laminated plan is nowhere to be seen. I give him a little kiss on his bald spot and go upstairs to admire my new bag.

17

Text from Dad.

> When you get in, please can you fondle the laundry?

> Sure, I can give it a quick kiss and cuddle.

> FOLD, I meant.

Woohoo, it's Friday night! Am I off to a gig, a club, a friend's house to watch zombie films? No ... you over-estimate La Brown, I am doing my English coursework at home in my room.

Although, massive plus side, my lovely boyfriend is helping me. I apologized for the vegetables and buildings in Gabe's PowerPoint, he apologized for his snotty tone (*TOO RIGHT*, I thought but didn't say) and now we're going through the finer points of metaphor and allegory. He seems more relaxed than he has done in ages – though he still looks too thin, with dark sleep-circles under his eyes.

Gabe and I are lying on my bed. We're allowed to sit on it if we keep the door open, and we began the evening that way but have honestly just slid down a bit. Lav and Roman aren't allowed to be on their own in her room AT ALL, ha ha. Lavender was furious, said it wasn't fair. But as Mum pointed out, if they're all over each other like cheese on pizza in public, what on EARTH would they do with privacy? Whereas Gabe and I don't even really hold hands when we're out. It's not our way.

It's lovely lying here with Gabe, though. So warm and cosy. I wish we were always like this, not misunderstanding each other and falling out and worrying about Hazel (OK, that's more me than him).

I tell him I understand how stressed he is, wanting to do well at school but then also risking a relapse through stress, so missing more school and feeling MORE stressed about having more to catch up on. Poor guy. I show him the calming breathing exercises that Hannah sent me, and we lie side-by-side, breathing loudly together.

Mum pops her head round the door. "What ARE you doing?"

"Breathing exercises."

"Oh. Good. It sounded... Never mind." And she goes as quickly as she came.

"I will cut down on the unicorn emojis and time the vegetable ones better," I tell Gabe, squeezing his hand. "And I'll read more."

"You don't have to do that."

"*Au contraire!* I WANT to be more mature. I have a keen, intelligent brain," I say, hoping this is true. I've not really tested the theory. "What's your next debate about?"

"The Middle East," he tells me.

"Like ... Birmingham?"

"The Middle East of the WORLD, Lou, not Britain."

"Oh, right, right," I say. "Yeah, like Iran, Iraq, Afghanistan, Blazakhstan..." I trail off, as this is all I know and I suspect Blazakhstan might not be a place.

Rain hammers down on the window and I'm so happy. I think guiltily of Dermot. I don't know why, I just imagine him in his damp-smelling house on his own. Although I said I'd go to Performance Class with him tomorrow morning, didn't I? Mustn't forget.

"How's Dermot?" says Gabe, interpreting my silence with unnerving accuracy. See? We're *made* for each other.

"He's OK. Deeply weird of course," I add, looking at Gabe with a smile but he doesn't smile back.

"Don't be mean," he says.

"I'm not! That's not fair. We're friends. I've been spending loads of time with him since the prom stole Han. Smell me." I hold out my arm. "I bet I smell of old corduroy."

"Hey," says Gabe. "He's a nice guy."

"I know. I like him. That's the sort of joke I'd make *in front* of him."

And there we go. Instantly, we switch from calm and peaceful to me feeling like he's judging me when I was only being silly.

"OK," Gabe says, doubtfully.

"Why, don't you trust me? I'm not a bully!" I say. I'm offended.

"Hey. I love you, Lou," says Gabe, "but..."

Breathe, Lou. He just told you he loves you. Your boyfriend just said he loves you. I cannot wait to tell Hannah!

"But sometimes you can be mean. You think you're being funny—"

"I AM being funny!" I say, my voice wobbling. He doesn't understand: funny is my thing. I'm not pretty, I'm not clever and now he wants to take my only skill away from me, like it's nothing?

Do not tell Hannah this bit.

My temper flares. "I'm sorry I'm not clever like your little debating team, snogging maps of the Middle East because my ... the –" I cast around wildly for an insult

– "because I'm deeply insecure and need everyone to know I'm SPESHUL."

"Hey," he says. "Now *that's* mean."

"Yes," I tell him. "I'm trying to be mean now. See the difference? This lot sound like –" so hard to insult people you've never met! – "like they're the sort of people who always have clammy hands."

Gabe bursts out laughing.

Tell Hannah this bit.

"Lou! That's nasty," he says, grabbing my ribs and tickling me.

"But you're laughing!" I say, slapping his hands off me. "So get off your high horse. Have you never seen the films? Girls do not change for boys. That is always the wrong thing they do first before they realize they're brilliant as they are."

I'm joking. But not a hundred per cent.

"I'm sorry," he says sincerely. "I know you're a kind person…"

"Thank you!" I say with dignity.

"Deep down. Really deep down. Maybe, level minus six."

I hook my legs around his and try to push him off my bed. He fights back. He's surprisingly strong and I don't manage it. He pulls himself up next to me again, holding my feet so I can't kick him.

I reckon it's THREE WHOLE MINUTES before we stop kissing. That was the best kiss I've ever had. Even if he was holding my feet the whole time.

Hannah will not want to hear that detail.

We both glance towards the open door and look guilty.

"Now," Gabe announces loudly, picking up his iPad. "Metaphors and allegory."

Dad pops his head into my bedroom, looking suspicious. "What are you doing in here?"

"Breathing exercises," I say, a little breathlessly.

Later, Roman comes to drop off Lav and pick up Gabe. I open the front door in time to see Ro leaning towards Lav for a kiss and puckering up to thin air because she's already out of the car. I feel Gabe's shoulder against mine. He saw it too. We exchange a mystified look.

"Hi, Lavender."

"Hey, Gabe."

"Bye, Lou."

"Bye," I say, giving him a fond high-five before he runs through the rain to his brother's car.

Lav heads straight upstairs, clearly in a right old mood. I decide to leave her to it. When she's cross with someone, it can spill out and splash an innocent bystander. I don't fancy that tonight. I want my happy mood to stay. I poke my head in the living room but it's empty, Mum and Dad must've gone to bed early. I don't know why they're tired, they don't do anything these days.

I go to grab a glass of water and see a gas bill lying on the kitchen counter, with red writing on. I feel bad for ever sneakily turning the heating on. I won't do that again.

I head to bed. Out the window I can see a light on in Dad's shed. The light is flickering in the little window. Why's it flickering?

Because he's dancing.

He's dancing alone in his shed, in the middle of a rainy night.

WORRY DIARY

✱ Dad (late night solo shed-dancing).

I wake up with a start. I fell asleep watching kitten videos on my phone. I wipe the dribble off it and see I have two texts. The vibrating must have woken me; the weak winter sun certainly wasn't going to.

One from Dermot, sent twenty minutes ago.

Want to come to mine before Perf Class? Or Aggy
could come get you? If you still want to come that is?

Perf? I think, groggily.

And one from Gabe, but in trying to read it, I accidentally call Dermot.

"Hey!"

"Oh hey! Sorry. I called you by mistake!"

"Shall I go?"

"No, no, no. I'll come to yours if you just give me your address. What time?"

"In, like, fifteen minutes?"

"How long will it take to get to you?"

"Um..."

"Fifteen minutes?"

I haul myself out of bed and dance around my cold bedroom, scribbling down Dermot's address.

"What shall I wear?"

"Anything!"

"Really? Not things I can stretch in or...?"

"It's not yoga!"

He sounds amused. But all I know about this class is that it *isn't* yoga. So unhelpful. Loads of things aren't yoga, like bowling or arson. I pull out the closest clothes to hand, jeans and a top with leopard-print elbow patches. I examine the top: it's suspiciously nice, too nice to be mine. It must be Lavender's. Mum's obviously put it in my room by mistake. *Technically* not my fault. I pull it on and sneak downstairs, hoping Lav doesn't catch me.

Shall I put on make-up? No, I don't have time to wipe it off when I get it wrong and give myself droopy sloth eyes. So I just bundle my coat on and I'm heading out the door when Mum appears in the doorway of the living room, still in her dressing gown. I suddenly feel bad being all, *Oooh, look at me, so busy – lots of things to do!*

On impulse I dart forward and give her a hug. She's smiling by the time I pull back.

"Where are you going?"

"Dermot's house. I'm going to this Performance Class with him. Do you know anything about it?"

"I think Aggy enrolled him in it to make some friends as he didn't have any."

"*Mother.*"

"What?"

"Poor Dermot."

"I meant … to get away from all the girls bothering him."

I shake my head and back out of the door. "Bye, *Mother.*"

"Coming straight home afterwards? Or do you need a lift?" She looks like she doesn't want me to say yes. I bet the car has, like, the barest *whisper* of petrol left in it.

"Don't worry," I say, closing the door behind me. "It'll be nice to get some –" hail hits me in the face, hard – "fresh – argh! – air."

I jog to Dermot's because I'm late and also because, honestly, if I stop I fear I'll freeze to the pavement. As I run, I realize Dad wasn't home. I don't know how I can be so sure, but he's a man of many noises, sighing when he sits down, humming when he's eating and snickering when he's reading. You know when he's home and when he isn't. He's doing "work" for Uncle Vinnie, isn't he.

After ten minutes, I slow to a walk. Then retrace my steps, turn back and walk up the road again, checking Dermot's address on my phone. This can't be it, it's a massive old house at the end of a long driveway. It looks like something out of a fairy tale.

It's probably divided into flats and he and Aggy live in a small part of it. The driveway is lined with grotesque gnomes, missing limbs and noses. Aggy definitely lives here. I crunch up to the front door. I can't see individual doorbells so I bang the huge claw door knocker and hope for the best.

There's a little scuffling behind the door and it opens very, very slowly. Dermot appears, out of breath but grinning. "Sorry, it swells in wet weather. And hot weather. In fact, it's only usable in a mild September."

"Are they your gnomes?" I ask.

"Aggy thinks they're funny and now people bring her any new ones they find. It terrifies the local kids." He gives me a quick sideways look. "Karl Ashton lives on this street."

"Oh..." I say.

"Yeah, he loves that. My mum, the crazy lady in the old house." He does spooky witch hands at me. "Let's find her, I haven't seen her in a while."

I follow him in, thinking, *How can you lose your mum in a flat?* Dermot is so odd.

And then I get it. We're standing in a gigantic hallway. At the far end, a huge staircase curves around up to the first floor. A chandelier the size of a small car hangs, dusty and browning, above us.

"This is all your house?"

"Yeah."

"All of it?"

"Except the floor. We can't touch that. But the rest is ours."

I stare at him. He stares back.

Dermot's funny. It's just an unusual brand of funny. I can see why it goes unappreciated in our school.

There are piles of boxes everywhere, draped in large white sheets. "Aggy's in here somewhere..." says Dermot. "But I lose her regularly."

"What about your dad?" I ask without thinking.

"Ah. We lost him, two years ago."

"Behind the fridge?"

"Cancer, but ... ah ... so."

"Dermot, I'm really—"

"That's all right. Come on." He leads me upstairs.

165

"I am sorry," I tell his back. Today he's dressed in a three-piece tweed suit with a cartoon T-shirt underneath. Even when we're talking about cancer, my brain notices stupid things.

"It's really OK," he says. "It was a long time coming and the last year was terrible."

"Oh!"

Aggy pops out from behind a tower of boxes and it's hard to say who's most surprised.

She clambers over the boxes to give me a dusty hug. Surprised, I hug her back.

She looks at me thoughtfully. "I've never seen you face-on, only profile," she tells me. "You have strong eyebrows."

I'm kind of thinking the same thought. Aggy's such a whirlwind of pink hair and noise in the morning, but from the front, without all the shouting, she has a lovely face. Like an apple.

"Mum." Dermot is clearly embarrassed and I decide to keep the apple thought to myself.

"Thank you!" I tell her, genuinely pleased. "I know they're big but I worry they're wonky."

"Oh yes." She examines my face. "They are, but I like that. It's different." She has price stickers all over her hand.

"Be careful none of the boxes topple over onto you,"

she says, pointing at us warningly. "You're very precious to me," she adds to Dermot, taking a £9.99 sticker off her hand and popping it on his jumper.

"Please, woman," he chastises. "Can we get a lift?"

"Yes. Five minutes. Show Louise the house?"

"She doesn't want to see a house."

"I do!" I blurt out. This is a RICH PERSON'S HOUSE. I follow Dermot up *another* big spiral staircase.

"Mind those steps." Dermot grabs my arm. "They might be rotten."

"This place is like a castle," I marvel, touching an embroidery hanging on the wall.

"A rotting castle. My parents always meant to do it up, but..."

"It's cool as it is," I say. "It has character."

I walk into a huge cobweb and stifle a scream.

We reach the first floor and go into a huge room with yellowing stripy wallpaper and windows looking front and back. There's a suit of armour leaning heavily to the left with a leg missing, but it sort of suits this house.

"What is this room?" I say.

"I suppose ... like a second living room?" Dermot says vaguely.

Two living rooms. I should feel jealous, but my eyes follow a crack from the floor up the wall to the ceiling. There's a lot of dust in the air, and the furniture is beautiful, but everything is stained or broken in some way.

The crack ends in the base of another huge, browning chandelier. I delicately step out from underneath it.

"So ... did you used to be rich?" I ask, more nosy than polite. Dermot nods.

"Yeah, my mum and dad were musicians. They were just starting to make money writing for adverts."

"Which ones?" I'm curious and he sings a couple. I recognize them but I don't know them well enough to sing along. I try anyway.

"It's OK." Dermot waves away my tuneless attempts. (*Meeeehhh bu bu da da da dooo-weeee Krispies?*) "They were big in Japan and India. But anyway, then Dad got sick – just after they bought this house."

"Could Aggy write music without your dad?" I ask.

"I hope so. She's just had a bad eighteen months."

"God, Derm," I say. "You've got a complicated life."

"I'm very, very brave," he deadpans.

The way he says that reminds me of Gabe and I realize I never read his text. I take out my phone. He sent it late last night, asking if I'd like to meet Hazel, Lara and Lisa tomorrow. And him, of course! (He doesn't usually indulge in an exclamation mark, but there's loads here. It's like he's trying to make the prospect of meeting them sound FUN.)

So I apologize to Dermot and quickly text back, I'd love to! Tell me where and when. And, I add, in a lovely display of maturity, I'm looking forward to meeting Hazel, Lara, Lisa, Llama, the whole lot of them. (Unicorn emoji, smiley face.)

I am a nice, non-jealous, calm gf.

Although. If he texted me late last night to invite me, was he texting *them* late at night to arrange it? I'm so petty. It doesn't matter if my boyfriend texts other girls late at night. You either trust someone not to flirt with other people or you don't. And I do. So shut UP, subconscious. If you work as I think you do.

I put my phone away. Dermot is showing me something. Aggy's art collection. "She only keeps the really ugly paintings," he says, waving a hand across a series of cross-eyed, double-chinned portraits propped against the wall.

"Think my mum dated a couple of these," I muse. Which is a BIT mean but he laughs and so does Aggy in the doorway so I feel it's OK.

"Right, ready to go?" she asks.

19

This is so weird. I am standing in a circle with people who ARE all wearing stretchy trousers, thank you, Dermot. In fact, it looks exactly like a yoga class.

Performance Class is held on the ground floor of a vast warehouse-type building, and we find the entrance down an alleyway next to a boxing club. It feels cool and edgy, walking past tattooed men with towels over their shoulders, then pushing open a vast steel door. However, as soon as you're actually *in* Performance Class, the edginess dribbles away in the presence of people in stretchy trousers flexing and talking about avocados.

A lithe man with a very complicated haircut greeted us at the door – "Hi, friends!" he cried. "You're new," he twinkled and pointed at me. "I'm Uliol."

I was trying to work out if he had a speech impediment but Dermot said, "Hi, Uliol!" So I guess not.

Everyone seems to know each other, and I stop feeling sorry for Dermot as the rest of this class clearly *love* him. It's like he's got a double life! They admire his clothes and ask after his mum. Dermot has mates in their fifties, with pierced lips, in dashikis. I feel so boring I might as well have turned up carrying a clipboard.

"OK!" Uliol bounces on his tiptoes and the circle gathers more closely. "We have a new member. Everyone, this is Lou. Lou, this is EVERYONE!"

I give them all a shy wave and get smiles and nods in return. "Everyone" is mainly adults and I'm glad I'm wearing Lav's cardigan. I probably look twenty-one.

"Do you know much about us?" Uliol asks and I shake my head.

"Quick, quick, super-quick," he says, still bouncing. Just bouncing while he talks, why not. "I set up Performance Class five years ago for troubled teens and the troubled teens told me to get stuffed. But it was actually a blessing, as the universe sent a ragtag collection of adults my way: sensitive souls, artists and oddballs, and now we're a happy family! And we've still got one or two teens," he says, pointing at Dermot, who bows.

"Now, let's go round, quick, quick, super-quick, and everyone say something they're proud of this week. Go!"

He points at me and I freeze. My mouth goes dry and I say, *"Bwah. Ah. Uh. Sha."*

"OK!" Uliol says, briskly. "That wasn't fair. We'll start *here*," and he points at a lady on the opposite side of the circle. I feel like I've let him down.

"Being honest with my mum!" she cries out.

"Yes!" everyone shouts at her, including me ... a bit late.

"Being more positive!" the man next to her calls out. Well, that's lowered the bar. I must've done something vaguely good this week.

"Yes!" I yell, racking my brains.

The attention is moving round the circle towards me. Dermot says, "Making friends!" and I'm sure this refers to Hannah and me. Which is sweet, but the naked honesty (and, let's be frank, uncoolness) of it makes me so glad no one from school is here.

Finally, my turn. My tongue feels thick again but I manage to stammer, "C-coming here!"

"Yes!" everyone shouts, pointing at me, and it's still so uncool but I feel good. I do a little double thumbs-up at them and think if Cammie ever saw this, I'd have to move schools.

I realize this is the sort of place where someone can put their hand up and say, super chill, "I've just written a poem about food and sexuality, if you wanna hear it, guys?", and rather than pinning him down and giving him a violent wedgie that he'll taste for a week, everyone stops what they're doing and listens to it.

It's wonderful and also terrible. This class gives people NONE of the defences they need in the real world. At school, caring about things is loser-ish, sincerity is pathetic and being different is more dangerous than weeing on an electric fence. Finally, I understand why Dermot is so terminally Dermotish.

"How long have you been coming here?" I ask him.

"YEARS, why?"

"Uh-huh. No reason," I nod.

Uliol stands in the middle of the circle and divides us into groups of five. I'm eyeing up my group: there's an unimpressed-looking black woman called Patrice, a gentle man called Eli with wispy blond hair and an extremely confident girl with long plaits who is called Star. (Well, she *says* she's called Star. I'd like to see her passport; I bet she's really a Pauline.)

This is like the time we tried Zumba, and Mum and I were forced to admit that we had no rhythm. Dad, on the other hand... The teacher moved him to the front of the class so everyone could learn from his "uninhibited grace" and "fluid hipwork" and he was SO smug on the drive home.

Anyway, while I'm sneaking a look at my group and hoping they can tolerate a weak link for one morning, the door clangs and Uliol sings, without looking around, "Better late than never!"

I glance across the room, towards the door, and see Pete.

Yes, *that* Pete. Surly, uncommunicative Pete. The boy least likely to ever sit in a circle and listen to someone's poem about food and sexuality. He must be lost, looking for the boxing club. Although ... next to me, Star gives him a salute and Patrice blows him a kiss. Huh.

I give Pete a little wave and he stares back at me, clearly horrified. Uliol puts him into another group and I don't get the chance to talk to him. I turn back to my group, where Star is taking charge.

"Guys," she says, in dreamy tones, "I'd like to work on my spontaneity."

"OK!" Dermot agrees, but I have questions. How can you work on your spontaneity? Surely that's the sort of thing that just happens?

Eli jumps straight into it, bouncing on his toes just like Uliol. I start bouncing too but feel like a tit and quickly stop.

"Name a place," Eli says, pointing at me. I have to stop myself from retorting, "No! YOU name a place, Bossy!"

"Essex," I say and the mood in the group seems to sag. What have I said? What've I done wrong?

"That's good," Patrice says. (Her face says, *It's not. It's rubbish.*) "But how about somewhere smaller?"

"A matchbox," I suggest, desperately trying to give them the answer they want.

"Something we could be inside?" Star's dreamy voice is getting a little terse. I get it, I'm annoying. SORRY.

"A sleeping bag!" I brainstorm, feeling like we're finally on the right lines. I even bounce again, I feel so confident.

"NO!"

Uliol looks over at us and Patrice apologizes for shouting. "I'm sorry. That's on me," she says. "But no, we need a place where three or four people –" she gestures round at us – "can stand and have a conversation, a scene, a conflict. Yeah?"

"Yeah," I say in a small voice. It's no fun being thrown into something you don't understand. I could be in bed right now. "How about a cupboard?"

Star massages the bridge of her nose and sighs.

I wish I *was* in bed right now.

"What's *in* the cupboard?" she asks.

"Nothing?" I reply.

"Can you see why that doesn't give us much to work with, dramatically?" Eli says in serious tones. Dermot hasn't said anything. I have a feeling he's holding in giggles.

"There's a … mop in there," I say, willing my brain to be creative. "It's wet."

"Great. A mop. We can work with a wet mop, right, guys?" says Dermot, trying to get the mood up.

So we establish that two spies are hiding in a cupboard.

With a mop. Which is wet. Star and Patrice pretend to be the spies, and they're so funny; they add all these extra little touches, like finding things on the shelves, miming it all.

Then Dermot steps forward, declaring, "Aha! It is me, Agent Milfoux, cunningly disguised as a wet mop!"

I'm laughing while the other two "spies" reel in shock and accuse him of lying. Eli nods at me and I realize I have to join in. I panic and yelp, "I'm a mop too!"

Star sighs and stops twirling her fake moustache. "I've had a long week," she says to no one in particular.

"Why don't we all just agree where it's set, and what's going to happen and write it down?" I finally say what I've been thinking all along.

"But improv is thinking in the moment, being responsive, saying *yes, and...* to everything your team members say," Eli explains. "Whereas writing is control."

"I like control," I say without thinking. And my team members nod. *Yeah, you can tell.*

"Let's try another one," Dermot says, keeping the peace. "It's set in zero gravity..."

So, an hour later, we're taking a break and I'm standing with Dermot, watching people stretching and chatting. Unlike school, I am GLUED to his side. He'd better not go to the toilet: everyone here intimidates the heck out of me.

Speaking of which... I tried to nip over to Pete and say hi, but each time he'd move away and start talking to someone else. After a few attempts, I gave up.

"Do you know him?" I say to Dermot. "He used to go to our school."

"Yeah," Dermot says. "He started coming here just before Christmas."

Just before Christmas. So, just *after* Lou Brown and the Aquarium Boys came to a wet and dangerous end. And around the time his two oldest friends started going out with The Stupid Brown Sisters™.

"Thanks for coming," says Dermot. "I thought you were going to drop out."

"If you'd told me what it was, I might've," I grouch.

"Yeah. That's why I didn't."

"Hmmm." I glower at him.

"By the way ... I have a present for you," he says, and I shut up whingeing immediately, because I am only human and I heart presents.

20

I position my little taxidermy mouse on the wall in our front garden, against a backdrop of primroses. I turn him gently so you can see his loafers and briefcase, and I take a photo. He is beautiful and I shall call him Mr Business.

I send the photo to Gabe and he replies immediately.

WHAT. IS. THAT?

Oh, this? Just an exquisite piece of taxidermy that Dermot gave me. NBD.

I'm so jealous. My otter is rotting.

Gutted, pal.

Swap?

Nerp.

So gutted. Don't bother coming tomorrow.
Just stay in, hang out with your mouse.

I put Mr Business on the kitchen table so Mum can enjoy him. She chokes on her soup.

"Off!" she shouts. "That's so unhygienic!"

"No, it's not. He's dead."

"Dead things are unhygienic, Lou."

"Then why did you make me kiss Grandpa when he died?" I ask.

Silence. I feel I've made a good point.

"I don't like cruelty to animals," Mum says, changing the subject.

"Animals aren't killed for taxidermy," I tell her, feeling embarrassed for her ignorance. "They're stuffed when they die!"

"Die of what?" she asks.

I blunder into her trap. "Well, like mouse illnesses. Or ... old age?"

"Does this mouse look old?" Mum demands, holding it up with a napkin.

"No. But. Well. It was probably ill."

"So you think taxidermists sit patiently in animal hospitals waiting for mice to pass away. Then they ask the mouse family gathered around the hospital bed if they'd like their uncle stuffed and dressed as a dainty stockbroker?"

She has ruined my present. I hadn't thought about it that way at all.

"Fine." I put Mr Business by my feet and go investigate the saucepan of soup on the hob.

"No way!" Mum says, pulling me back by my jeans pocket. "You wash your hands first."

I do but I grumble so she doesn't think she's won. "Where's Lav?"

"In her room."

"And Dad?" I ask and she holds her hands up.

"I don't know actually. He's not answering his phone, or texting back."

"Is he out with Uncle Vinnie?"

"I don't know. I think he might be doing that job Uncle Vinnie got him, or waiting to do it."

"Whatever that job might be…" I say slowly.

"Lou, please. I have more than enough to worry about right now."

Please, she should peek in my Worry Diary. I've got enough to open a shop.

We spend the afternoon together watching *The BFG*. I don't think Mum's paying attention. She sighs. "I don't know why Sophie's parents let her out so late."

"Mum. He nicked her from an orphanage."

She keeps her phone next to her in case Dad calls, but nothing.

As the film is reaching the end, I hear a thudding noise in the back garden, like someone's kicking our sticky back gate open. Mum hears it too and we both turn our heads like meerkats.

Burglars? I mouth at her and she looks baffled and shrugs.

"In Dad's shed?"

We get up silently and creep into the kitchen. All the lights are off, so we can see the back garden clearly by the light of a nearby street lamp. There's someone in Dad's shed, and the light is off, as if they're trying not to attract attention.

I pull a long, sharp knife out of the knife block.

Mum looks at me.

I put the knife back.

Mum wrenches open the back door and says, in a steadier voice than I could have managed, "Hello?"

"Excuse me!" I chirp from behind her, trying to sound adult and threatening. I fail.

"Who's out there?"

"Me!" Dad pops his head out of the shed, and we both shriek with surprise. "Who else would it be?"

"A burglar?"

"How much do you think they'd get for my radio, two spades and a small stash of beer?"

"A small stash of what?"

"Nothing."

When Dad comes in, he smells as if he's been out in the cold for hours. Mum and I keep asking him how his day was, but his answers are all very vague and deliberately boring. His day was fine, the work was fine, he did fine, he might go back again. At least he's clear about how much he earned – a hundred pounds, which he stuffs in the teapot with pride.

I want to know what he was up to, but at the same time I can see that Mum's annoyed at him for not answering her texts and is looking to start an argument. As I much prefer my parents on friendly terms, I change the subject. I tell them I'm meeting Gabe and his new Debating Club friends tomorrow but they're very serious and clever and I'm worried I'm going to look like a dimwit. So what can I do?

"They'll love you, no matter what," says Mum, smiling.

"Yes!" Dad agrees. "And you're not stupid; you're super bright and FUN."

I blink at the pair of them. I wasn't expecting much, tbh, but that useless response did a limbo boogie under my low bar of expectations.

They smile back at me. *You're welcome! We just did some parentings!* I'm surprised they don't high-five each other.

No wonder I'm not clever. This is what I come from. I bet Gabe's family are discussing the Middle East RIGHT NOW. "Just to play devil's advocate, Gabriel, what about the Treaty of Blahbaddy-Blah-Blah..."

I go upstairs to try and get more practical help off Lav. She's in bed, reading. Her hair is greasy, she's not wearing any make-up AND she doesn't even yell at me when I accidentally knock a pile of her clothes off her chair. All very un-Lav.

"What are you reading?" I plonk myself next to her on the bed. "Sorry, I just knocked a mascara behind your bedside table."

She ignores it and shows me a book on feminism. "Megan says that profiting from your looks is anti-feminist and playing into the patriarchy. But I think she's wrong, so I'm reading up on it so I can tell her to eff off."

"Good thinking," I say, wondering how soon I can change the subject onto *my* problems without sounding selfish.

"Um? I'm meeting Gabe's Debating Club friends tomorrow?"

"Oh, yeah, you said. They sound dry."

"Can I borrow some clothes?"

"Do you promise not to spill anything down them?"

"I promise to *try* not to?"

In bed that night, I feel really nervous, though I know I shouldn't. I look over at my chair, where Lavender has laid out my outfit for tomorrow. Nothing fancy: skinny jeans, T-shirt, cardigan and trainers... BUT the secret ingredient is Lavender's actual genuine vintage leather jacket. The most expensive thing she owns apart from orthodontist-straightened teeth.

I offered her Mr Business as a thank you but she said she didn't want a dead mouse in her bedroom – no matter how formally dressed.

I meant *to borrow* not *to keep*, so I'm secretly very glad that was her answer. Lucky escape there.

Narrow squeak, I think and smile to myself in the darkness. That's the spirit – upbeat. Nothing to be nervous about. Look at my lovely witty personality. I am super fun.

Look forward to seeing you tomorrow! I text Gabe. No emojis, all words. Mature texting.

I lie in the darkness waiting for him to reply. My palm begins to sweat. I put my phone down and wipe my hand dry. He's probably busy. Or asleep.

When did having a boyfriend get difficult? I didn't sign up for this. The first two months were a breeze; it was less stress than having a goldfish. I pick my phone up again and google *Blazakhstan*. Sigh. It's not a place.

I can see Lav's reading light is still on. On an impulse, I get out of bed and rummage around on my desk till I find a piece of paper. I scribble a quick note to her: *If there's anything I can do to help, let me know?* I stare at it, wondering what I could do. Reach something high up? Tell her a funny secret about Pete? Turn *another* team of dancers into synchronized swimmers who destroy a TV studio and become briefly famous?

I sneak out into the hallway, avoiding the creaky floorboards I know are lurking underneath the carpet. I push the folded note under her door. I turn to go to bed when I hear a soft scooting noise and see my note by my feet with something written on the back.

Thanks x

I go back to bed and scroll around on my phone until I find what I'm looking for. A podcast called "The Middle East for Dimwits". That's me! Maybe I can get up to speed by tomorrow. Worth a try.

I wake up the next morning – it feels like seconds later – my headphones tangled around my neck again. I don't feel much more informed about world politics, but ... I run my fingers quickly across my face. No spots, anyway.

After twenty minutes in the bathroom, I can no longer ignore Dad's banging on the door. "FINE, I am DONE!" I tell him.

"Water doesn't grow on trees, Lou," he says.

"No, it falls off them after rain, so…"

"So?"

"I'm just saying it's not a great saying … *moody*," I add under my breath as I head to my bedroom.

I start the podcast again while I'm getting dressed. As I'm putting the T-shirt on, something incredibly complicated happens in the 1980s and I don't hear it all, so I'm confused. I sit, frowning at my phone. Sad to think Dad finds things on his phone this baffling EVERY day.

At least my clothes look good. Lavender's a genius – somehow I look ten times cooler than in my usual efforts. I look at myself in the mirror and stand a little straighter.

Should I put some eyeliner on? Best not risk it, quit while I'm ahead. I carefully pick up my bottle of hair oil. There's only a tiny amount left. I was going to save it for prom but my hair is huge and frizzy today so I need a bit to help me feel confident. I apply it, enjoying the unusual feeling of my fingers going *through* my hair, rather than getting snagged so hard I have to call for help.

Great, now my appearance is sorted, I'll walk into town to meet Gabe and the boffins, listen to my podcast, get educated on the way.

I knock softly on Lavender's door as I pass.

"Lav?"

Silence.

"Thanks for the clothes, Lav. Do you want to see how I look?"

Silence. So I take a photo and WhatsApp it to her. I can hear her phone chirp in her room and I wait a minute in case that woke her up.

Nothing.

21

WORRY DIARY

* Lav is sad.
* When she's sad, she's more lenient about lending clothes. Am I a bad person to enjoy this side-effect of the sadness?
* Stupid boffins, making me feel thick.
* But seriously, a lot of places end in -stan and I can't remember them all!

It's a half-hour walk into town, so I set off at my usual striding pace. The one that everyone except Hannah complains about. I keep zoning in and out of the podcast but I REFUSE to let it get me down. It's a very complicated issue; no one could get on top of it in thirty minutes. All I'm aiming for is not to say "Blazakhstan".

My phone buzzes. Text from Dad.

Good lunge!
Luge.
L U C K.

Ha ha. Autocorrect really hates him.
Then again. This one is from Gabe:

Aargh. Change of plan. Not meeting in town after
all, Hazel's at the coffee shop in the park. xx

Great. Gabe knows my feelings on coffee – I can't
stand it when people sit around in cafes sucking on latte
frappé half-fats all day as if we're not teenagers, we're
just small lawyers with bad skin.

Make mine a venti skinny-soy half-froth
sugar-free caramel flat white! xx

(I'm joking! Obviously I'm joking. But he'll know that,
we're a very LOL laid-back pair.)

Sorry. Everyone wants to go there now.
Shall we just do this another time?

I'm joking! I text, feeling wrong-footed. I'll come have a tea. Which cafe, the one near the bandstand? xx

He doesn't reply immediately. Perhaps Hazel wants to do something else now. *Everyone to the skate park, Hazel's had a whim!* I'm not getting a good feeling about this girl. But she's Gabe's new friend and I am going to be nice.

They'll be in the cafe by the bandstand. Everyone goes there, they give out free cake and there's always seats. The one near the pond is dingy and dark. I feel shy and annoyed. Why do I have to run around, chasing Gabe's friends, listening to podcasts and hoping I'm good enough for them?

Also, Lav's skinny jeans are so tight it's quite painful to walk and not helping my mood. I daren't put my phone in my pocket or else it'll crack into dust. I reach the bandstand cafe and look around for Gabe, nervously smoothing my hair and T-shirt. I look down, realizing I've smeared hair oil down Lav's top. Oops. You can only see it if you squint at it in bright light ... which she will when I bring it back.

I order the smallest, cheapest thing I can see – an espresso. I take the teensy weensy cup to a table and stare at it. That's like two thimblefuls of coffee. Who's it for, pixies?

The first sip hits me like a smack around the face. I put the cup back on the saucer and push it firmly away from me. So I'm done with that for ever, thank you, bye.

But once I swallow it, weird noises start coming from my stomach. Fine, not my stomach, my BOWELS. Because I am made of sexy and cool. I text Gabe.

Heyo, I'm at the cafe? Xx

I opt for breezy, though what I really want to say is, I feel left-out! And I might poo myself. (He does NOT need to know that.)

Thought you weren't coming. Only just seen
your text. We're in the cafe. Where are you? X

I look around the almost-deserted cafe.

Unless you're all hiding in the toilet,
I think we're in two different cafes.

No kiss. I don't know if he noticed, but I've been double x-ing here like a chump and he's been going single x or no x at all! Plus, with all this toilet chat, I would've ordinarily made a pun like "Is that the one *urine*?", but I'm not feeling particularly LOL. Absent-mindedly, I take another sip of coffee and wince as my guts do noisy roly-polys.

My phone buzzes again.

We're at the cafe by the pond, it's where everyone goes.

Coming.

Sorry. X

22

I cross the park again. It's now raining, my trousers are tight, my guts are loud and I'm feeling sorry for myself. There's another noisy rumble from my stomach just as I reach the cafe, and I have to wait for it to stop before I can go in. Oh, PLEASE, I hope this cafe has loud background music ... drum'n'bass, a marching band weaving between tables. Anything.

The door makes an exuberant dinging noise as I enter the quietest cafe I have ever visited in my life. I've been to more raucous funerals. (Mum's family, obvs.)

I can see Gabe and three girls sitting on sofas in the corner. The girls all have their legs curled up on the seats in a way that looks cute and arty but, come on, it's rude to put your feet on someone else's furniture.

"Hey!" Gabe gets to his feet and does look, I am pleased to note, happy to see me. I hug him hard. He is brilliant, and I'm so happy he's my boyfriend. So he might have a dodgy taste in friends; no one's perfect. One of the girls stands up when Gabe does. She has long blonde hair and thick black-rimmed glasses. She smiles and gives me a hug.

"Hi, I'm Lara! I've heard so much about you!" she says, friendly but not all fake gushy, and I'm grateful that she's here. Plus she has really bad skin but seems confident in herself, so I feel better about my hair. Even though I can feel it reaching for the ceiling in dramatic wisps.

The other two girls don't get up, so I give them a little wave. They stare at me coolly.

"Hey, you," one of them says, a girl with short black curly hair and a lot of ear piercings.

"Lou," I say.

"Lisa." She holds her hand out, frowning, mock formal. I shake it, feeling like I'm being made fun of but I can't work out why.

"And you must be Hazel," I say to the third girl, who has started chatting to Gabe again, and if I don't say something, I'll just be stuck waiting for her to stop.

Hazel is wearing a black tutu, red boots and a green jumper. She looks like a stuck-up gnome. Her body is angled towards where Gabriel was sitting and her arm is on the back of the sofa so that when he sits down, she'll basically have her arm around him.

She is *exactly* as annoying as I thought she'd be.

I'm not sure what comes over me, but as Hazel looks me slowly up and down (a classic bully move – Nicole can reduce someone to tears with a well-timed up-and-down), I mentally blow my coach whistle at myself.

Come on, Lou! Don't let yourself feel small. I channel my inner coach, a splash of Lav, Dermot's unself-consciousness, Hannah's bluntness and a bit of Patrice's YES and I sit down right next to Hazel – under her arm.

"Ooh," I say. "Cosy!" The look on her face is priceless. "What have I missed?" I say, and they start telling me about this debating club that they're in and the debates they're having about social media and the impact on print journalism. And I don't know ANYTHING about these topics. So I say, "That sounds really interesting," (polite lie) and ask loads of questions.

People love being asked about themselves, so I do that for half an hour and by the end we are all chatting quite happily. Hazel keeps her body twisted towards Gabe the whole time, and she talks over me a lot, and never gives me eye contact. There are so many subtle ways you can shut a person out of a conversation. But Lara is nice; she and Gabe laugh at my jokes.

At one point, I get hot and take off Lav's jacket. Hazel looks at my T-shirt as if she's struggling to keep a straight face.

"Oh *God*. Remember last year when everyone wore that top?" she remarks and Lisa cracks up laughing. Lara smiles awkwardly.

"Anyway." Gabe steers the conversation back on track so smoothly that I don't register how rude that was. But five minutes later, I'm steaming angry at her. Of course, it's too late now – we're all talking about some article online that everyone except me has read – and I can't yell "IT'S MY SISTER'S T-SHIRT. IT'S NICE! SHE'S NICE! AND YOU'RE A COW, YOU COW."

AND everyone in your year wore that top because my sister wore it first and she's so cool EVERYONE copied her. So that's how that happened.

While I'm stewing on that, Hazel throws me another curveball. "Are you up to speed on the Leveson Report?" she says. And obviously I'm not. I have no idea what she's on about. But thanks to Dermot and two hours of improv practice with Perf Class, I keep my cool and pull a face as if I'm mentally sorting through the vast library of things I *do* know to see if Leveson is in there.

And would you know, he's not. Or she. Or it. Whatever.

Forty minutes in, I head to the toilet feeling pleased with myself but exhausted. I don't know why I have to work so hard to make these three like me when they're just having a relaxing Sunday coffee (I rub my sore stomach). Also, they are très dull. Give me Dermot any day.

I exhale deeply as I sit on the toilet and have a little rest. My cheeks hurt from smiling so much and my neck is stiff from nodding keenly to show everyone how interested in them I am. No one's asked me anything about myself.

That's good, I guess? I haven't got anything very interesting to tell them. Except Perf Class, but I can only imagine how Hazel would react to that. She'd sneer herself inside out.

When I get back, Gabe has bought coffees for everyone. They all just take their drinks off him, casually, without offering any money. Like of course it's fine for him to buy five coffees, cos we all have huge allowances, right?

Gabe offers me a mug.

"Oh no, I'm fine, thanks!" I say.

"Well, I got it for you."

Right. So I guess I'm going to have to drink another mug of muck. I take it from him. "How much do I owe?" I say, trying to buy time.

"Two pounds ten." He takes my money but no one else offers. You shouldn't get free things for being rude. Also... The girls are all sipping theirs like sophisticated women of the world. I stare at my coffee and I don't know what to do. If I drink that, my guts will go crazy.

Maybe it'll be OK. I smile at them and take a gulp.

Instantly, I feel my stomach clench and I know it's going to make a terrible noise. I panic. I fumble my phone out of my pocket, hold it up to everyone and press play. The podcast about the Middle East blares out and my stomach grumbles underneath, unheard.

Everyone in the cafe stares at me in surprise.

"Have you heard this?" I shout over it. "It's about the Middle East!"

Hazel's mouth twitches, and she looks at Gabe as if for an explanation. Lara looks surprised and Lisa, well, she is definitely laughing at me. But I don't care. I'd rather sound pretentious than like I'm about to soil myself, so the joke's on her.

"And the … ah … Middle East?" says Hazel delicately. "What do *you* think of that whole sitch?" she pursues, with a "secretive" sideways look at Gabe. It's cleverly done – it makes it look like she and Gabe have a private joke about how thick I am.

"I don't know," I say miserably. "I missed the ending."

I'm still holding my phone up like a wally so I stuff it back in my bag. Everyone starts talking about this big competition. They've just got through to the semi-finals.

"Are you coming to watch us?" Lara asks.

But the semi-finals are the same date as the prom, I suddenly notice.

"Oh. My. God," Hazel drawls at Gabriel,

jokingnotjoking. "*You're* not going to prom, are you? What kind of basic b are you?"

Not even a question, just a flat statement: of course he's not going to prom. And I know what that b stands for.

"Yeah, I don't think I'll be able to come," Gabe says, wincing as if he's worried I'll be upset. Hazel smirks. So of course, *I* say, "That's cool." I shrug, with a nonchalance I don't feel. "Hannah's organizing it, so I have to go – but you don't."

"Cool, thanks," says Gabe, looking relieved. "But I will try to come! Afterwards if not for the whole thing."

I shrug and smile like I could NOT care less. Breezy breezy meezy. That's who I am.

No you're not, my stomach says with a tight clench. *You're annoyed.*

"That's so nice of you to support your friend," says Lara sweetly and I feel like hugging her. Right now, I like her more than my arse of a boyfriend. Gabe always stood up for me last year when Roman and Pete were making fun of me. Where did that brave guy go?

"Oh, wow!" Hazel checks her watch. "Guys, we need to study for tomorrow's debate. Sorry, Lou."

I feel dismissed.

Hazel says firmly, "I've decided Gabe should give the opening speech instead of Lara ..."

Lara looks disappointed about this but clearly Hazel makes the rules.

"… so he has to study with us about … ah … half an hour ago!" Hazel taps her watch.

Gabe walks me outside to say goodbye. Lara hugs me, Lisa gives me a languid, faux tragic farewell wave that makes me feel silly and Hazel barely registers that I'm leaving.

"So, how was that?" he asks.

I stare at him, trying to work out if he's being deliberately dense. "Yeah, they all seem lovely," I say sarcastically. BUT HE TAKES IT SERIOUSLY!

"Right? I knew you'd like them, once you stopped worrying about not being clever enough," he teases and dips in to kiss me.

I have never kissed Gabe while sarcastically rolling my eyes, but there's a first time for everything.

"I know Hazel can be a bit…"

I nod. Yeah. Does he want me to put the adjective in here? Because I have lots.

"But it's just what she's like." He shrugs, like it's funny, really.

Is it funny, really? Is it? *Oh, well, if that's just what she's like…* I seethe to myself as I stomp home. *Don't mind Hazel, she's just slapped your gran, kicked your cat and set fire to your curtains. That's just what she's like, LOL!*

I need to go home, spend about half an hour on the toilet and then air my views on Hazel loudly to my sympathetic family. Except … as I finally turn into our road, I realize this Sunday is turning into an unparalleled cowpat of a day. I've forgotten my house keys. No one is answering the door or their phones, but I can see lights on – my dozy family have clearly got headphones on or the TV up loud. All the things they tell me off for. The hypocrisy rankles.

When I sneaked out a few months ago, I just climbed out onto the roof and down via the water butt. But sneaking in is harder, especially as I was fitter then and my stomach wasn't cramping with caffeine. But, with no other options, I clamber onto the water butt and wobble there for a bit. Once I'm steady, I reach up to the garage roof and haul myself up there. It's not an elegant climb and I find myself face down in a puddle full of rotten leaves. They cling to my cheek like long-lost friends.

Ah, Hazel, it's just what she's like, I gripe to myself, anger giving me a useful burst of strength. I scoop the leaves off my face and slowly stand. *She's horrible and she dresses like she lost a bet! If she was a bit shorter, she could join the other gnomes on Aggy's drive.*

I edge along the roof towards my bedroom window. My locked bedroom window. It starts to rain again.

I scrabble at the edges, but this window cannot be opened by a burglar having a tentative pick with cold fingers. Dad will be pleased the house is secure. Even if he finds my frozen dead body on the roof like a nasty Christmas decoration.

I walk onwards to Lavender's window, which I can see is open a crack. I peer in and find myself face-to-face with her. She looks furious. I recoil before I realize she's not mad at me, she's on the phone and mid-argument. She jumps when she sees me and holds her heart. I give her a sad, wet little wave. She shakes her head at me. *What are you doing?* she mouths.

"Climbing into your bedroom?" I say, hopefully.

She opens her window and lets me in, wrapping up her conversation on the phone. "You're not listening to me, Ro. If you're not listening, there's no point in me— NO, that's how *you* feel about it. Not how I feel! You know, I'm going to go, it's like talking to a brick wall and Lou is wet on my floor." She hangs up.

Lou is wet on my floor. Thanks, Lav.

Still, she's very helpful pulling me out of her skin-tight wet skinny jeans; it's like trying to peel a grape. "Are you and Ro arguing?" I wheeze.

"Yeah," she struggles. "He thinks this modelling thing is great: I should get a portfolio together, start an online campaign to get people voting for me..."

"Do you *want* to be a model?" I ask, doubtfully.

She stops pulling at my jeans and points at me.

"Exactly! Thank you!"

I'm not sure what I've said that's so brilliant but I'm definitely doing better than Roman.

"I *don't* want to. I have never wanted to. I want to get some money for Mum and Dad and go back to my normal life where girls don't shoulder-barge me in the corridor and boys don't draw penises on my face."

I'm horrified.

"On PHOTOS of my face."

"Oh, right. Yes, of course. Phew."

"But he's not listening!"

"He's always been a bit ... what's a nice way of saying fame-hungry?" I ask, squirming on the floor, twisting to get the jeans past my knees.

"There is no nice way," she concludes, whipping them off my ankles and onto the radiator.

I wrap myself in her dressing gown and sit on her floor and tell her about today. She agrees with me about everything and it is hugely satisfying. This is where Gabe lets me down. He isn't so easy to complain to – he's too thoughtful. He'll say things like, "But what if...?" and, "Just throwing this theory out there..." Which is annoying when all you want to do is rant about the heinous injustice of your life.

"What can I do?" I say pathetically at the end of my story.

"Hope that he's just a bit intimidated by her right now but soon he'll remember how much he likes you. Give him some time."

"So, bite my tongue for a few weeks and don't tell him I think his new friend is one of the worst people I've ever met in my life?"

"Yes. No. Really don't do that. You don't want to have a fight with him where he's defending her against you. Think how jealous that would make you feel."

I imagine it. My stomach clenches.

"Excuse me," I say demurely and disappear to the bathroom. I am gone some time.

Everyone is in such a bad mood that Sunday evening that Dad sneaks out. We spend ten minutes wondering if he's left us for good because we're all so grouchy when he reappears with pizza and ice cream.

"Mark!" Mum says, but he stops her before she can worry about the expense.

"Supermarket pizza. I promise. But I think we all need a treat?"

"We do!" I say, tugging the boxes out of Dad's hands and shouting out instructions to Lavender, who is already crouched by the oven, hands poised over the dial. We are such an efficient team.

WORRY DIARY

* Must bite my tongue every time I want to say something nasty about Hazel.
* Is tongue re-attachment surgery expensive?

"You're getting better!" Dermot is yelling at me one morning over the rattling of Aggy's van.

I turn a steady gaze on him. "How could I have got worse?"

...

"Tell me one way I could've been worse than my first time."

"Hang on! I'm trying to think. Well. You. You didn't hurt anyone's feelings?"

"What?"

"On her first week, Star made a girl cry."

"Which girl?"

"You don't know her. She doesn't come any more."

"Not surprised. Bloody Star."

I have now been going to Perf Class for four weeks. Hannah's always busy with prom stuff these days and Gabe is working hard with his debating team, so my weekends are empty, bare deserts without so much as a camel to chat to.

It's nice to have something to do every Saturday morning. And I am getting *slightly* less rubbish. The last three times I have worn stretchy trousers and not ruined the improv by trying to set scenes in a matchbox. Star has stopped sighing and massaging her temples every time I speak, Patrice is rolling her eyes at me less and I've stopped sweating uncontrollably. Although last Saturday Uliol twinkled at me and said he was going to push me out of my comfort zone next time, which sounds awful.

Pete still avoids speaking to me, although two weeks ago, he showed off some dance he'd been working on, slow and acrobatic like the stuff we used to do underwater last year. He looked delighted by all the whooping and applause. When I texted him afterwards to say well done, I got a Pete-like Cheers, mate in return.

"I couldn't do it!" Aggy bellows. "GEAR CHANGE.

Performing and getting up in front of people terrifies me. He doesn't care at all." She nods at Dermot.

"That's because he doesn't feel shame!" I shout.

"Do you think?" Dermot looks thoughtful.

I gesture at his outfit. He's in culottes and a little jacket. I'm pretty sure these clothes are meant to be worn by a lady playing tennis on a hot day. As it's late February, he's layered them up with multi-coloured jumpers and a pair of leggings.

Aggy laughs, but stops when Dermot turns to look at her. "I don't know what she means, the girl's talking nonsense," she promises him.

Ugh. That reminds me. "It's prom soon and I've got nothing to wear.

I've decided to ask Hannah if I can borrow something. I bet Barbra's bought her three different dresses "just in case", so I'm hoping to swoop in and nab whichever one she doesn't want. I don't mind what I wear. I don't think I'll even have a date, as Gabe is still saying he can't come. It doesn't matter but it does feel like a tug of war between me and Hazel. Gabe is the rope and I'm losing him.

Dermot and I hurry across the car park to school and I can see Lavender has got here before us. She's sitting on the steps with her friends, swamped in a big duffel coat. All her friends are loud and boisterous. Any time I talk to them, they always talk over me or throw things at each other. Last term I got hit in the face with half an apple, so now I give them a wide berth.

Dermot gets out his phone and turns it on silent – school rules. He holds it up, struggling slightly as his fingerless golf gloves don't give him much grip.

"Uh. Excuse me?" One of Lav's friends stands and points at him. We both freeze. Jessica has short white-blonde hair, loads of piercings and is the only person I've ever met who can wear black lipstick and not look like a pen exploded in her mouth. She is intimidating and knows it. More so when she's yelling and pointing, like now.

"What are you doing?" she continues across the yard. Lavender pulls Jessica by the sleeve to make her sit down but Jessica's having none of it.

"Are you taking photos of her?" she continues, pointing at Lav. "Do you think you can just invade her privacy and take photos of her, you creep? What is WRONG with you?"

Lavender snaps. "Jess. Shut UP! He is not taking my photo. He's a family friend! Stop it, please."

Jess sits down again, grudgingly, giving Dermot a look, like, *You're lucky ... THIS time.*

Dermot and I hurry into school.

A couple of boys shoulder-barge Dermot as they overtake us in the corridor. But for once, it doesn't send him sprawling. I think it might be a friendly shoulder-barge.

"Ignore her, mate," one boy, Jared, tells him. "Jess accused me of the same thing yesterday. I was taking a selfie of my coldsore."

Dermot looks relieved. "I'm not a creep," he tells Jared, anxiously tightening the straps of his satchel and getting one of his gloves caught in the buckle in the process. Jared watches Dermot untangle his glove from his bag without laughing and goes way up in my estimation.

We reach our form room to find Hannah sitting in her old seat next to me. I head for the two empty seats behind her so the three of us can sit together. If Hannah minds, she doesn't say. Across the room, I can see Melia shooting her evil looks and the other two whispering to each other. Hannah pulls her towel out of her swimming bag and dries the ends of her hair, using her towel to hide her face from them.

"You all right?" I ask. She mouths something at me but I can't catch it. Dermot and I lean in.

"We've found bands, we've seen venues, we've looked at decorations online. Nothing is good enough for Cammie. Everything must be perfect, and I don't have enough hours in the day to make everything as perfect as she wants it to be. And she has to have the final decision on everything!" Hannah hisses furiously.

I try to hide how pleased I feel. What's the word, *vinaigrette*?

No! *Vindicated*. I feel vindicated.

"What about the other two?" I whisper.

"Melia is obsessed with finding the perfect dress, Nicole is obsessed with finding the perfect date!" she hisses back.

Dermot and I snigger.

"I'm not even joking! They have a shortlist – ten of each. They're driving me up the wall."

"Are you going to ask Dan?" I say, without thinking.

Hannah does huge, horrified eyes and shushes me like I'm shouting her crush's name from the rooftops.

"Which Dan?" Dermot asks.

See? I mouth at her. "I can say it. There are like eleven Daniels, Dannys and Dans in school, it could be any one of them."

Hannah has a crush on a lifeguard at the swimming pool called Dan. She spends about four hours training every day, and he's there most of the time. She's been in his company about a hundred hours this term and still hasn't worked up the courage to say so much as hello to him.

In fairness, he is ridiculously good-looking and very aloof. It's an intimidating combination.

Before Mr Peters takes the register, he perches on the front of his desk and addresses the class.

"Now I know everyone is very busy with schoolwork

and extracurricular activities," he begins. Hannah makes a little huffy noise as she stuffs her swimming towel back in her bag. "So I thought, as we're all here now, we could have an update from the Prom Committee about how everything is coming along?" He raises his eyebrows at Cammie, Nicole and Melia. In one swift movement, they all look at Hannah.

Mr Peters follows their gaze. "Hannah?"

Those three are good. They work as a pack, like wolves.

"We... The.... So..." I can hear how dry Hannah's mouth has gone and I feel for her. She needs a bit of Uliol's improv. There's a long, heavy silence, broken by the most unlikely of people.

"Hannah was just—"

"Sorry, Dermot, can't hear you?" Mr Peters says.

Heads turn towards Dermot and the sniggering starts as everyone takes in his outfit: half 1920s lady tennis player, half gym-bunny. Dermot ploughs on.

"Hannah was just saying that they're considering venues and bands and decorations but they probably need to make a decision soon?"

"Ideally," Mr Peters says drily. "Prom is now two weeks away."

Cammie looks stony-faced. I'm pretty sure Melia gives a dry heave.

"Um, so maybe," says Dermot, donning the faraway Thinking On His Feet look I recognize from Perf Class, "maybe it would be helpful if you gave the committee a deadline for making the decision. Maybe they have to tell the rest of the year ... or ... something." His bravery abandons him, melting away under Cammie's steely glare.

I squeeze his arm quickly. *Well done!*

"OK?" Mr Peters seems surprised. "Whatever works. I want to make sure you haven't blown the budget on clothes and gigs!" he laughs, but Nicole squirms guiltily and I am *so* glad none of this is my problem. "So, how about you tell us about it tomorrow?" he concludes.

The bell for first lesson goes and immediately Hannah is summoned from the other side of the room with hisses of "HAN!" She shoulders her bag and trudges over to them, giving Dermot a quick mouthed *THANK YOU*.

"Good thinking!" I turn to Dermot. He does a little curtsy and I ignore Karl making faces at him behind his back.

We make our way to maths, leaving Hannah to her passive-aggressive argument in the form room. They're all calling each other *honey* and asking about hurt feelings, but I know this is when they're at their most dangerous. Poor Hannah. She's a fish finger in a sea of sharks.

At lunchtime I grab Dermot before he does his usual disappearing act.

"Where do you go every lunch time?" I ask him and he looks shifty.

"Just … the library."

"Because you don't have anyone to sit with?" I guess, with more accuracy than tact. "Sorry!" I say. "I mean, want to have lunch with me?"

"OK," he says but he doesn't look keen.

"I don't chew with my mouth open," I tell him.

"No, no, that's cool," he says and follows me to the lunch hall.

Weird.

Well, I think it's weird until he pulls out the fanciest packed lunch I've ever seen. "Is that…? What IS that?" I squeak at him.

"Tempura."

"I see." (I don't see. I'll need to look that up later.)

"My aunt has this food ordering service from Selfridges that she sends Mum and me." He looks uncomfortable.

"It's OK that you're rich," I tell him graciously, through a mouthful of his tempura. "Couscous?"

"Brilliant," he lies.

When I get home from school, I dump my bag in the hallway and head to the kitchen for a snack, although these days there is not much to actually snack on. Mum and Dad have stopped buying chocolate and biscuits, and even the fruit is getting sparse. I examine a brown banana on its last legs. I shall show it out in style, I decide, peeling it, dotting the last of the peanut butter along it and heading upstairs to eat it.

As I pass the living room, I can see Mum napping on the sofa. She's sleeping so much more than usual at the moment. I feel a prickle of impatience. How tiring can job-hunting be?

It's Monday, so in an hour Hannah will be heading off to therapy with Hari. I text her.

How much are you going to slag off
the Prom Committee to Hari?

(Now YES, this is mean but I'm taking advantage of their new friendship falling apart. I can't have her being best friends with that lot. Melia at a push but not the other two.)

SO MUCH... she replies, with a string of planet emojis. Anything you want me to ask him? she offers, and I think.

I'm worried about my mum.

OK.

She seems down and tired all the time.

So, just to recap: I'm getting therapy from my
therapist on YOUR behalf, about your mum.

Too much?

I don't think I'll be able to keep my stories straight.

Fairy nuff.

x

x

I bet I know what Hannah's going to spend her hour
talking about. Our English lesson, first thing tomorrow,
when the Prom Committee have to make some decisions
about the venue, the theme, the band, the food. I am so
glad I'm not them, I think, stretching out in bed. My feet
dangle off the end. I think I've grown AGAIN. I'll add it
to the Worry Diary, but right now I'm so happy to not be
"Cams", "Mell" or "Nic". Or Hannah, I think, with a
prickle of guilt.

For once, I'm going to get a good night's sleep.

24

WORRY DIARY

✱ I've definitely grown again. I banged my head
on the bathroom ceiling this morning. Never
done that before.

In English the next day, Dermot and I are sitting together
and, across the room, Hannah is sitting with Cammie
and Melia. I can't see Nicole anywhere.

"So!" Mr Peters bounds into the room, late as always.
"Before we get back to Toni Morrison, let's have a quick
catch-up on the prom!" he says brightly. "I know a couple
of the teachers are getting a bit anxious that we haven't
got details yet, but I have full faith in my team!"

I don't believe him for a second. He fiddles nervously
with his cardigan buttons. Uliol tells us that ninety-three

per cent of communication is non-verbal, so always watch people's bodies. Not like that.

"So, who wants to put an anxious teacher out of his misery and tell him that the prom is all organized? Anyone...? Aaaanyone."

I glance at Hannah, whose face looks frozen, like the one time we tried to play Poker. Behind her, Cammie and Melia don't look much better.

"Um, Mr Peters." Cammie has her hand up but as always it seems less like a request to talk than a lazy formality. *FYI, babez. Chattin' here.* "We can take you through it in a couple of days. We're just finessing a few details."

"No." Mr Peters is smiling but firm. "I haven't been able to get any information out of you guys in weeks, so why don't you share what you have with the class today and *finesse* those few details later."

"No, because..."

Cammie is insistent but Mr Peters pulls rank.

"Yes, because...!" he echoes her. "It's two weeks away. It's time you opened up the organization a bit. If you're struggling, I'm sure the class would be happy to help."

"The Class" look a little sly and cross their arms, as if they're smelling the possibility of a disastrous prom and a humiliated Cammie and the most help they're willing to offer is watching the carnage while eating popcorn.

I share this feeling one hundred per cent.

Out of respect for my friend and cowardice in the face of Cammie, I hide my smirk in my jumper sleeve. Before I feel too guilty, I remind myself of a conversation with Hannah a few days ago.

"How's your mum and dad, are they back in work?"

"No," I said, baffled. It's the biggest problem in my life right now, and if it had suddenly gone away, *I would've mentioned it*.

"Argh," she said with a brief sad look on her face that reminded me of her mum. Then we were onto something else. This was poor BFF work on Hannah's part. So I let myself enjoy the next twenty minutes while she, Cammie and Melia have to field questions from the class.

"Where's Nicole?" asks Mr Peters.

"She felt sick and went to the nurse," says Melia with a sour look on her face. I bet she's furious she didn't think of that trick first.

"So, firstly, WHERE is the prom going to be?" Mr Peters settles in with an easy question.

"You know where Dreezy shot his last video?" Cammie says.

"What do you think, Camilla?" says Mr Peters, gesturing at his cardigan and sensible trousers.

"The nightclub scene. With the exposed brick walls and the tigers."

"Cammie."

"OK," she says, eyes wide like she can't believe someone so ignorant is allowed to teach. "The Rothermere Estate. The ballroom. My father hooked us up."

A couple of people say *wow!* and Cammie looks smug. Yeah guys, prit-ty cool. NBD.

A hand goes up, an Indian girl I don't know very well called Sasha. "How are we getting there?"

Melia shrugs at her. "How do you get *anywhere*?"

Some people laugh, but Sasha's not letting it go. I mentally salute her. "I walk, Melia. Shall I walk the ten miles from here to the Rothermere Estate?"

"I don't know," Cammie says, rudely. "You sort it out."

"Cam-*illa*." Mr Peters is looking weary.

Camilla throws her hands in the air, like, *Why are you making this difficult?* "Get your parents to drive you, get a cab," she says to Sasha, without bothering to turn her head to look at her.

Mr Peters is shaking his head. "You can't expect the whole year group to get cabs both ways. You'll need to find money in the budget for coaches."

Cammie is scathing. "Coaches aren't allowed at the Rothermere. It's not that sort of place." She seems to think that's the end of the discussion, but Mr Peters does not.

"Then you need to rethink your venue, Cammie. This prom is for everyone, not just people who can travel ten miles on a whim."

Hannah is staring out of the window. Her jaw is flexing and I think she's chewing on her brace.

Sasha puts her hand up again; she seems to be designated spokesperson for the class. She's probably fearless because she has a very large brother in sixth form. "OK. How about entertainment?"

"Are you wondering how *they're* going to get there?" asks Melia, sarcastically, and there's some snickering.

"I'm wondering if they exist, Melia. Let's *finesse* the details later."

HAHAHA! (I laugh inside my head.) The rest of the class does it out loud.

"We're still auditioning," says Cammie, smoothly.

"My cousin? He's in a band so we have a back-up. He says he's happy to help." Hannah says, shyly.

"Excellent." Mr Peters is grateful for *any* good news.

"No, it *sounds* excellent when you say your cousin's in a band," Cammie snaps. "Then you find out it's a Christian rock band and they sing about the Lamb of God."

"Cam-*illa*," Mr Peters warns.

"After you've travelled out of town to see them play at a gig which turns out to be in a church," adds Melia, bitterly.

"That's awful," I say, sincerely. "How far did you have to travel? Five miles, *ten*?"

At this point, the class starts hooting with laughter again. I can't believe I said that, the words were out of my mouth before I knew it. I blame Uliol. I'm dangerous now I can think on my feet. "I'd hate to travel a twenty-mile round trip to something rubbish," I hear myself adding and the room explodes with a fresh gale of laughter. My ears flush hot and I have to hide a pleased smile. I don't dare look in Hannah's direction.

Mr Peters gestures with his hands to bring the class under control and is about to speak when Cammie, as ever, gets the last word. "And it's fancy dress. Nu-Grunge and bling. If you don't look tight, you're not coming in." She looks right at me, knowing I have never looked *tight* in my life.

"Do you think that instead of working on rhymes, you should've focused more on organizing the prom?" comes a fake concerned voice from the back of the room. We're all getting witty now. Uliol would love this. Next to me Dermot shakes with quiet laughter and poor Mr Peters flaps a copy of *Beloved*, trying to bring his English class under control.

25

WORRY DIARY

* Spotted Dad yesterday, hurrying into town carrying a huge grip bag. Mysterious.
* We'll have to visit Dad in prison every weekend – I'll never see Gabe and I won't get to go to Perf Class any more.
* Just realized I like Perf Class. I'm terminally uncool.

When I get home from school, I find the house strangely quiet. I hang my coat up and see Lavender's duffel coat already hanging there. "Laaaav!" I yell up the stairs but no reply. Her coat is sticky. I feel down the arms and there are gross flecks on it.

I think I'm looking at a choice combination of hair

wax, spit and gum. This is something you learn from being friends with Dermot: Things Bullies Like to Flick at You. In a moment of sisterly tenderness, I take Lav's coat into the kitchen and start to sponge off the nasty bits. It's dark in the kitchen and as I look out of the window, I can see Dad's back in his shed, working on something. What is it? Crime homework?

You can always tell when someone's looking at you. Dad's head bobs up at the shed window and he gives me a little wave, which I return with soapy fingers. He turns off the light in his shed, secures the three locks and comes into the house.

"What did you spill on your sister's coat?"

"Nothing. I ... er... Foundation," I say, quickly. God, I've NEVER had to do so much thinking on my feet.

"Get it cleaned up, quick!" he says, anxiously.

"Why?"

"She'll kill you."

"She will?"

"Louise. The sister you know and love is gone. A monster has taken her place."

"Not being a teeny bit dramatic?"

"Nope. After Roman dropped her off this evening, I heard thwacking."

"Thwacking?"

"I think that's the word. She had her umbrella out and

was *thwacking* away at our bushes in the front garden. It's not funny!"

"It's a bit funny. What did the bushes ever do to her?"

"The neighbours were staring. She was whacking chunks out of the lavender bush."

I keep scrubbing at the coat.

"Did you say something to her, Dad?"

"No. I stayed in the back garden until she'd gone in, then when she went to her room, I hid her umbrella."

"You're a hero. Where's Mum?"

"She's helping Nicky at the salon. She's short-staffed and offered to pay her, for once."

Dad grabs Lav's coat off me and takes over scrubbing.

"I'm gonna go see Lav." I leave him to it.

"Good luck."

I'd usually barge into Lav's room but now I'm hesitating outside with my hand on the doorknob. I'm sure Dad is exaggerating but I suddenly feel nervous about going in. Sometimes Lav feels a lot more than a year older than me, and now is one of those times. I open her door a crack and slide my nose around it, then slowly more of my face. She's sitting on her bed surrounded by homework.

"All right?"

"Pffft," she says non-committally.

I sit on her bed, knocking several textbooks off and

224

giving her my best listening face. To my surprise, she opens up a bit.

"My stupid friends. They think they're protecting me! I can't wait for this competition to be over, someone else to win and everything to go back to normal."

"Huh," I say.

We sit in a heavy silence for a while. Then she finally gives in. "What, Lou? What does *huh* mean?"

"You might win?"

"It's a public vote. You have to promote it to get people voting and I haven't."

"Huh."

I catch a look off her and say, "No, nothing! Ignore me!" It's not nothing, but I don't want to stress her out any more. It's just that I was on Roman's Facebook page earlier and he is a one-man PR team, drumming up support and votes. He's lucky Lav's been avoiding social media lately.

I go into my room and lie down on my bed. I should do my homework but my arms and legs feel rubbery at the thought of work.

I'll have a small nap, five minutes. Ten, at most...

An hour later, Mum pops her head around the door.

"When did you get back?" I ask. "And why is your head stripy?"

"It's not, is it?" Mum looks horrified and my sleepy brain registers that only Evil Grandma would think that a good thing to say aloud.

"No, no!" I assure her. "Probably just the dim light."

She touches her hair and looks unconvinced. "Anyway, come down for dinner. It's soup.'"

Lav joins us at the kitchen table. Dad eyes her suspiciously, as if expecting her to start thwacking things again.

"It *is* stripy, isn't it?" says Mum, touching her hair. I shake my head but Lav is nodding, so I give up.

"Nicky said she'd give me highlights and then halfway through said she wouldn't *charge* me—"

"I should think not!" Now Dad's listening.

"She just wouldn't pay me for the day's work, and that would even out, financially."

"Oh Mum..."

"And I got upset, I said I need the money, and we argued a bit, and she finally saw my point of view."

"Good! Too right!" we all say, indignant on Mum's behalf.

"So I got paid, but we'd lost track of time arguing, so the bleach had been on my hair too long. And now I look like a skunk."

We stare at her. I'm struggling to think what to say, because she's nailed it. She has skunk hair.

"The prettiest skunk in all the world," Dad says

finally, leaning in for a kiss. Mum smiles and I refrain from giving that the retching noise it deserves.

Now look, I like ketchup, but this is a three-bottle pack from the pound shop and it smells remarkably vinegary. Plus, I've never *held* a fistful of it before.

"It's not going to stain, is it?" Mum asks in muffled tones from under her ketchup-slathered hair.

"You or the bath?" Lav asks.

"Both!" Mum snaps. "And will you get off your phone!"

Lav looks wounded by this injustice. "I am *googling* how this works, thank you. You cover your hair in ketchup, wrap it in cling film and leave it for an hour."

"And it'll make me less skunky?" Mum asks.

"It'll take the brassiness out of the bleached— Yes," Lav interrupts herself to keep it simple. "It'll make you less skunky."

"I still think you look pretty," says Dad absent-mindedly. He's sitting on the toilet (as a chair, thankfully), also on his phone, licking ketchup off his fingers.

"What are *you* watching?" Mum asks.

"Kittens fighting their reflection," says Dad, gently putting his phone under Mum's curtain of hair.

Lav and I roll our eyes. What would she do without us? All Dad would do is eat the excess ketchup and google kittens.

26

WORRY DIARY

* Nothing new – hurray!
* LITERALLY NONE of the old worries have
  been resolved – boo.

I'm just cleaning my teeth when there's a banging on the
bathroom door.

"Lou, out!" Mum shouts and I open the door to her.
She tumbles into the room and hops into the shower.

"Don't panic," I tell her as she whisks the shower curtain across. "You won't miss anything on TV, with the
plus one channels."

"Oh, ha ha," she says. "Your dad and I are due at the
Jobcentre in forty minutes. If you're late, they sanction
you."

"What does sanction mean?"

"Cut your benefits off," Dad puffs at me as he squeezes into the bathroom to clean his teeth and neaten his hair. "And we're down to half a cauliflower for dinner."

"That sounds better than a whole one, tbh."

"I hope we don't get that horrible woman again," Mum snarks from the shower. "She says I need to 'think outside the box' with my job goals. I'm a teacher! She acts like I do something weird and niche like juggling."

"She'll be glad to see you're dipping a toe in hairdressing," says Dad.

Mum laughs. "Now, *hairdressing* ... that's a profession people will always need."

"No, you're doing it wrong," Dad jumps in with an even more prim, clipped accent. "Hairdressing is an 'all-weather' line of work as I like to call it. Not like teaching, which is a more vulnerable vocation in the current climate."

I leave them to it, because there is nothing more boring than listening to people do impressions of someone you've never met.

I open the front door to see if Aggy is coming and, to my surprise, the van is sitting demurely at the end of the drive. Aggy gives me a smug wave as I jog down to join them.

"Good luck, Mum and Dad!" I yell over my shoulder. "What's this?" I ask as I climb up next to Dermot.

"I sold a table for seven hundred quid, picked it up for next to nothing!" Aggy tells me. "So I thought I'd treat us all and get the van serviced. Listen!"

She turns on the engine and it purrs into life. Like a tiger, we agree, and ride to school feeling like royalty, especially as Aggy's thumb is better so she's changing her own gears now.

Dermot tells me as we head to school that he and Aggy often finds loads of designer clothes in her clearances – he could help me find something for prom? I look down at his trousers, which seem to be made of wetsuit material. Then I look from his gigantic hobnailed boots to his garishly patterned mohair cardigan and his tie made of plastic. I do a lot of looking, as I think that makes my point more clearly than having to say it.

"I won't dress you in anything I would wear," he says good-humouredly. "I'll find you something boring if you like."

"Yes, please!" I say, relieved. "Like maybe dark blue? Plain dark blue?"

He sighs dramatically. "Fine."

We arrive at our form room to find Hannah sitting at our shared desk again, so I guess the Prom Committee haven't kissed and made up yet.

Mr Peters closes the door behind us and turns to the

class. "Nice to see you back, Nicole," he says. "I trust you're feeling better?"

"Yah, it was like one of those twenty-four-hour things," she says, giving Melia a smirk that she doesn't return. Nicole can be so dense. She faked an illness to leave her friends in the lurch and then expects them to high-five her for it later? Her smile flickers and fades.

"Right, well. I wanted to talk to you all about bullying on social media. It's come to the school's attention that there's been a lot of … activity … online around a modelling competition?"

All eyes in the class swivel to look at me. It's not a nice feeling and I examine my fingernails with interest. These cuticles need pushing back and there's no time like the present!

"I understand that there are two local finalists in the competition, one is from this school and one is the –" Mr Peters looks up, as if he's trying to remember – "the girlfriend of a cousin of someone's auntie's dog-manicurist."

Everyone stares at him blankly. Dermot grins. Mr Peters points at him. "Thank you, Dermot. If it wasn't for you, I'd start to doubt my wit. God forbid. The point is, one of the other finalists has a tenuous relationship to someone else at the school and I understand that feelings are running high. Can you just do me a favour, guys? I'm a nice teacher, aren't I? Lenient on punctuality, turning a blind eye to nose rings – *yes, Sasha, I have noticed* – listening to your myriad problems... In return, can you just not get involved in this? It's all getting a bit silly, as I think we saw in the canteen the other day."

"You got it, Mr Peters," says Sasha and there's a murmur of agreement. I imagine this talk is going on in all the other classrooms and feel grateful that school's stepping in. I hope this makes Lav's life a little easier. It's just a couple more weeks till they announce the winner and then everything should calm down.

"Thank you," he says. "I mean it. I'll be looking online, and if I get any sense of bullying behaviour from anyone in my form, I'll be handing out a whole term of detention... And you won't be able to go to prom," he says as an afterthought. I see Cammie bristle. Clearly Mr Peters doesn't think banning someone from prom is much of a punishment. I'm inclined to agree with him.

Hannah makes a beeline for Dermot and me at break-time. She looks desperate to get away from the other three, but keeps getting dragged into argumentative huddles. Cammie is always grabbing her friends, pushing and pulling them around with elegant, slender hands that are bizarrely strong. Melia and Nicole must be covered in tiny bruises. Hannah isn't taking her intimidation any more, though. I hear her say, "Stop hissing at me, Cammie! You're spitting in my mouth."

Obviously, it's nice to have my friend back but I am staying well out of this drama. I've had enough this term, especially with Lavender's problems on top. I see her at lunchtime, sitting with Roman, huddled in a massive hoodie. Roman on the other hand, is chatting away animatedly, trying to get her to look at something he's discreetly showing her on his phone. (Seriously, no one pays attention to the phone ban any more – they're going to have to start ripping them out of our hands at the school gates.)

I don't usually go and chat to them at lunchtime. I don't want Ro to think I'm trying to form some kind of gang of the four of us. But I wander over, to see if I can inject some cheeriness.

"What up, dawgs?" I greet them breezily. Lav doesn't look up, Ro frowns at me like I'm mad and a girl I don't know laughs at me. Thanks, guys.

Nevertheless, I persist.

"Everything OK?" I ask.

"Yeah." Ro looks his usual cocky self. "Less than two weeks to go."

"To the—"

"The announcement of the winner?" He nods at Lav. "I think she's got a great chance. She's easily the hottest of the lot."

"The lot?" Lav finally looks up. Yeah, I'm not loving this tone either. "I'm not a prize cow," she snaps at him.

Ro looks baffled, so I expand.

"In a cow competition?" I say. "And you're not her farmer," I add helpfully.

"I have no idea what's wrong with either of you," says Ro, laughing. "This is the most exciting thing to happen to us ever. Can you stop being so sour about it?"

Lav says nothing, just looks sour.

"By the way, I've been meaning to ask, what are you going to wear to the ceremony?" Ro asks and Lav looks panicked.

"I don't know," she says. "Do we have to go?"

He ignores her question. "That's cool," he says, "I'm talking to some brands."

"Bran? Bran Flakes?" I ask and he just shakes his head slowly at me as if he doesn't have time to explain to Idiot McThick. I was trying to lighten the mood, sor-ree.

"Don't try and get free stuff, it's embarrassing," Lav tells him.

"No, it's an *opportunity*," he corrects her. "Who wouldn't want to dress the winner of a national modelling competition? They'd PAY for a chance like that. I'll make some calls now. See you in class." And he gives Lav a kiss and leaves us to it. She looks ready to hit him. Or anything near by. So I back away too.

Everyone around me is having such a fractious day, I'm glad to clamber into Aggy's van at four thirty and leave

Hannah to her prom problems and Lav to her enthusiastically shallow boyfriend. Even the smell of mouldy old furniture is soothing.

"I might sort through some clothes tonight," Dermot says. "Pick out some things for you?"

"If you're sure?" I say doubtfully. "Won't that be hugely boring?"

He shakes his head. "I like stuff like that. How do you feel about sequins?"

"Like I do about skydiving: queasy and scared."

I drop out of the van when I get home and wave goodbye to my new stylist. As soon as I'm through the door, I can feel something is wrong. All the lights are off and there's an unfamiliar bleeping sound coming from upstairs.

"Mum?" I call out softly. There's no answer, so I creep upstairs towards the sound, not bothering to take off my coat or bag. It's dark apart from a flashing red light in Mum and Dad's bedroom, accompanied by the bleeping. The room smells sour and Mum is asleep in bed. Her phone is flashing with an alarm that says, *Girls*. Is it to make sure she's awake when we come home? I turn the alarm off and sit next to her for a while.

We never ask her how her day has gone any more. When she worked at the university, she always had funny stories about her students and their awful sex-obsessed poetry. But these days, we don't bother, because all she's doing is staying at home, watching TV or applying for jobs online.

There's a noise behind me and I look around to see Lavender beckoning me out of the room. I follow her downstairs. She makes me beans on toast and we eat it in front of the TV.

"It's nice," I tell her.

"I put chilli and paprika in it."

"Ooh, fancy."

"I think the paprika went off in 2009, but..."

"It's red dust. What harm can it do?"

"Right?"

"Right!"

There's some sleepy movement upstairs and eventually, Mum comes down. She's washed and dressed and seems to be making an effort, though she looks a bit watery-eyed. I'm glad when the front door bangs and Dad is home.

"How's my flower?" he asks, bending over to kiss her. "Looking completely deskunked, may I say?" he teases and she takes the compliment with a little preen.

"Worrying?" he asks in a quiet voice meant just for her and she nods a bit. He looks thoughtful and goes into the kitchen, rattling around as he makes a cup of tea.

"I want to talk to you about my job!" he calls from the kitchen.

"Oh, yeah," Mum says warily and I turn the volume down on the TV. I think we'd all like to hear about this so-called "job".

"So, I'm actually quite good at it!" he shouts through the door. I get the feeling he'd rather talk like this than face-to-face.

"Is it project management?" Mum asks.

"Sort of. More marketing, really!" he says.

"And legal?" Lav and I jump in at the same time with the question we've been worrying about most.

"Yes!" He sounds exasperated. "Have a little faith in me. Anyway. I'm actually quite good at it and I've been offered the job for as long as I want it."

"That's amazing!" I shout and even Mum brightens up.

"It's not much money," he warns. "We can keep on top of the main bills but we still need to make some decisions about the house and where we live."

"Yeah, yeah, yeah…" Mum waves away his caution for now, and I'm with her. Just knowing there's some money coming in cheers us all up. Lav and I lean against Mum and she pulls a blanket over our legs. Mum's wearing her nice perfume again – she smells of herself.

"It doesn't matter what the job is," Mum says quietly, turning to us. "Cleaning toilets, a paper round, deliveries. It doesn't matter what the job is, right, girls?"

"Right," we say, and I mean it.

She glances behind her, to check Dad isn't coming. "You must never be ashamed of your dad, because he's doing his best for you two."

"I wouldn't!" I say, genuinely.

The patio lights flick on, illuminating the back garden and I see Dad scurry across the lawn to the shed. Mum doesn't notice.

"Mum," Lav says, firmly, "we're not snobs."

"Yeah!" I feel the same. "We would never be embarrassed by Dad's job."

As Dad staggers across the lawn, he seems to be hopping into a pair of ... massive black boots.

"I'm ... I'm proud of him," I carry on, slightly distracted, "for finding work. Not that... I know you're going to find a great job too!" I add hastily. Dad marches back into his shed, in his big black boots.

"Good." Mum looks relieved. "I'm glad to hear it. Being cool means nothing when you're an adult. Anyway, I *always* think your dad's cool."

Now Dad strides out of his shed, fully dressed, dramatically silhouetted in the back garden, and all Lav and I can do is stare. Mum finally turns to see what we're looking at.

"Oh, hell, no," she says.

On our patio, a massive bumblebee stands, legs apart,

hips rocking in rhythm to Lady Gaga's "Applause". I don't know where the music is coming from, but the sound quality is fantastic. The bee shoots his arms in the air and launches into a flawless dance routine. Despite the boots, he moves with uninhibited grace and fluid hip-work. I recognize some Zumba moves.

"I think he's got speakers in his bottom," Lav says, going to the patio door to admire him more closely.

"What am I looking at?" says Mum.

"The mascot for the local football club." I suddenly recognize the costume. "The Bumbles."

The bee flicks his stinger at us in a sassy fashion.

So, Dad is a big bee.

27

WORRY DIARY

* ~~Dad is out of work~~
* Dad is a big bee.

This is progress. It's the first worry I've crossed off all term.

Mum and Dad are still asleep as I head downstairs for breakfast. I can't get used to this, it's weird. Mum and Dad were always the first up, racing around pulling on their work clothes and shouting about laptop chargers. First Dad stopped doing it, now Mum too, and Lavender and I are the only ones up most mornings. I feel like I need more parenting than this, I think, as I tip out my own cereal. Hannah's mum still gives her a French plait every morning while she eats high-protein slow-release grains or whatever Debs decrees now.

I'm wolfing down the rubbish emu cereal before it collapses into mush when Lav comes into the kitchen.

"Hey, Lav, now Dad has a job – of sorts – do you think we can go back to the old cereal?"

"Maybe. What's wrong with this one?"

I tip the bowl up and show her my soggy emu shapes.

"Ew."

"Are you not gonna eat breakfast?"

"Nah... What? Lou, why are you staring at me like that?"

"Nothing. You're just looking a bit scrawny these days."

"I'm stressed."

"Well, if you lose too much weight, everyone will think you're trying to get model-sized because you love modelling and want to be a model and—"

Lav glares at me and starts shaking out a bowl of cereal. Result. I am a good sister, caring and manipulative. But this really is the sort of thing Mum or Dad should be up and keeping an eye on.

Lav's phone vibrates: Toot toot, from Ro. She looks unenthused. "Can I swap and take the van?" she asks.

"Are you still annoyed with him?" I ask.

"Yep. Not sure he's even noticed – he's been talking to *brands*."

I tip my bowl into the sink and hurry out of the house to see if Gabe is with Ro this morning. He is!

"Hello, stranger." I go round to his window to chat.

"I'm sorry." He looks mortified. "I'm so buried in schoolwork and extra classes and debating practice... I know I've been a bit quiet."

"That's OK! I've been busy too," I say, and immediately regret it. I don't want to tell him too much about Perf Class in case it gets back to Hazel. Thankfully, he's already looking at his school books again and I see Aggy's van trundling round the corner, right on time.

"I'll see you later." I wave and Gabe blows me a kiss. A few seconds later, I clamber into the van, and Dermot hands me his phone.

"I've got lots of potential dresses for you," he announces.

I scroll through the photos.

"For you to get an idea of what they'll look like on..." he says, unnecessarily.

I'm looking at ten photos of Dermot wearing vintage dresses.

"Dermot," I say seriously, because this is very serious. "Don't ever let your phone fall into the hands of someone at school."

"OK."

"No, I don't think you're taking this as seriously as

you need to. Look at me. If Karl Ashton got his hands on this, he would make your life HELL."

"He's been doing that for years."

"This would give him fresh ammunition. He'll be picking on you till you're thirty."

"I'll be a fashion designer by then, so my security will deal with him." Dermot folds his arms, looking stubborn.

"Fairy nuff."

I flick through the photos. Some of these are very, very cool. There's one that's way too weird for me, but I can think of someone who'd look good in it.

"Could Lav borrow one of these?" I ask, and Aggy nods.

"Of course! Just be careful – some of them are worth a lot of money."

"How much?" I ask. Bit uncouth but that's how I roll.

"Several hundred," Aggy says. Wow.

"Can I borrow one that *isn't*, please?" I say, thinking of my own clothes, dotted with various meals.

As Dermot and I pass the NO MOBILE PHONES ON SCHOOL PROPERTY sign by the entrance, I remember I need to send a text. I join several people standing by the sign, tapping on their phones. I'm not sure this warning has the desired effect.

Lav! If you need a dress for the
competition ceremony thing, Aggy's got
a beautiful one you can borrow!

Dots pop up to show Lav's replying and I suddenly
worry I've been tactless, so I add, but you might not want
to go. Her reply surprises me.

Well, maybe.

You're going?

Did you know that Amelia B's cousin's
girlfriend is in the final too?

No? (Although I guess that must have been what Mr
Peters was talking about...)

I really hate Amelia B.

Lav really hates Amelia B. For good reason. Amelia
B is a gossip machine and is also not above throwing
someone's bra out of a window when they're getting
changed for netball. Last term, poor Lav had to go and
retrieve a bright orange bra from the middle of the yard,
with about three classes watching. Since then, Lav has

nurtured a strong and lasting hatred of Amelia B.

Well, Ro'll be happy you're going! Looking on the bright side.

Lav gives me the emoji with a flat look on its face. I always wondered what that one meant, and now I see it's a fond irritable weariness.

I stop texting as I realize Dermot is waiting for me and we head into school.

"I wonder if Hannah's sitting with us today?" he says. "It's always a sign of how well or badly the prom is going."

Dermot gets to the form room ahead of me then looks back with a comical *Eek!* face. Hannah is sitting with us, reading a history book as if it's the most fascinating thing she's ever read. When we both know it isn't.

Dermot sits behind and I flump down next to her.

"Nice evening?" I ask.

"Nope," she says quietly, eyes on her book.

"Thought not," I say. "I texted but you never—"

"I'm sorry!" She gives me a quick glance. "I'm jus—"

"So busy, I know."

She shakes her head, still pretending to read the history book so the Prom Committee don't know she's talking about them. "It's such a mess," she whispers. Dermot leans forward to hear. "We spent so much money going to gigs to 'scout' bands and we used prom money."

"Han!" I say, scandalized.

"I KNOW! It wasn't my idea, obviously. Cammie said it was *research*. Now Mr Peters says we can't put it on at the Rothermere Estate because it's too far away. So we have no venue, no entertainment..."

"Well," says Dermot, trying to be positive, "what *have* you got?"

Bless him. Hannah stares down at the history book, thinking. There's a long, long silence. Dermot and I exchange a look.

"We have ... food!" she whispers finally. "Melia's family are doing the catering. They're not happy about it but Cammie bulldozed them into it. And we have a sound system from Cammie's uncle."

"Is that the VJ thingy?" I ask and she nods.

We sit and think.

"You're a bit stuffed," Dermot whispers.

"Thank you," Hannah says sarcastically.

"OK, guys!" Mr Peters runs into the classroom, even later than usual. "Adams!"

"What have I done?" Pima Adams looks like a rabbit caught in the headlights.

"Nothing! High-speed register. Come on, class, look lively. Alexandrous!"

"Yeah!"

"Anderson!"

The bell goes, and we all start packing up our bags.

"Au Yong! Stop moving. I need to get a look at you, see who's here." Mr Peters is trying to be heard over the noise. He gives up. "Fine, just tell me if you notice someone is missing – we'll do it that way!" he shouts as we leave.

Cammie, Melia and Nicole are more subdued than I've ever seen them. At lunchtime a kid in the year below trips and lands with his face buried in his tray and they say nothing. This is usually the sort of thing they would elevate into a school-wide snark-off until the kid has to change schools, dye his hair and adopt a new name. But they just sit, silently eating their salads.

Roman steps forward and helps the kid up, offering him a tissue. I get the impression, from the way he keeps glancing back at her, that he's trying to get in Lav's good books. She's sitting with her friends, not with him, and does seem to be treating him to her chilly side. Which, as someone who once used her tweezers to unblock a plughole, I can attest is pretty fricking cold.

Just then, I spot Gabriel. It's rare to see him at lunch – he's usually in some extra class or dweeby club – so I bounce on over to see him. "Heyo!" I say, with more enthusiasm than cool.

"Hey!" he says. "I was coming to find you."

We sit down at the nearest table. Gabriel says he's

taking a break from Debating Club; he's getting a bit fed up with Hazel.

"Oh no," I say, SUPER-MATURELY. "That's a shame." I don't start listing possible reasons why. Is it her controlling personality? Her rudeness? The way she dresses like a stuck-up gnome and you feel like popping a miniature fishing rod in her hands? Hopefully I'll be able to cross her off my Worry Diary list soon enough. I am *racing* through these!

I spot Hannah and Dermot over Gabe's shoulder, looking a little lost. "Hey!" I wave them over. There's not much room at the table; they have to squeeze in where they can.

"Yeah, I, er..." Gabe continues. "I think she was hoping me and Lara would ... um..."

"Would *um...*?" I ask, but with a nasty feeling I know what he means.

"You know, go out."

"But what about me?" I say, more baffled than angry. Though angry will probably come later.

"I don't know if she really thinks about other people's feelings," he says, slowly, like he's cracking a complicated mystery.

"And how did Lara feel about the matchmaking?"

"I'm not sure she even knew what was going on. I think Hazel just likes to manipulate people for the fun of it. She can be a bit mean, actually."

"You. Don't. Say," I reply, in tones drier than Mum's couscous.

Gabe turns a wondering look on me. "Did you not *like* her?"

"Gabe." I can't kiss him in school or there would be wolf-whistles and detention, so I put a hand on his shoulder. "I don't think you're smart enough for Lara. You should stick with your basic b girlfriend."

The bell goes for end of lunch. PERFECT TIMING. I flash him a smile and head to class, Hannah and Dermot in tow. Just occasionally, once in every blue moon, Lou P. Brown is cool.

The rest of the day is surprisingly good. Without constant snarky quips from Cammie and her lot, I speak up in class a lot more, and thanks to Dermot, I actually know the answers. I even get a test back in history that's eighty-six per cent!

Eighty-six! This is the highest mark I've ever got, I tell Dermot excitedly. I see him subtly cover up his ninety-two per cent. It's like my emotions are on a seesaw with Cammie's and we can only be happy when the other one is miserable (a theory I have LONG HELD).

"Eighty-six!" Mum is crowing that evening as she dishes out dinner. "My clever girl. Just for that, you can pick out the courgettes."

Woohoo! I loathe and despise courgettes – they're soggy, evil and taste of dishwater. "Can I spoon them onto Lav's plate?" I ask.

"No," Lav says firmly.

"Did *you* get eighty-six per cent?" I ask. "Because if you didn't, I think you should eat my courgettes."

"Give them to me," Dad says. "Fatherhood is nothing but eating the stuff no one else likes."

"And dancing in a bee costume," Lav reminds him. He gives her a wink.

My phone rings with an unknown number.

"Ignore it," Mum advises. I turn it on silent but the Unknown Number calls again and again. By the fourth time, Dad wipes his hands on a tea towel and holds his hand out for my phone. I pass it over.

"Hello?" Dad answers in chilly tones. "Well, yes, she is here. She's eating right now... Well, OK. I mean, I'd rather *not* but ... if you insist..."

I watch him basically being bullied over the phone. I can't think of anyone who would be so instantly controlling, except...

"Cammie?" Dad says to me.

I freeze. "What does she want?" I hiss.

"She wants to come over," Dad answers in a whisper, looking scared.

"WHY?"

Dad shrugs, and hands the phone over as if he's glad it's not his problem.

"Hello?" I say nervously.

"Hey, babes. Listen, we're coming round."

"Oh *God*, no."

Mum, Lav and Dad have stopped eating and are all watching me squirm on the phone. I'm sweating like it's my first Perf Class.

"What?" Cammie demands.

"Coughing, I was coughing. Um, why … are you … coming round?"

"See you in ten." And she hangs up.

I put down the phone and turn to my family to tell them to brace for the worst, flee for their lives.

"What?" says Mum.

"Something wicked this way comes."

WORRY DIARY

* Cammie in my house! Everywhere I look, I see uncool things that I will be mocked for.

Mum and Dad finish dinner and clear away the plates while I scurry around the living room, scooping up every embarrassing photo of me (which is EVERY photo of me) and shoving them under the sofa. I spot a horrible deformed clay cat with **MUmMy** scraped into it and hide it under a cushion.

A sense of doom settles over me and spreads to my family.

"Do I still have skunk hair?" Mum asks, examining her reflection in the kettle.

"Stop. She's just a girl from school," Dad says. "I'm

sure she's nice deep down."

"Maybe she has nice bone marrow," says Lav. "But the rest of her is a bi—"

"*Lavender.*"

I don't know what Cammie wants from me. But whatever it is, she'll just demand it and I'll do it, if that wimpy little phone call is anything to go by. The doorbell rings.

"Your friends are here!" Mum calls from the living room.

Does no one listen to me? That is not what's happening.

I open the door. "Hi! Cammie. Melia. Nicole." They push past me as if they own the place. Following behind is Hannah, mouthing, *I am so sorry*, and shaking her head. She hugs me, and whispers in my ear, "I didn't think – I told them about your dad."

WHAT about my dad? My insides go a little watery. They don't know that my dad is the football mascot, do they? Why would they need a big bee? Why would *anyone* need a big bee?

"Mark?" Hannah calls. "Can we speak to you? Please."

Dad pops his head out of the living room, looking wary.

Melia jumps in and gets down to business. "Mr Brown."

"Hello … uh."

"Melia. Hannah said you had a plan for prom."

"Oh! Well … I *did*."

There's a silence. Dad examines his fingernails. "But Hannah felt my help was not wanted, so…"

Cammie, Melia and Nicole swivel unfriendly eyes on Hannah.

"I'm sorry, Mark," Hannah says. He looks up.

"And?"

Hannah looks blank. I take pity on her and whisper something in her ear. She frowns but I shrug at her like, *If you want his help.*

"And project management is an art form?"

"Yesssss." Dad does the guns at her with his fingers and I make a mental note to die of shame later.

"Please step into my office," he tells them.

WORRY DIARY

✱ If Cammie, Melia or Nicole breathe a word
   about what my dad is like at home, I will never
   live it down.

"Do take a seat," says Dad, perching on his work-bench in his little shed and gesturing grandly towards paint cans on the floor.

To my surprise, all four girls grab a paint can and sit down. They must be desperate.

Dad gently kicks a four-pack of beer under his work

bench, out of sight, unrolls his laminated prom plan and pins it on the wall. He kept hold of it. Of course he did. He's adorable.

Click.

He has a little device that shines a pinprick of light at the plan. He's using it as a pointer, though the laminate is so shiny we're all getting lasers reflecting at our eyeballs.

"Now, if you had accepted my help, we would have begun work in Week One."

I flinch from a wobbling beam of bright light. He's not adorable; he's incredibly annoying.

"It is now Week Six. Can you see the problem we're facing?"

"Yes, Mr Brown," says Cammie, repressing her snappy instincts admirably. I'm very impressed.

"As you can see, the workload in Week One is light. Weeks Two to Five are heavier but manageable and then it intensifies in one final focused week. However, you rejected my offer of help in – please be quiet, Louise – in Week One and now your options are greatly reduced."

He clicks off his pointing light like the whole thing is a lost cause.

"So you can't help us?" Cammie says, betraying a hint of impatience. Dad looks into the middle distance. I imagine rock music is playing in his head.

"Luckily for you, I'm the best of the best," he tells the middle distance. Nicole peers out into the garden to see if there's anything there. Nope. Nothing but Dad's love of drama.

"Your challenges are threefold," Dad says, putting one foot up on a paint can and knocking Melia over with his knee. "I am so sorry." He pulls her out of a pile of wellies.

"You need to host a prom. You need…"

"No, no, that's it, Mr Brown," says Hannah. "We just need to host a prom."

"Hannah, Hannah, Hannah…" Dad says shaking his head. "Challenges are just opportunities to achieve."

"I don't think that makes sense," she says stubbornly.

"At Lou's sixth birthday, you came dressed as a plum and wet yourself."

There's a silence. Nicole tries to hide her sniggering beneath a dainty cough.

"I don't see how that's relevant," Hannah mutters.

"It isn't. I just wanted to share it with the room and remind you I have plenty more where that came from."

That shuts Hannah up.

"You're looking at a threefold issue: host a prom, which contains three subdivisons. Namely, find a venue for the prom, arrange transport to the prom and hire some entertainment for the prom. If you find a venue closer to town, you instantly knock one task off that list."

Melia and Nicole look at Cammie, who shakes her head and mumbles something.

"What was that?" says Dad.

"Fine," says Cammie, ungraciously. "No Dreezy mansion."

"No Dreezy whatsit," Dad agrees, chirpy at winning an early battle. "Now, *this* is your school." He pins up a map next to the six-week plan and points at something in the middle. "And this is a four-mile radius around it, which I think is a reasonable distance to expect people to travel under their own steam. So let's pick a venue within that circle and within reason. As you're going to lose your deposit on the first place – ten miles away, woefully impractical and painfully expensive – there's not much money left to play with. Wouldn't have happened on my watch," he mutters to himself.

Cammie, Melia and Nicole get up to peer at the map. They look unimpressed.

"Uh ... Bowlarama?" says Melia, sarcastically.

"It smells of feet but has good square footage," Dad says.

"I was joking," she says.

"Well, we don't really have time for that, do we? Because you're awful at project management."

I look at Melia silently swallowing her rage and plotting ways to make my life hell later. I spot Dad's bee costume folded up beside me and lean forward to block it from view. Everyone looks at me, as if I've leaned forward with a great idea.

"Um, the Town Hall?" I say, squinting desperately at the map.

"Hardly cool," tuts Dad.

Fine. Last time I help you. "Well, this isn't really my prom, or my problem," I say, standing up. Hannah turns big pleading eyes on me. I sigh and sit back down. Ugh, I hate being a nice person. If I was heartless, I'd be in my cosy bedroom watching YouTube right now, without a care in the world. Maybe unravelling the mysteries of contouring.

"A local celebrity would also be a good idea, make an appearance sorta thing," says Dad, twinkling at me like we share a delightful secret. *No way*, my stony expression says. No oversized bee is dragging his musical arse to my prom. Thankfully, the others ignore him.

"We want somewhere impressive, somewhere with a bit of class," says Melia, desperately.

"Glamour!" Nicole pleads.

"On a budget," Hannah adds quietly.

"Perhaps..." says Dad, staring at the map like a maverick cop who's just about to crack a serial killer's identity. "Just maybe..."

There's a long silence. Cammie massages her temples

like, *Am I really so desperate I'll put up with this?* Clearly she is, as the five of us stay perched on our paint cans, knees by our chins.

"Wait here," says Dad, and hurries out to make a call. The darkness of the garden swallows him up and we can just hear the murmuring of him talking into his mobile.

"Thanks, Lou," says Hannah, gratefully, and to my surprise the others murmur agreement.

"He'll help you," I tell them. "But he's going to be really annoying about it."

"Same," says Melia. "My mum and aunt are catering the whole thing at cost price and I'm never going to hear the end of it."

Behind her back, Cammie rolls her eyes and I realize this Prom Committee may be even less harmonious than I thought.

Dad is still out there on his phone, and everyone is getting cold.

"How long will he be?" Nicole asks me. I shrug. How should I know? He's full of unpleasant surprises.

Finally, he comes back to the shed, breathing on his hands to warm them but looking very pleased with himself. "I have a surprise for YOU!" he announces. "Just ten more minutes. Help is on its way."

Lav knocks on the shed door – carrying a tray. "Mum made me bring you out tea."

"I don't want tea." Cammie waves Lav away like she's a waitress. Lav stares at her like she's seriously considering dumping the tray on her head. Instead, she pours Cammie a large mug and says, "I. Brought. Tea." And stomps off back to the house.

"So, how's swimming?" Dad asks and Hannah launches into talk about Personal Bests and resistance training, assuming he remembers it all from when I was a swimmer. Dad's eyes glaze over, but he says, "Uh-huh... Great stuff... No way?" at various intervals and I think he gets away with it.

There's another knock on the shed door. "Better not be more tea," Cammie mutters. To my surprise, the door swings open to reveal Dermot standing there.

"What?" Melia says, looking from Dad to Dermot and back again. "What's this?"

"The answer to all your problems, so be polite," Dad tells her. "Come in, son. Come in. How's Aggy? Want to sit on a paint can?"

"Actually, Mr Brown, my trousers don't really bend so I'll just lean against this if that's all right."

"Against what? NO!"

Dermot leans against a sturdy-looking sheet of MDF that instantly snaps, collapses and swallows him whole. Dust billows up and fills the shed.

"Evacuate!"

Spluttering, blinded by dust, we all stagger out into the garden. Dad pulls Dermot to his feet and pats his back while he coughs and spits into a flower bed.

"I'm sorry," he croaks. "They're my least flexible item of clothing."

Once we're all settled back in the shed and Dermot is resting semi-comfortably against the wall, Dad outlines his great plan.

"We host the prom at Dermot's house," Dad beams, smugly.

"You can't host two hundred people in a house." Nicole looks exasperated.

"You can in this one," says Dad and the Prom Committee eye up Dermot, intrigued.

"We pay Aggy and Dermot the cost of venue hire, cheaper than Bowlarama hopefully?" Dermot nods gravely. "And you can use Aggy's house clearance items to dress the whole thing."

"Mmm-yeah-no. We were going for a Nu-Grunge and bling vibe," Cammie says.

"Whatever you were *going for*, you've missed by some way," Dad slaps her down. Wow, he's really feisty when he's project-managing. "You were going for an absence-of-any-guests-because-they're-ten-miles-away vibe. And now you will have an antiquey ... ah..."

"Baroque," Dermot helps him out. I'll have to google that word later.

"That sort of thing," Dad concludes. "It will have the real Wow Factor." (He has been learning new words from daytime TV.)

Everyone ponders this. It's actually a brilliant idea. Dad smooths his workflow spreadsheet, lovingly.

"Do you mind people from school in your house, Dermot? What if they don't behave?" I say, anxiously. The thought of Karl playing some cruel prank on Dermot in his own home makes me feel sick.

"AS IF I would trust a load of teenagers to behave! No offence," says Dad. "This is where your mother's thuggish relatives finally come in handy."

I congratulate him on his cleverness and he bows. Cammie, Melia and Nicole add their praise. Hannah follows up a little more grudgingly. Dad notices.

"Your plum costume was so heavy with wee you staggered around in circles and fell into a bush," he reminisces.

"DAD."

"Sorry. Now onto entertainment. This would have been a Week One decision, but there's no point crying over spilt milk because *you* forgot to order milk." He chuckles to himself.

"Actually," says Dermot, "I have one condition for

using our house: we provide the entertainment."

I have a horrible queasy feeling I know what he's going to say next.

"You ... and your mum?" says Nicole slowly.

"Me and my Perf Class," he says proudly. "We're really good. We improvise scenarios, dance and do poetry."

"Oh. Oh God..." says Melia faintly.

I'm just imagining the Perf Class onstage, taking suggestions from the audience – all smutty, obviously. If they're even listening. While Eli and Patrice bicker over motivation, and Star does a handstand. No way. I will talk him out of this as soon as I get him alone.

"Lou's in it too," says Dermot.

Melia, Nicole and Cammie look at me as if all their Christmases have come at once. I give them a watery smile, to match the feeling in my guts.

29

WORRY DIARY

* After I'm humiliated at prom and run away to
  start a new life somewhere, what name shall
  I choose?
* Samantha Finglebrink?
* Effie Nimplestick.
* Beverly Amplebank the Fourth?

We go to Aggy's that weekend. She finds the whole
thing hilarious. She's delighted that the house is getting
spruced up and seems unbothered by the thought of 200
teenagers trying to get drunk and get off with each other.

"It's too quiet, just Dermot and me," she says with a
shrug when Dad strides through her second living room,
gesticulating dramatically and painting a lurid picture

of vomit bouncing down the staircase, fights breaking out in the fourth bathroom and bras hanging off oil paintings.

"All right, Mark," Mum says, slightly alarmed as he stands on a chair to demonstrate the more dramatic parts.

"Well," he says, tucking his shirt back in, "I just want Aggy to be fully forewarned. Teenagers are disgusting animals— Hello, kids."

"Hello, Mark," say Roman and Gabriel.

It's Friday after school and Dad has drawn up plans of the whole of Dermot's house. We now have a list to take to the hardware store and we have roped everyone in to help. This was a slightly bigger job than I realized. Even Pete has agreed to come along. Not enthusiastically, sure, but he's here. Gabriel was debating this evening but offered to cancel it for us.

"Are you sure?" I asked. (Not that I wasn't delighted.) "Don't they need you for the semi-final, practising and stuff?"

"Hazel keeps changing her mind as to who's going to actually debate in the semi-finals," Gabe said. I bet she does. I imagine that's how she wields her power, promoting people and demoting them.

If Hazel and Cammie ever joined forces, they'd rule the world. Let's hope they never meet.

I love this weary, irritable tone Gabe now gets when

he's talking about Hazel, but I wisely kept that to myself and said, "Well, if you can come, that would be great. I know Hannah will appreciate it."

"Oh, *he's* here," is actually what Hannah says. But I am determined I will make my boyfriend and best friend BE friends. At least I don't have to worry about Gabe and Dermot, who get on brilliantly. Give Gabe an exquisitely detailed stuffed otter, and you've got a friend for life.

When Dermot tells Roman and Gabriel about Perf Class, they struggle to keep a straight face at the thought of me being "spontaneous" and not in charge. They collapse into giggles when I tell them we're the entertainment for the prom. I look at Pete; he refuses to make eye contact with me. But that's cool, Dermot and I haven't told anyone he's in Perf Class and I'm not gonna snitch on him now. He should have a bit more faith in me!

Me, Gabe, Pete, Lav and Roman squeeze into Pete's Mini. It's a tight fit. I'm spooning Lavender with a dead left leg.

"Am I sitting on you?" Gabe asks, concerned.

"Everyone's sitting on me," I reply, muffled.

I only ever trail behind Mum and Dad in the hardware store. I've never had to navigate it myself, and Lavender's never been. When we get there, she looks around in awe.

"Wow," she remarks, "a shop this big and there's nothing I want to buy! Ooh, Hello Kitty doorknobs?"

We grab a shop assistant. "What is a sprocket?" Gabe asks her, as if he's new to the English language.

"Does that say *widget*? Is that a thing?" demands Pete, pointing at Dad's list. "If I said *widget* to you, what would you think?"

We spend a hundred pounds in the hardware store, then with a groan I fold myself back into Pete's Mini. Someone pats me comfortingly on my thigh.

"That was me, by the way," Lavender says.

"Glad to hear it."

We drive to Dermot's house to find that Mum's family have already taken over. They're moving furniture, sweeping, rewiring – I'm extremely impressed. We carry our bags through to the kitchen, where we find Aggy inexplicably charmed by my uncle Eddie, who's explaining to her how you can build your own septic tank in a normal suburban back garden. I have no idea why.

"Right, gather round!" Dad gets his bossy voice on and we obediently cluster into a semi-circle around him. "We are cleaning all the surfaces, removing all dainty ornaments, dusting the robust ones and sponging down the walls – brightening the whole place up. But then and only then do we clean the floor – LOUISE, ARE YOU LISTENING TO ME? STOP LOOKING AT YOUR PHONE! – and we go room by room. Door closed means: *Not done yet.* Open door means: *Behold my achievements!* Anything you find that you think will be suitable set-dressing for the prom, pile it in the conservatory. This includes beautiful things or hilariously ugly things, nothing too expensive because teenagers will destroy them like wild pigs. OK? Gooooooo..."

Dad puts his hand in the middle of our semi-circle. I frown at it. No one moves.

"Please," says Dad. *Oh fine.* We all put our hands on his hand and yell, "GOOOOOO, TEAM!!" then shoot our hands in the air. I think Dad has picked this up from the football club. I'm glad Cammie, Melia and Nicole aren't here to see it. They're helping Melia's family with the catering. Apparently, they have a huge draughty lock-up just out of town and the Prom Committee are there all weekend getting a crash course in hospitality. Whatever that means.

Everyone branches off to find a room to clean. I can hear Dad relaying instructions somewhere in the house, and I follow his voice. Which is hard as the house is so big it actually has an echo. I'm roaming around for ages, uncovering room after room. Each with the same familiar musty smell.

I can hear worrying sparking noises coming from the second living room. Mum's cousins are doing the electrics. According to her they know what they're doing, but I'm not so sure – I can hear them playing YouTube tutorial videos.

Dad is now in a bedroom putting forth a controversial idea. He wants to nail shut all the rooms we don't want prom attendees to go in. Aggy isn't sure.

"Aggy, listen to me. They're teenagers. Basically, undomesticated animals with push-up bras and a sense of entitlement."

"Dad." Lavender emerges from a nearby room with a sponge in hand. "I am RIGHT here."

"I know you don't have a sense of entitlement, pet." Dad pats her on the head. "We haven't got the money."

If he makes it to the end of the day without getting a slap, I'll be amazed.

I leave Dad and Gabe hammering planks to one of the bedroom doorframes so the door can't be opened. I hope I'm within earshot when they realize they're blocking themselves in.

Half of us are splashing soapy water around, the other half are doing electrics. It's a high-risk combination, so we agree to start at different ends of the house and meet in the middle. With a big electrical fire and lots of screaming.

Aggy is such a magpie. She's gathered loads of weird and wonderful stuff over the years from house clearances and travelling. The whole first floor is full of amazing things like suits of armour and velvet chaises longues. (I know what they are now.)

Hannah tries to "tidy away" Aggy's gnomes, but it turns her from gentle oddball to steely-eyed negotiator in seconds.

"There's one with no arms and legs and a crack in his nose," says Hannah. "Can I get rid of that one at least?"

"No! He's my favourite – he has character!"

I carry some seriously old fashion magazines out to the recycling, just in time to see Dad clambering gingerly out of a bedroom window and shuffling along the roof. For a project manager he really doesn't think ahead.

Later, with dust in my hair and aches in my bones, I wander to the kitchen to find Aggy and Dermot cooking pasta sauce in a pot so big I could get in it and invite a friend.

"Where did you get the pot?" I ask, taking a seat at the kitchen table.

"Robin, Dermot's dad, brought it back from a jazz tour in Spain."

"Did you go?" I ask Dermot and he nods.

"I'd be onstage in a papoose," he says.

"Do you remember that?" Angie says, surprised.

"No," he admits and his mum drops a kiss on his arm.

This tender moment is ruined by my dad, very much alive and back in the house, screaming, "YOU DON'T SCARE ME!" a few floors above.

"I think he found a spider," I tell them and chop onions to be helpful. Which makes us all cry, but I think Aggy was heading that way anyway.

By the end of the night I'm picking dust out of my eyelashes as I sit on the stairs, exhausted, to catch my breath. I don't think I've worked that hard in a long time. Aggy brings us dinner. It's delicious, and there's enough food for everyone but not enough things to eat off, so I have a pint glass of hot tomato pasta and Dad has five dainty teacups full.

As I eat, I watch Pete mucking around with Roman in the front garden, trying to hit him in the face with a filthy rag. Their breath is puffing out, visible clouds in the cold air. Pete seems in a great mood – it's like old times again.

I'm glad Pete is happy. For purely selfish reasons, cos I need to ask him a big favour.

30

WORRY DIARY

✱ Why does NO ONE recognize a terrible idea
when it's staring them in the face?

My last hope was that Uliol would realize it was emotional masochism to put his class of sensitive artistes in front of a rowdy mob of schoolkids, but...

"*Children!*" He beams. "How delightful."

"Well..." Dermot begins.

"Not children," I inform the class firmly. "Our age. My age." I gesture at us. "Bigger in some cases, and definitely louder."

"I think it'll be brilliant," says Patrice, looking enthused.

Really? Everything I've tried for the last five weeks,

she's given me this unimpressed face, but somehow the thought of public humiliation gets her all twinkly-eyed?

You're weird, Patrice.

Uliol is squatting on the floor, legs wide. "OK, let's brainstorm. Dermot, is there a fee?"

"Sorry." Dermot gives me a glance to check, then shakes his head.

"Fine, no glitter cannon," says Uliol. "We'll just have to create entertainment with our bodies and minds. Thankfully, they're the most powerful things in the world, right, guys?"

Everyone's nodding as if they haven't heard of nuclear bombs or elephants.

We decide to do a fifteen-minute improv set. I allow myself to start breathing a little. Fifteen minutes, that doesn't seem so long – that's like half an episode of TV. Maybe if I wear my hair differently, no one will know it's me.

They'll think it's that *other* six-foot fifteen-year-old girl in our school. Terrible idea.

"I want to perform my latest poem," says Eli self-importantly. "It's about the fragility of democracy in a world where media is becoming increasingly untrustworthy."

That'll have the kids dancing, Eli.

We break away into our usual groups. For all their grumbling, Eli and Patrice have stuck with me, so I can't be *that* bad. And today, for the first time, Pete joins us. It's gone from him refusing to make eye contact with me, to the two of us discussing an imaginary pineapple that I've brought to the vet because I think it's not well.

"He's been so listless lately," I say to Pete, who squeezes the air, miming feeling a pineapple and looking concerned.

"Are you feeding him anything different?" he asks, seriously.

"No," I say, leaving a pause, then adding, "just popcorn."

Everyone in the group starts laughing so I demonstrate. "I poke one on each of his spikes."

They laugh harder and I love this! But I do wonder if 200 teenagers from school are going to find it quite as funny as we do.

Eli reads his poem and it's actually even worse than I thought. Excessively long – and I'm no poetry expert, but it does sound a lot like whingeing. I peek around the room and I can see quite a few people glazing over, clearly thinking about what they're going to have for dinner but disguising it behind nods and thoughtful fingers-on-lips. Uliol looks *thrilled* by it, but enthusiasm *is* his default mode.

As we fetch our coats at the end of the session, I put Phase One of my plan into motion. "Hi, Pineapple Vet!" I say to Pete.

He gives me an unamused look. Fair.

"Um, ah, could Dermot and I get a lift home? Or, just to your home and we can walk to ours? Aggy can't pick us up today."

(She can't pick us up because I asked her not to pick us up. Cunning as a weasel, Lou P. Brown.)

"I don't have room, I've got a load of wood in the car."

"Wood? Why?"

"We're decking the garden."

"Oh, uh." This isn't going well. "Can we sit on top of the wood?"

"No, you'll bend it."

"Can we sit *underneath* it?"

"Suit yourself."

"Ow ow ow ow ow ow ow ow," Dermot whispers from the back seat.

The wood is in big rough planks, and every time Pete takes a corner with his usual reckless speed, it shifts, depositing jagged rows of splinters across my skin. From Dermot's squeaks, I think we have the same problem.

Pete seems oblivious to our pain. "Is Lavender looking forward to the awards ceremony?"

"What?" I say, baffled. "Not particularly. Pete, can I ask you a favour?"

"Is she nervous she's not going to win?"

"No! She doesn't want to be a model. She never even entered the competition, she only stayed in it because we need the money. Hey, can I ask you a favour?"

He turns left. *Ow ow ow ow ow ow ow ow ow.* I think I've got a splinter on my forehead. I hope I can get it out in time for prom.

Pete says, "I thought she'd be excited."

"Not really, no. Lav doesn't like being the centre of attention. That's more of a Ro thing."

"Ha. True."

I can see we're nearly at Pete's house so I have to ask my favour quickly. "Pete, will you perform with Perf Class at our prom?"

"No way."

"But we need you! You used to be so cool—"

"What's that supposed to mean?"

"I hadn't *finished*," I say, struggling to explain myself from beneath a pile of planks. "When you were at school, everyone thought you were cool, and *now* you're cool in a different way..."

"Is that right?" he says moodily. "That's Ro and Gabe you're thinking of. I'm flunking a college course."

"Not everyone can be academic," comes Dermot's squashed voice from the back. Pete turns to look at him.

"Are you academic?" he asks.

Dermot hesitates. "Um, well..."

"Exactly. It's always smart people who say you don't need to be smart."

"Pete," I tell him, "I'm rubbish at school. If I ever get above a D, my family melts with pride."

"Really?"

"Yes. So you and me need to stick together!"

"You're being manipulative."

"Pleeeaase!!"

Pete is now hauling planks of wood off me so I can get out of his car, and I'm resorting to desperate begging. I'm convinced that if Pete's with us, we won't be humiliated so badly. Everyone still remembers him as the cool guy from sixth form, with the car and the attitude. They won't dare give us trouble if he's onstage.

At the very least, I'm hoping they spend fifteen minutes murmuring "Is that...? No way...? IS it...? It looks like him, but..." before they think to start heckling.

"Nope!" says Pete cheerfully. "I am not humiliating myself for the sake of your prom."

"It's not MY prom!!" I'm going to have to get that tattooed on my forehead soon.

"Even less reason to do it," says Pete with a wolfish grin. It starts to rain and he heads indoors with the wood. "BYE-BYE!" he says pointedly as he bangs the front door shut after him.

I slump, pull my hood up and start walking home. Dermot catches me up, pulling a splinter out of his face. "Your plan..." he deadpans. "Does it end with you and me walking home in the rain?"

"I want to say no," I tell him. "But that would be a lie. I didn't think it all the way through."

As we walk, I get a text from Gabe that cheers me up.

Do you want me to come to prom with you?

"Dermot! Steer me while I text?" He helpfully grabs my coat and pulls me away from approaching lampposts.

It's OK if you want to do Debating, I reply. Again, so maturely!

Really?

Yeah. And I mean it. It's not like everyone has a date for prom. Hannah doesn't, Dermot doesn't.

Really? You're not just saying that and then when I don't come to prom, you'll be sad?

No!

Dots appear. He's typing. Then they stop. Start again. Dermot pulls me hard left as I'm about to march into a postbox.

Gabe finally replies.

I'm thinking of dropping out of Debating
Club and using you as an excuse.

Et two, brutal!

It's Et tu, Bruté! You say it when someone's
betrayed you. Which I haven't!

Is it from The Simpsons or Shakespeare?

Oh. My. God.

What? Well, anyway, that. You. If the
sock fits, Bruté. (Sock emoji.)

Good grief, Lou P.

So... I text, feigning casualness. Not enjoying Debating
Club?

Hazel's still being a bit...

I have to put my phone away at this point, as I'm so
tempted to finish that sentence for him with some robust
honesty.

We reach the end of Dermot's road. I wave him

goodbye and then head to mine at a run, with my hands in my pockets because it is so cold! I don't know how Dermot survives in his retro threads. I'm freezing in layers of practical knits.

I get home to find Dad in full project management mode, taking Mum through his daily chart now we're down to what he's calling Crunch Point. I close the front door quietly and go hide in my room to finish my chat with Gabe.

Difficult is the word he finally came up with.

Yeah, I reply, wondering if my sarcasm is obvious.

Manipulative.

Keep 'em coming.

Bit mean?

Dresses like she lost a bet.

Lou!

Sorrynotsorry.

So I can come to prom? If you'd still like me there.

Sometimes words are not enough. So I send him a gif of a dog delighted by snow. Because I'm going to prom with my boyfriend! And also: I WAS RIGHT ABOUT HAZEL.

I wander into the living room, where Mum is watching Dad dancing. Is it more or less weird that he's in his bee costume?

"I feel like the penultimate spin needs to—"

"That one?" He demonstrates.

"No, the one that starts low and – look." She stands next to him and does a spin. "That one, I feel it could move more seamlessly into the next move? If you went anti-clockwise, your weight would be on the other foot, which would help."

Dad grooves slowly, pacing out his dance moves. "You know –" he takes his bee head off and twinkles at Mum – "there's a spare costume. I could sew a little bow on it and you could—"

"No, Mark."

"No, Dad," I add from the doorway. He looks up, surprised to see me.

"We're on track, Lou!" he says. "With your prom."

"It's not *my* prom!" I say for the hundredth time since Cammie turned up on our doorstep. "They're so lucky you're helping them."

Dad waves a big insect mitt at me. "I don't do it for thanks."

"That's good," I tell him. "Cos you won't get it. They're very rude."

"Right." Dad is now hopping around to get out of his bee trousers. Is he wearing a pair of Mum's thick tights underneath? Actually, I don't want to know. "I need to get to the football grounds nice and early to meet some fans," he adds.

He drops that in like it's nothing.

"Have you *got* fans, Dad?"

"Oh it's nothing, really. It's more Monty than me."

Monty? I mouth at Mum.

"Monty the bee," she whispers. "He has a Facebook fan page."

Dad hurries out of the house. "Tomorrow, Lou, I want to talk the last week of pre-prom planning!"

We sit watching rubbish TV together for a couple of hours. I know it's not a great way to spend a Saturday night, but it's hailing outside. Once your parents can't afford to drive you places and you have to walk everywhere, you get very picky about what social plans you make.

Two drag queens twirl around on TV. "That reminds me," Mum says. "Aggy invited you and Lavender to try on dresses tomorrow? You have to PROMISE not to damage them, though, Lou. She needs to sell them on afterwards."

I think my face says how I feel about that because she gives my foot a squeeze. "We'll pick out something dark."

I do the guns at her in an impression of Dad. She shakes her head. "He's having such a nice time. Good thing your Prom Committee is..."

"Rubbish?"

"Yeah. Will you see if Lav wants to come tomorrow?"

"Lav!" I call upstairs. Nothing. "I'll go up."

I creep upstairs, as if I'm sneaking up on a dragon having a nap. Standing outside Lavender's room, I give myself a little mental blow on my coach whistle. *Come on, Lou. Don't be a wimp.*

I knock on the door. I can hear her inside but she's not answering. I poke my head in and come face-to-face with my sister, arm drawn back as if she's about to attack me.

"AARRGH!" I shout and she yelps the same back at me and pulls her headphones out.

"What are you DOING?" I demand.

"Teach Yourself Tai-Chi."

"Fairy nuff." I wait for my heart to stop hammering against my ribs. "Listen, do you want to go to Aggy's and try on some of her old dresses tomorrow? Vintage, I mean – not her old personal dresses."

"Yeah, I'd love to." She winds her headphones around her phone and puts it away. "Was that Dermot's idea? I guess you're friends now."

"Yeah. It's cool, I just have to remember that … many artists and great thinkers were bullied at school."

"Brilliant. I should be Picasso soon."

"You'd imagine everyone would want to suck up to you if they thought you were going to be a famous model."

"Maybe in an old film. These days, it's *basic*."

"You're not basic," I comfort her. "You're actually very tricky."

Lav's trying to push me off the bed when we hear Mum laughing loudly from the living room. We go down to see what's up and she swivels the computer round to show us that Monty the Bee is trending on Twitter. Apparently, there was a fight between a couple of rival fans, and as they started swinging punches, Monty (aka Dad) got between them and danced as the punches rained down helplessly on his padded costume. We click on *#monty-forworldpeace* and scroll down. There's so much love for Dad! Not sure I've ever been on Twitter for so long without seeing a single snarky comment. But hey, who can hate a pacifist bee?

I can answer that. We can hate a pacifist bee when he goes out for drinks after his triumphant game, gets home late and manages to crash into everything in the house before finally finding his way to bed. Where he proceeds to snore loudly for seven hours.

31

WORRY DIARY

* Did you know that every generation is bigger than the last one? Me neither! Till I tried on dresses from the 1950s... WEEP!
* Hatty Wimplekickers? Maybe that's what I'll change my name to when Perf Class gets shamed at prom.

"I can't wear a strapless dress, I'll basically be naked!" I say, panicking and trapped in another dress that's too small on the shoulders. "Calm down, Lou," says Mum. "Or you'll get hot and swell and we'll have to cut you out." I feel like a monster.

"Breathe out. All the way out," Aggy commands me.

"Eeeeerrrrrrrrrrr," I breathe, trying to deflate as much

as possible. I get my arms out and the top of the dress hangs around my waist. The bottom half clings so tightly I feel like a mermaid.

Lavender stands next to me, looking like a queen in a long, flowing yellow dress with a delicately beaded corset. Even Mum got involved and she looks like a dainty flower in a purple A-line dress. I think she's got tired of saying, "No, Lou. You're perfect as you are," because she's starting to say it in a sort of distracted, robotic way. All these dresses are tiny on me. Did nobody *eat* back in the nineteen-fifties? Maybe they were all ill with olden-days diseases.

Perhaps I need to be withered with smallpox to fit into these. The trouble is, I don't have a waist. I have a middle where I bend, but it doesn't go in. I never have to think about this until I'm trying on clothes.

"How's it going?" Dermot calls from the other side of the door.

"Lav looks nice!" I shout back, full of self-pity. "And I hate my shoulders."

"What about—"

"Don't say strapless! It's basically naked."

"A jumpsuit?" he says, his arm appearing around the door draped in a navy-blue velvety thing. I waddle over hastily in my super-tight dress and examine it. It has long legs and long sleeves and is covered in lots of tiny embroidered copper-coloured stars. It's beautiful.

"Go on, Lou," says Mum and I decide to give it one last shot. It's a bit of a hassle to get on – it zips up at the side and has a tie around the waist that I lose up my sleeve for a while – but the moment I straighten up, Mum, Aggy and Lav's eyes brighten.

"Yes! That one!" Lav says, clapping.

"Really?"

"Look." Aggy pushes me in front of a large mirror. And for the first time all morning, I look like me – not me stuffed into a fussy dress or fidgeting in a corset and skirt. I look like me, with my hands in my pockets (it has pockets!), lounging elegantly in a gorgeous soft waterfall of a jumpsuit.

"And these?" Dermot's hand appears around the door again, this time holding a pair of coppery cowboy boots.

"Shoes never fit me," I say, my good mood deflating a little.

"These are men's."

"Oh, maybe." I hurry to pull them on and they fit perfectly! And they've even got high heels. Well, about three inches, which is high for me but apparently normal for cowboys. You'd think if you spent all day on horseback chasing cows, you'd do it in sensible flats, but the Past is a funny old place.

I stand in front of the mirror in my new outfit and

feel fantastic. I feel even better when Aggy says, "You've managed to pick the least expensive items I own."

"So I don't need to worry about spilling food down me?"

"Or giving them back. They're yours."

I have never squealed over an item of clothing before, but there's a first time for everything. Lavender tries on more dresses while I dance in front of the mirror in my jumpsuit. Now I can't wait to wear this to the prom; I'm actually really excited about it. This must be how people like Cammie feel all the time. I could see myself getting into clothes now. When Mum and Dad both have jobs, I remind myself.

Lavender has taken off her yellow dress and is now trying on a long slinky green one, with a feathery jacket over the top. "Yes," Mum, Aggy and I agree. This is THE dress. Lav looks at herself in the mirror, pleased.

"OK," she says. "I think I can do this awards ceremony. It'll be fun, right?"

"Right!" I say, glad to see her looking happier.

"And Roman will love all the glamour!" says Mum, brightly. I do a *Shush!* face at her.

"You know what I'm looking forward to?" Lav says.

"Little food on trays?" says Dermot from the other side of the door.

"Yes, but also," Lav says, "once the ceremony is done,

I won't have to think about this competition ever again."

"Unless you win," I point out and her face falls. "Then you get that one-year modelling contract. Sorry!"

We spend all day at Dermot's house – it's lovely now it's been repaired and cleaned up for prom, although Dad did nail shut a couple of rooms that Aggy actually needs, like the bathroom and the cupboard where she keeps the vacuum cleaner. "But his heart's in the right place!" she assures us.

"Hmmm," I say, thinking of the hungover man we left at home, drinking green tea and accusing me of walking too loudly.

I still think the prom is a load of old fuss over nothing, and I *still* think the Prom Committee couldn't organize a fruit salad in a fruit bowl, but it's actually been pretty good for Dermot.

Until ... everyone watches the Perf Class improvise "comedic scenarios" to utter silence. Followed by Eli's terrible poem. Oh well. Dermot will have had a good week anyway. Nothing lasts for ever.

I dance in my new jumpsuit, feeling the slinky fabric against my legs. Some good things last a while though.

I finally take it off and Lav, Mum and I head home to show Dad our new outfits. Dad is lying on the sofa, acting as if he's ill and not hungover. Mum, Lav and I swank around in our fancy new clothes, treating the living room like a catwalk while Dad tries to squint around us at the TV. "You look lovely." He finally gives up and pays us some attention. "But why are you all dolled up?" he asks Mum.

"I've offered to help chaperone the prom," Mum reminds him, "with some of Lou's teachers. I thought I might as well look nice."

"Oh yeah," Dad grouches. "Mr Peters and his *lovely eyes*."

This was a chance remark Mum made last year and Dad will not let it go. Mum gives him a hard stare. "At least his eyes aren't bloodshot, *Monty*."

Just then, Hannah calls, asking for a favour. She's timed that well.

"Lou, will you come help me ask Dan to prom? You know, the lifeguard at the pool."

Of course I remember who Dan is. "Well, he wouldn't be a lifeguard at the library," I chuckle.

Dead silence from Hannah. Oh God, I'm not funny. I'm going to be SO unfunny at the prom.

"Anyway," Hannah presses on. "Help me?"

"OK, but how? We can't do it together."

"I don't want to do it by myself! Could you just help me out?" she snaps, clearly forgetting how much me AND my dad have already helped her out.

"Have you just had your brace tightened?"

Her tone goes ice-cold. "Yes, why?"

"No reason. All right, just tell me when."

"Tomorrow after school. I have a training session."

Oh, great. I have to go and face my horrible former coach, Debs. Hannah got into the swimming training camp, so Debs loves Hannah. I didn't, so she treats me like a bad smell.

WORRY DIARY

* All my funny has gone. Chased away by fear.
* Will being in the swimming pool make me sad?
  Will I end up sobbing over verruca socks?
* I have no faith in Hannah's plan. But she's not
  asking for opinions.
* Debs. Eurgh.

The swimming pool is right next to school. I used to practically live here when I was a swimmer, but I've avoided it this term. It feels odd to be going back. I just hope I don't bump into Debs. I hurry to the pool after school, looking around as if I'm on a military manoeuvre.

I can't see Debs anywhere, thank goodness. Not that

I'm scared of her. Just … happier if she's not there. I feel the same about wasps.

Dan is sitting on the tall lifeguard chair. He's very handsome and a terrible lifeguard – he's on his phone.

Hannah is in the fast lane, ploughing her way up and down at speeds that seem crazy to me. I was this fast only last year, but it's hard to imagine. The girl's a MACHINE.

You can always tell when someone's looking at you, can't you? Hannah gives me a little wave and swims over. I squat to talk to her.

"You look nice!" I say. "Have you done something to your hair?" Google suggests complimenting your friend and hopefully their crush will join in, if you make it look fun enough.

"Yeah," Hannah says sarcastically. "Dragged it up and down a swimming pool. Please try and focus."

Dunno why I bother.

"Is he looking at me?" she whispers.

"Dan?"

"Yeah."

"No."

"He never does."

"Right."

"Think he's playing hard to get?"

"Uh…" I say, trying and failing to sound encouraging.

"Uh, *what*? You think asking him to prom is a bad idea? He's too good for me?"

"No! I'm not saying that. And you know best if you should ask him. You know him better than I do."

"I don't know him at all. We've never spoken. I've just stared at him from a distance."

"Hannah!"

This is such a bad idea.

"I'm going to do it anyway," she tells me. Typical stubborn Hannah. "I keep swimming here hoping he'll talk to me. My parents are going nuts. They built a swimming pool so I didn't have to leave the house to train."

She catches the look on my face. "Sorry. Rich people problems. Just … stick around, OK? I'm going to talk to him any minute now. Please don't embarrass me."

"I'm not the person you need to talk to about that," I say, looking past her. Hannah glances over her shoulder.

"You brought Dermot?"

I shrug. "He fancied a swim."

Dermot's emerged from the changing room and is now walking towards us. Finally, something to make Dan look up from his phone.

"So…" Hannah hauls herself out of the water for a closer look.

"Talk us through this?" I ask Dermot, studying his choice of swimming attire.

"Love to." Dermot is enthusiastic about his creation. "I took an old wetsuit that my mum found in a house clearance, and I cut it off at the knees and hips to create a pair of tight knee-length shorts. Because when I wore the whole thing it felt like being buried alive. *Then* I took the bit that covers the head to make myself a little hat."

"And sewed cat ears onto the hat?" I ask.

"No!" He laughs at the ludicrousness of that idea. "Raccoon ears."

"Silly me."

"And..." Hannah points at his hands.

"I used the leftover fabric to make myself webbed gloves for go-faster-ness."

"Sensible. And the tail?"

"Bit of fun."

Dermot twists his body to make his long tail swing. There's a clicking sound from behind us. I look around to see who's taking photos of Batman's burlesque cousin. Across the pool, Dan pockets his phone and tries to look innocent.

Hannah whispers urgently to us, "Is Dan looking at me?"

Dermot and I peek around her at Dan.

"Subtly!" she hisses.

"Well," I say, "he's looking in this direction, but..."

"Oh my God!" She looks thrilled. "Will you fall in so I can rescue you?"

"No way!" I'm indignant. "I was an Olympic … a near-Olympic swimmer six months ago. And now, what, I suddenly can't stay afloat?"

"This isn't about *you*, Lou," Hannah sulks.

"*And,*" I say, "it's such a contrived romantic meeting thing. If it was in a film, you'd scoff at it."

"FINE! Forget it."

"Shall I pretend *I* can't swim?" Dermot asks.

Hannah brightens up. "That *is* more believable!" she says.

"Totally believable," says Dermot. "Cos I can't."

He jumps in the pool and sinks like a stone.

Hannah looks worried. "He's being funny," I reassure her. But he doesn't come back up. We stand by the side of the pool, staring at the raccoon lying on the bottom. He looks so small.

"I'm sure he's absolutely fine…" A cluster of bubbles break the surface.

"Dermot!" I shout, and Hannah and I jump in, feet first, no grace or style, just pure panic.

I hit the water with a roaring in my ears, and I can't see anything because I haven't got my goggles on and it's nothing but bubbles around mine and Hannah's flailing arms. Her fingernail catches my face and scratches me, a jagged stinging smile on my forehead.

No sooner do I get my bearings and start swimming towards Dermot than there's another explosion of noise and bubbles above me and I can feel strong hands grabbing me painfully hard under the armpits and hauling me upwards. I try to fight back – I've got to get to Dermot – but this person is far too strong and my arms feel useless and rubbery, as if I'm flapping through custard.

I break the surface of the water with a gasp and find I'm being dragged towards the ladder steps. I look up, Dan is trying to pull me bodily out of the pool, scraping my back against every step on the way out. *Ow, Dan! There must be less painful ways to get Hannah a date.*

(OK, I'm not thinking that at the time. I'm thinking, *Ow! What? Ow! Nose fizzy! Armpit sore! Dermot?*)

I'm struggling to breathe because I haven't had a chance to tie my hair back and it's formed a wet heavy helmet over my head.

"You're OK. Relax, relax," Dan soothes me, unnecessarily. He lies me down. I try to sit back up, because I'm fine, but Hannah appears and kneels beside me. She puts her hand on my forehead. Right on my cut. OW! Plus, this hand-on-forehead business may look caring, but she's pushing down to make me shut up and stay still.

"You were so brave!" she quivers at Dan. Steady on.

He just jumped in a pool. That's only brave if he's dissolvable in water. Plus, he's a lifeguard – *that's what he's for.*

"Where's Dermot?" I gasp.

"Sh-sh-sh," she says.

"Don't shush me! Is he OK?"

"I'm fine!" Dermot waves at me from the pool, bobbing happily in the deep end. "Only joking."

"A pool is no place to joke around," says Dan, self-importantly.

Such a square. "Thank you, Mr Safety."

"Hannah?" A horribly familiar voice appears from … somewhere. I can't see because Hannah is *still* holding me down by my flipping head. I don't need to, though. A mile of muscular leg appears beside me, ending in a tiny pair of shorts.

"Hello, Debs," I say, without enthusiasm.

"Louise, can't you swim *at all* now?" my old coach asks, genuinely baffled.

Ugh. Hannah had better ask Dan out quick. They'd better have the greatest prom ever and get married and live happily ever after or NONE of this embarrassment is worth it.

Debs wanders off into her office. I hear the door shut. Nice to know she cares.

"She's my best friend!" says Hannah irrelevantly to Dan. Is her voice wobbling? *Is she making her voice wobble?* This is excruciating, watching two idiots flirt while I lie on the floor beneath them. I can see right up their noses.

"Hey, are you OK?" Dan says, putting a manly protective hand on Hannah's shoulder.

I cross my arms and sigh loudly.

Hannah nods bravely, eyes fixed on Dan. "Wouldyouliketogotopromwithme?" she blurts out.

It's not elegant but it is quick.

"What?" he says. *Come on, Dan, keep the pace up, this floor is cold.*

"Oh." He's finally deciphered what she said. "I'm already going with someone, sorry."

"Who?" Hannah says. It sounds like she's going to try and argue Dan out of his prom date. I don't think this is how romance works.

"Brendon?"

"Oh."

I can't take the awkward silence any longer so I join in from the floor. "He's an excellent hockey player."

"Yeah! Isn't he great? So quick on the wing!" Dan says.

Ten minutes later, Hannah, Dermot and I are huddled by the exit waiting for our lifts. Hannah wanted to get out of there as soon as possible so we barely got to dry ourselves before hastily scrambling into our clothes. I run my hand over my damp neck.

"That's what you need, though," I tell her.

"What?"

"Someone who glows like that when they hear you praised."

Hannah just sighs.

My back is throbbing and I have a cut on my face, so my sympathy is limited.

"Han, you hadn't ever spoken to him. It was always going to be a long shot."

"Had you ever even seen him at ground level?" Dermot chips in.

"Shut up. Both of you."

"No. YOU shut up. I ache all over and you haven't said thank you yet."

"It didn't work!"

"That's not the point! I tried."

"Thank you for pretending to drown so I could humiliate myself," she says grudgingly.

"Thank you both for trying to rescue me," Dermot pipes up. Even Hannah has to smile at that.

"You're welcome," she tells him. "You have a very subtle sense of humour sometimes."

"It has been said," he agrees.

Aggy and Barbra arrive at the swimming pool at the

same time. I can see Barbra giving Aggy's old van a horrified look. I'll tell her the rat story one day, I say to myself, as we all wave goodbye to each other.

I rest my head on the seat as Aggy drives me home. I'm being rude – I should make conversation and say thank you for the lift – but I think I might be sick if I open my eyes and see everything whooshing past. I must look as bad as I feel because Aggy puts a lovely cool hand on my forehead while we're idling at the lights. I keep my eyes closed until the van stops and then Dermot helps me gently out.

"Thank you for me being quiet," I mumble, nonsensically.

"Thank *you* for not being sick," he says, holding me up as he rings the doorbell. Mum opens the door and makes concerned noises at me. They might be words but I'm not really listening. I feel Dermot give me a pat on the back before he runs back to the van. I flap a clumsy goodbye wave over my shoulder.

I think lying on the cold poolside with a scraped back was a bad idea. My head hurts, I'm hot and cold and I drag myself to bed wrapped in several layers of pyjamas. *Such a good friend to Hannah,* I grouse to myself as I shiver under the covers. *So unappreciated. She'll be sorry if I die – or, worse, can't go to prom.*

At the thought of my lovely new jumpsuit hanging in my wardrobe never to be worn, my eyes fill with hot tears. I must be feverish.

There's a soft tapping at my door. "Are you all right, Lou?" says Mum, coming in. I shake my head sadly beneath the cover. She crouches next to the bed. I feel her rubbing my shoulder and I lift the side of the duvet to tell her about my night, in a husky croak.

Mum's annoyed. "When did Hannah get so selfish?" she asks.

"She's just had her brace tightened," I defend her. "Top and bottom."

"Well, still... Would you like something to eat?"

"No, thank you."

"Boiled egg with its head off and toast to dip in?"

"Maybe."

I manage half an egg before I burrow back under the covers, feeling sick. I hear Dad come in and sit at my desk.

"How's Lou?"

"Eeeuuurgh."

"Can I finish your egg? Waste not, want not."

33

WORRY DIARY

✱ Bhvbfrkoijpgtko¡els nifhnui di djeiowf

I wake up at about five in the morning feeling like something is very wrong. I stand in the bathroom for ten minutes, shivering and wondering if I'm going to be sick. I don't want to be sick; I hate being sick. I breathe deeply until the feeling passes and creep back to bed, but I lie awake for a while, not quite trusting my body.

The next time I open my eyes it's to find Lavender and Mum standing beside my bed. "Lou?" Mum says, "do you think you'll feel better if you eat? Cereal, toast, another egg?"

My mouth fills with spit and my chin wobbles. I croak, "Please stop naming food. It's not helping."

"OK, then have a shower? See if you're up to going to school?"

I sit up, feeling groggy, and let them manhandle (womanhandle) me into the bathroom. I sit in the shower as my legs are too wobbly to stand. Mum stands over me and tuts. "I've a good mind to send Hannah a photo of you."

I look up at her, squinting as the light hurts my eyes. "Please don't, Mum."

Once I'm "clean", I go back to bed. I do feel better actually. In an ideal world, I'd rather my showers weren't team efforts, but this one was needed. I text replies to Dermot, Gabe and Hannah all asking where/how I am – Hannah gets a slightly terser reply than the others, *as she deserves*, but she sounds so sorry that I relent. I have a sudden thought.

Did you tell Cammie etc that you asked Dan out?

OF COURSE NOT.

Still Number One! I'm still Number One! I do a weak little air punch from my bed.

My phone buzzes. You're not going to tell them, are you?

Yes, I reply. Cos I'm evil.

I saw Dan at lunch.

It's lunchtime *already*? Time flies when you're sweating and aching in bed.

He let me queue-jump. And complimented my shoes.

Not a complete loss then – you made a friend!

But who will I go to prom with?

It's OK. I was going to go by myself.

… She's typing. I rearrange the cold wet flannel on my forehead. I also have a hot-water bottle on my feet, to accommodate my many different temperatures. One benefit of Mum being unemployed is dedicated full-time nursing.

You're not NOW, Hannah texts, with a dogged grip on facts.

No, I concede. But I WAS.

NOT THE SAME!

I can't win an argument with Hannah even when I'm at full-strength, so this is useless. I snuggle back under the duvet for a nap. I wake up to Mum stroking my hair off my clammy forehead.

"Hey, Goldfish, I'm just popping out."

"Where?" I demand, struggling to sit up. "What if I need soup or a fresh flannel? Where's Dad?"

"He's with Vinnie at a work thing, and if you've got the energy to be annoying, you must be feeling better," she says wryly. "I have to go to the Jobcentre. I don't really want to. It was all right with your dad – you know how chatty he is. But now he's a bee, I'm on my own."

She looks so sad … I rub my eyes to make them less bleary. "OK, so I'm coming with you."

"There isn't time. And you're ill. And we'll be walking MILES."

"How many miles?"

"Well, two."

I haul myself out of bed. "How long've I got?"

"FIVE MINUTES."

"Fine."

I pull on some clothes and spritz body spray all over myself, to hide the musty sick-bed smell. Then add a little hairspray for extra camouflage.

"Lovely," Mum says, watching this.

"Shush, I'm helping," I say, pulling my socks on with

difficulty as I'm still quite stiff.

Mum makes me bundle up warm before she lets me out of the house, despite my insistence that I'm too hot anyway. So by the time we reach the end of the driveway, I'm already sweating buckets.

"It's good," Mum tells me. "Sweat the fever out."

I give her a disgruntled look. The hood of my jacket is lined in bright pink fake fur (a hand-me-down from Nicky) and I can feel it sticking to my clammy face. I'm trying to be thoughtful and helpful, but so far it's a massive faff.

Am I going to be sick? I pause... No. The feeling passes, and we carry on down the road.

The feeling returns a couple more times as Mum hurries me to the Jobcentre. It's a half-hour walk, and it's a horrible route, along main roads, with cars and lorries roaring past. Today, as an added treat, sleety rain seems to be blowing upwards, snatching our hoods off our heads. We finally stumble through the doors of the Jobcentre, gasping and dishevelled. Around us, people are shaking their coats and knocking umbrellas dry.

"Do that outside, if you don't mind." An official-looking man is berating a lady bashing her umbrella on the floor. She straightens up and looks at him as if he's an idiot.

"I do mind!" she says. "It's wet out there. How am

I going to get my umbrella dry in the rain?" She catches my eye and shakes her head at me, like, *This guy?*

I don't want to get involved so I stare into the distance and pick pink fluff off my face. Mum starts hunting through her pockets while the official-looking man sighs and stares at her like she's holding EVERYONE up.

"Sorrysorry," she's murmuring, patting through her pockets and trying to pull out a small green card. The rain has soaked into her pocket and the card is dissolving. She holds it up to him, floppy and fragile. "I've got Claudette at three-thirty?"

"Well, I can't read it, can I?" he says.

He looks up as a breeze lifts the hair around his face. I avoid his eye. Because that was me blowing on him to give him my germs. *Evil sickly cackle…*

He jerks his head at the staircase and Mum hurries towards it, pulling me behind her.

"Are you nervous, Mum?" I ask as we climb the stairs two at a time.

"If you're late for appointments, they cut your benefits. Come on, Lou. Quicker."

"Is Dad's job not enough?"

"No, darling," she says. "He's a part-time bee."

I start laughing and by the time we reach the top floor, we're both cackling. It's dead silent up there so everyone stares at us. We shut up immediately. Mum pushes me gently towards a bank of sofas and makes her way to a desk in the far corner, saying, "Hello, Claudette!" I sit on a sofa and look around. Dad's right, it *is* like a shop that sells chairs and sadness.

Around me, damp people sit waiting. It's very hot in here and we're all steaming gently. The man next to me has glasses that keep fogging up. He cleans them twice then gives up.

Mum told me to bring a book as she might be a while, so I grabbed the first thing that came to hand as we left. I pull it out of an internal pocket on my coat. It's about the only thing that stayed dry.

Good old Worry Diary. I give the front cover another look. A cake and the word "worry". What a daft design. Stationery for someone with an eating disorder.

Anyway, I flick through it and examine my lists. I take great pride in crossing off some of the items.

* ~~Nothing to wear for prom.~~ (Bye-bye!)
* ~~Hazel~~ (Ha! See ya.)
* Does Lav have a horrible creepy stalker?

I haven't thought about that one for a while. I should, though. It was weird for someone to enter the competition pretending to be her. I still feel uneasy about that.

✱ Mum needs a job.

✱ Mum is sad.

I look up at her, being lectured by a lady with a no-nonsense bob. I guess this is the woman she was impersonating the other day, but Mum doesn't seem to find her so funny now.

I circle my Mum Worries. And snap the book shut when suddenly she's in front of me.

"OK!" she says, all fake cheery. "That's that done for another two weeks!"

"Are you all right, Mum?" I say.

"I'm fine. Come on." And she pulls me up by my big coat and bundles me back out of the Jobcentre.

As we're walking back, rush hour is starting. We're constantly splattered with dirty water as cars whiz through puddles on the road. A car hoots and pulls in ahead of us on the hard shoulder. Mum spots the driver and groans.

"Hi, Barb!"

Hannah's mum gets out of her big fancy car and gestures for us to get in. "You're soaking!" she exclaims, a little unnecessarily, tbh. "Get your wet clothes off and hop in!" She pops the boot. Hannah gives us a little wave through the back window.

"I, uh…" Mum looks at me, I look at Mum.

Barbra gets back into the warmth of the car, shouting, "Just coats, shoes and outer layers off, so you don't damage the upholstery!"

Mum and I end up stripping off on the hard shoulder while the rain pours and cars tear past us. It's all very well for Barbra to say just take off your wet layers, but as soon as you take something off, the item of clothing beneath it gets wet, so...

"That's enough," says Mum, when we're down to T-shirts, and we hop in the car.

"Oh!" Barbra looks concerned. "You're still a *bit* wet. The leather seats aren't really meant to—"

"Mum." Hannah is firm.

"Yes, right. Well, something for the valeting company to deal with, I suppose," Barbra chirps to herself.

"How are you feeling? Any better?" Hannah looks concerned.

"Oh Louise, are you ill?" Barbra turns a worried face on me in the rear view mirror.

"A bit feveriiiiii-sh-ah!!" I say as Barbra winds down my window and a howling blast of hail wallops me round the face.

"I have to keep Hannah away from germs. She has national time trials in a month," Barbra explains. I nod understandingly, although my whole head is numb.

"Mum, it's fine, I'm fine." Hannah leans over me and

fiddles with the switches on my door to make my window go back up.

"Hannah!" Barbra presses the button in her door to make it go down again. I'm shivering, then warm, shivering, then warm. It's a good thing I'm already feverish.

I'm so glad when we pull up outside our house.

"Thanks. Bye, Hannah, Barbra!" I say, jumping out of the car. Mum and I gather armfuls of our clothes and shoes out of Barbra's boot and waddle awkwardly to our front door, trying not to drop things.

"Oh, glove!" says Mum, trying to kick a mitten in the air for me to catch. I grab for it and drop a jumper.

Dad opens the door and watches us struggle.

"You know you'll be warmer if you actually wear that stuff?"

"Put the kettle on, Mark."

He makes up for it by bringing me soup and sandwiches while I warm up on the sofa, and Mum fetches my bedcovers. I'm never usually allowed to do this. They say if I got a taste of life with food, a duvet and the TV, I'd never get off my bum and go to school. Quite right, too, I think, dipping a sandwich into my soup and channel-hopping. This is the life.

"Oh, Dermot stopped by! No, wait, the other one," Dad says, popping his head around the door. "I can't keep up with all your gentleman callers."

I count them off on my fingers. "Dad, I have ONE boyfriend. And ONE friend who's a boy."

"They're similar, though. Small and serious. Anyway it was Gabe."

Aaah, he probably missed me at school. So romantic.

A load of paper lands on my lap, almost spilling my soup.

"He dropped off your homework," says Dad.

Sigh. *Thanks, Gabe.* Heaven forbid I go ONE day without schoolwork. He would've had to go round all my teachers to gather this, I marvel, flicking through it. It's very sweet but so flipping diligent. I know why, though: there have been times when Gabe has spent months stuck at home thanks to ME, and schoolwork means a lot when it's your only link to normal life.

My English homework has a note on it:

No way you'll actually do this.
I'm humouring him.
Get well soon. Mr P.

Ha ha, Mr Peters knows me so well. But I'm going to do it first, just to prove him wrong. I set to work on an essay about Shakespeare's *Othello*. After about thirty minutes, I realize Mr Peters probably wrote that note as a ... thingy, reverse parallel parking.

Reverse psychology! That's what I mean. And it's worked! Look at this essay, it's actually good. Damn Mr Peters, he's sneakier than Iago.

WORRY DIARY

* Feel so bad for Mum going to the Jobcentre by herself.
* Bump on my chin. Threatening to become spot JUST in time for prom. (I know this is less important than Mum, but it's a really big bump.)
* Asked Uliol if we should practise before prom and he said, "No! Keep the spontaneity!" Great.

When I was coaching Gabe, Ro and Pete in synchronized swimming last term, we rehearsed every spare second we could find. Uliol has a much more laid-back approach and it is freaking me out. We're going to meet for half an hour before prom and "have a chat". *They* can have a chat; *I* will have a panic attack.

By Tuesday night, I feel better and I'm so bored of being at home. So on Wednesday morning I'm waiting for Aggy and Dermot. I kiss Mum goodbye, feeling a bit guilty about leaving her, and race outside as soon as I see the van.

Aggy slows down as she approaches, but doesn't stop. "THE ENGINE'S PLAYING UP AGAIN!" she yells past Dermot, who flinches delicately at the volume. At least I know what to do now. I trot alongside, Dermot kicks open the door and I scrabble up to my seat.

"What did I miss at school?" I ask.

"People are starting to panic and ask anyone to prom," he says. "At first, no one needed a date – they were so over trad ideas like that. Now it's three days away, they're panicking. Even I've had an offer! Girls are getting desperate."

"Hey!" Aggy and I slap him affectionately. "Don't put yourself down, Derm. You're the host!" I say.

"And HANDSOME," his mum adds.

"With an exciting fashion sense," I tell him. "So, who did you say yes to?"

He looks shy. "I had to say no. I'm going to be so busy on the night I don't think I'll be a good date."

"Shame," I say. "I was going to ask you to ask Hannah. But duty before love. I respect that."

As we're pulling into the car park, my phone buzzes with a WhatsApp message. Dermot gets the same a second later. It's a fancy digital invitation to prom.

"Better late than never." He grins.

It's so obvious that Cammie wrote the invitation. It says at the bottom:

No latecomers.
Dress to impress.
Admittance not guaranteed.

"Of course it's guaranteed!" I laugh. "It's *our* prom. And YOUR house. And who's going to turn latecomers away? My uncles are the doormen."

"I can't wait to meet these girls," says Aggy. "They sound like a trip."

"Hmmm, yeah, something like that."

Naturally, Dermot's address is on the invitation, and Karl Ashton recognizes it straight away. The moment we walk into our form room, people start interrogating Dermot.

"Is that your house?" Sasha demands, pointing at her phone.

"Um, yes?" says Dermot.

"Your house that you live in?" another girl asks. "Or

like a community home thing or something?"

"No, just me and my mum."

"You can have a *prom* in your *house*?" Sasha says slowly.

"It's not that big a deal," Cammie says airily.

"Two hundred people in one house? Yeah it is."

"You should see the state of it, though," says Karl, bluntly. Mr Peters walks in just in time to catch that. *Bad timing.*

"I'll see you later today, Karl?" he says, and when Karl looks blank, he adds, "In detention."

BOOM!

Hannah arrives and Cammie gestures her urgently over to their table. Hannah gives me an exasperated face and goes to join them. She takes a minute to mouth, *Feeling better?* and I give her a thumbs-up.

I don't feel jealous as the Prom Committee huddle and whisper throughout registration. I know Hannah would rather be sitting with us. Still...

"What are they talking about?" I remark to Dermot, a little louder than is strictly sensible. "My dad organized the prom, Hannah got the band and you're hosting it. There's nothing left for them to actually do."

The four of them stop talking and look over at me. Even Mr Peters glances up.

"Is that true?" he asks. I shrug and nod. It must be the

last gasps of my fever making me reckless!

Mr Peters looks at the Prom Committe. "Anything to add?" They look surly.

Except Hannah, who says, with a rueful laugh, "That's pretty much it."

"Cammie, Melia, Nicole and Hannah, can you sit there, there, there and there for English? I've turned a blind eye to talking in class as I assumed you were busy organizing. Guess not."

Cammie thumps me in the back with her bag as she walks past but I do not care. They all owe Dermot and me HUGE for digging them out of their prom mess. Cammie sits down and fixes me with a cold stare, which I return with a big smile. After a long couple of seconds, she turns away.

Dermot grabs my arm. "Lou, I think the fever's gone to your brain."

"I think it has too." I feel my clammy forehead. "Good thing it's half-term next week."

"Yeah, you can spend it changing your identity."

Ha. I'll be doing that anyway after Perf Class at the prom. For a moment, I imagine myself back in bed with a flannel on my head – "Wish I could be there, Uliol, but I'm ill! Genuinely ill, legitimate excuse!"

"I'll be glad when this weekend is over," I say to Hannah as we head to our second lesson. She agrees fervently.

"Because Lav will have won twenty-five thousand pounds?" Dermot says, always optimistic.

"Yeeaahh … that's it."

However, the rest of our year seems to be getting excited about prom, now they've finally got their invitations. Cammie, Nicole, Melia and Hannah are surrounded at lunchtime by people asking excited questions about what they have planned. I watch this from a distance, stabbing at my packed lunch as if it's wronged me.

"Who cares?" Lav has joined me, with Roman. I'm glad to see they're getting on better.

"I cares!" I splutter. "They wouldn't even HAVE a prom if it wasn't for Dad. They'd better thank him."

"They won't." Lav is confident, and probably right.

Over on Cammie's table, she's telling a long and flamboyant story and I bet it does not involve her perched on a paint can in my dad's shed begging for his help.

Between the prom and the awards ceremony, everyone's talking outfits on our table. Roman is showing Dermot numerous photos of him posing in suits. He's doing his selfie face again.

"Very slim fit, that one." Dermot's pointing at Roman's phone.

"I'm going to do a juice cleanse Thursday and Friday then fast on Saturday."

Lav looks up at that. "What, just starve all day?"

Ro's nodding like this is totes normal.

"So you won't chew anything for three days. Seventy-two hours."

"S'pose not, no. Come on, Lav. Nothing tastes as good as skinny feels."

"Ahem-hem-hem," I say. BFF right next to me, very recent eating disorder? *"Ahem-hem?"* I keep coughing but he's not getting it. Lav boots him firmly in the shin.

"Anyway," Ro prattles on, "we get a car to and from the ceremony so it's cool if I'm lightheaded."

"From starvation," Lavender says, flatly. Roman does the guns at her.

35

WORRY DIARY

* Star has dropped out of the prom.
  Apparently, there's "something going round".
  (Yes, Star: cowardice.)
* It's contagious! Eight more drop out. Now
  it's just me, Dermot, Patrice, Eli and his awful
  poem.

Even Mum and Dad are getting nervous about me performing at the prom. Over breakfast on Saturday, Dad says, "I'll bring Monty, in the boot of the car. Just say the word and I'll groove onstage and rescue you."

"I won't need rescuing," I say, nettled.

"You've never seen me work my magic on a crowd, Louise. I'm extremely charismatic."

"I bet."

"I put myself in mind of a young Michael Jackson."

"Do you now?"

"The strength of JFK."

"I'm happy for you."

"The charm of Take That."

"What?"

"And the twinkle of—"

"Mum, make him stop."

"No, but seriously," Mum says, "you might need him."

"Mum!" I'm outraged. "You're meant to have faith in me even when you don't. That's basic mothering."

"I know! I do! But I'm also realistic. There was an improv group at my old university, and gigs could go very ... badly. Once people are drunk, bad improv can make them riot."

"*Bad?* Thanks for that. For starters, they won't be drunk. It's a school prom – there'll be teachers there."

"Someone will spike the punch," Mum says, and Dad scoffs.

"They can *try*," he says. "Let's see little Harry Hipflask and Gennifer Supermarket Gin get past me."

There's a long silence. Mum strokes my hair.

"What are you thinking, Goldfish?"

I'm thinking, *When Harry and Gennifer Whatsit get past Dad and the whole party gets drunk and riots at my terrible Perf Class performance and I have to run away and start a new life, I'll go with Effie Nimplestick as my new name. It's fun and ethnically vague.*

"Nothing," I lie.

"Anyway..." Mum clearly feels she hasn't been very helpful here. (I second that.) "Who wants *pancakes*?" she says, like I'm five.

Me, I want pancakes.

There's a thumping noise from the hall as Lav bounds downstairs with some of her old exuberance. "Did I hear *pancakes*?"

"I'm actually kind of looking forward to the ceremony now," she confesses, stabbing at the hard bits in the sugar tin. "There'll be loads of cool people there. As long as Ro behaves himself and doesn't try to hog the limelight, it should be quite fun."

There's a silence. I think we're all imagining Ro sashaying up and down the red carpet, trying to get photographed.

"He's too weak to be any trouble," I say. Which is true. The juice cleanse on Thursday and Friday left him sluggish and (I didn't mention it) with bad breath. I saw him yesterday at lunchtime, his long frame folded languidly over a table, trying not to look at everyone's food. Mine in particular as I was stealing Dermot's packed-lunch pad thai.

"It's a shame Roman's not in the competition," Dad muses. "He'd have enjoyed it more than you."

"I know, right?" says Lav.

"Lav, will you do my make-up?" I ask. "I can do my right eye fine but I really struggle with my left."

"Tell you what, why don't I do both? Like normal people."

"Actually, Lou, what are you doing today?" Dad asks.

There's no Perf Class so I've been looking forward to a lazy day. "Have a bath, slap on a face mask. Maybe go see Pete, do some last-minute begging and pleading—"

"TRICK QUESTION. You're spending the day with me, pre-prepping the prom."

"That's a lot of Ps."

"Sorry I spat on you."

"What is pre-prepping?"

"You're going to find out!" he twinkles, as if it's an exciting, magical experience when we both know it won't be.

"Fine," I say. "On ONE condition."

Twenty-five minutes later, Dad's sitting in the car, reading the newspaper. I don't blame him, this is dragging on a bit.

"Pleeeeeease!" I call up again.

Pete's face appears at a window on the second floor. "Go away."

"Aha! I knew you were still there. Please come tonight."

"Nope." His face disappears again.

"No one will dare heckle you! They'll behave if you're onstage! WE NEED YOU!" I carry on begging. I'm standing on Pete's family's driveway calling up at the windows since Pete shut the front door on me, saying, "Never gonna happen."

I'm getting a sore throat.

I look back at Dad, who shrugs without looking up from his paper. I'll remember this when he wants opinions from me about "pre-prepping".

"Peeeete…" I'm getting whiney now. "I could've turned my back on you when you needed someone to train you last year. I could've said, *No way, you're not swimmers, you're dancers. I can't help you.*" I'm getting dramatic now. This is like the closing speech of a courtroom drama. "But I didn't." I slap my chest. "I ploughed time, heart and blood, sweat and tears into you guys."

"Sounds disgusting," Dad pipes up from the car.

"I helped you, Pete!"

His dad is now watching me from another window. Possibly – but hopefully not – the toilet.

"We *paid* you." Pete opens the window and leans his arms on the windowsill, with the complacency of a man who knows he's won an argument.

This is a good point. I forgot about that. "Do you *want* me to pay you?" I say desperately.

"*Can* you?"

"No," says the voice behind me.

"Dad, PLEASE," I shout over my shoulder.

Pete's dad sniggers from his window.

"Bye-bye." Pete shuts the window and draws the curtains.

I get back in the car and Dad starts the engine. "Hey, funny thing. Some girls from your school just walked past and it looked like you were begging Pete to go to prom with you!" He chuckles, as if this is a nice story and not totally humiliating.

36

WORRY DIARY

* Girls from school think I was begging Pete for a date.
* This humiliation will seem tiny compared to the Massive Big Shame this evening.

We pull up at Dermot's house, which looks neater than I've ever seen it. Aggy's gnomes stand clean and straight along the driveway, waiting to solemnly salute guests as they arrive.

Dad gets out of the car. I follow.

"Where did the clipboard come from?" I ask.

"When you're made redundant, you steal office supplies on your last day," he tells me, heading for the front door. "It's like a tradition. I've got a laminating machine in the shed."

Dad dings the doorbell, and Aggy answers, eating a piece of toast. "Oh! Totally forgot you were coming."

Dad gives a little shake of his head, and I KNOW he's thinking, *What would they do without me?*

May I answer that? I'd be relaxing in a bath right now, wearing a face mask and it would be brilliant.

We walk into the hallway and admire the results of all our cleaning work. When we left last weekend, Aggy and Dermot kept working. There are feathers hanging from the chandelier, and fairy lights woven up the banisters. It's proper Hogwartsy.

I wish I was seeing it for the first time this evening, that would be breathtaking. But, as Dad is marching me through every step of the prom, minute by minute, it's completely ruining any magic.

"Where's the actual Prom Committee?" I interrupt Dad as I'm walking up the stairs, pretending to be my whole year group. (It's difficult, even with weeks of Perf Class behind me, to embody 200 people.)

"Don't worry, they're working hard," he says, eyes on a stopwatch.

"Better be."

"Right. So: arriving at eight, three minutes of milling around in the foyer, add two minutes for cloakroom queuing and depositing..." Dad clicks on his stopwatch. "And by the way, you're manning the cloakroom."

"Oh what?"

"*Womanning* then."

"How long do I have to do it for?"

"Only half an hour, ninety minutes tops. It'll be fun."

"How will it be fun?"

"You'll be able to look at everyone's coats. And you can have a friend to help you."

He has a very sketchy idea of fun. I can't believe he's in charge.

"Now can you go in the living room and mingle?"

"Mingle with myself?"

"Yes."

Sigh. I head off to make small talk with myself.

"Where's Dermot?" I shout back at him.

"Sewing his outfit. He's busy."

"Fine," I mutter.

"I CAN'T HEAR MINGLING!" Dad shouts. I start complimenting myself about my excellent contouring. "Thank you," I answer myself. "I've been watching a lot of videos online and there's been some trial and error…"

Dad comes into the room and walks around me in a figure of eight. "Waitresses, waitresses, waitresses…"

"Waitresses? Ooh, fancy."

"And now –" he clicks his stopwatch – "it's nine twenty-five. And your … 'comedy thing' will be up on the stage at nine thirty."

"Comedy," I interrupt.

"Eh?"

"Not *'comedy thing'* like you said it, in air quotes, like it's *allegedly* comedy. It'll be funny; it *is* funny."

"Yes, dear."

"Hang on, an *actual* stage?"

"I'm going to build a stage." Aggy reappears.

"Oh, wow, that's really... Wow. How high will it be?" I ask nervously. "Just out of interest?"

"About four foot?"

Well, there goes that last shred of hope. I was thinking, if I managed to push our performance back a bit, everyone would be getting rowdy and by the time we started "Perfing" we might get lost in the crowd. Fat chance, if we're on an actual stage.

My stomach squeezes a bit and I do some Hari breathing exercises. It's hard to do these subtly.

"You all right?" Dad glances up from his clipboard. "Are you going to be sick?"

"N-yes. Yes, I am. Unless I go home and get a face mask on."

"Oh, fine. I'm pretty much done. Aggy! We're heading off."

"That's cool!" She looks up from chalking where the stage will go. "Anything else I can do tonight?"

"Actually, yes. I was going to ask you and Flora to

check the girls' toilet every fifteen minutes for drink, drugs and general illegal activity."

Aggy pauses, a measuring tape in her mouth. "I thought they were fifteen and sixteen years old? Not hardened criminals."

"It doesn't matter when it comes to event planning. Always expect the worse."

"Gotcha. I think I've got an electric cattle prod here somewhere."

37

WORRY DIARY

* It's 5 p.m. and we've only just got home.
  I have to get my make-up and hair done AND
  my outfit on.
* Probably should stop complaining about it and
  actually get started.

"Lav!"

"AARGH!"

"Sorry."

I'm wearing a lumpy orange face mask, I look like a squashed Wotsit. I'm enjoying creeping up on my family and scaring them. Although I should stop annoying Lav – I need her help. She is all dressed and ready, with green eyeshadow to match her dress and some loose curls through her shiny dark hair. She looks astonishing – if this competition was up to me I'd give her the twenty-five thousand on the spot.

And now it's my turn.

"Go and wash that off your face," she tells me. "Get dressed and I'll do your make-up."

I put my jumpsuit on. It's so soft and silky! I add the cowboy boots to admire the full effect, although we're not supposed to have shoes on upstairs at home so I have to tiptoe quietly into Lav's room. I look like the world's most stylish burglar.

Lav plaits my hair and piles it on the top of my head. It looks elegant and "out of the way", she says, making it sound like a naughty dog. I sit on the end of her bed and bounce with excitement as she unpacks her make-up kit next to me. She drapes something over my shoulders and gets to work. It's a lovely feeling, the soft make-up brush gently dusting my face. Then she comes at me with an eyeliner pencil. Not so nice.

"Stop flinching," she tells me.

"I'm not doing it on purpose!"

"You have to control yourself or you're gonna get zig-zags over your face."

"Are you decent?" When we shout out that we are, Dad pokes his head around Lav's door and watches her. "You look nice, Louise. Although…"

"Although..."

"I'm not sure about that – cape thing?"

"I'm wearing a tea towel round my shoulders, Dad. So I don't get make-up on my jumpsuit."

"That's good cos it looks a bit frumpy."

Mum appears in the doorway and does a twirl.

"Lovely, Mum!" We all make *ooh* noises at her, which is the sound you *must* produce if someone does that in front of you. Only a monster lets someone twirl in silence.

She's wearing a long slouchy trouser suit, all tailored and androgynous. Neither word I would ever have used before I knew Dermot. I'm starting to appreciate clothes. Although my main criteria for dresses are still: 1) Dark enough to hide stains, and 2) Pockets.

"I'm sure Mr Peters will enjoy looking at you with his lovely eyes," Dad mutters, pettily.

"I'm sure he will," Mum preens. She is in a better mood than I've seen her in for ages. I'm so glad the prom is good for someone. "Now what are you wearing?"

"I don't know." He frowns.

"Something you feel comfortable and confident in," she suggests, helpfully.

"That would be the bee outfit."

"Dad."

"No, Mark."

"I think it's the best version of me," he says. "When

I'm wearing it, I feel liberated. There's a spare su—"

"You already said. But no, thank you," I tell him.

Dad stares at Mum's feet. "Will you be wearing heels?"

"Why?" Mum is confused by this sudden interest in her footwear.

"You don't want your trousers to drag on the floor. It'll be a sea of alcopops, hair wax and hormones."

Mum, Lav and I stare at him. Lav says what we're all thinking: "Dad, HOW disgusting were you as a teenager? Because you have a really warped view of ages thirteen to nineteen."

Thankfully, before he goes into detail about his grotty teenage behaviour, Lav's phone buzzes on her desk.

TOOT TOOT!

Gabe and Roman are here! We squeeze past Mum and Dad and dash downstairs, as quickly as we dare. Lav's dress makes a proper bustling noise like in a period drama. We enjoy this so much that we bustle in and out of the dining room a few times.

The boys start knocking impatiently. "Let us in! The wind's messing up our hair!"

We take pity on them and open the door. Gabriel looks gorgeous in a navy blue suit that matches his eyes and a grey shirt. I can't help but notice that Roman is dressed very similarly, but he waves it away. "It's fine. We're going to different places, so FOR ONCE he's allowed to copy my style."

"I'm not copying his style," Gabe says, kissing me hello and admiring my jumpsuit.

"Look!" I show him. "Pockets!"

I do a twirl and he says *ooh* because he knows the rules.

"And..." Gabe presents me with a flower. Um...

"Thanks?" I say, panicking. "I, uh, didn't get you one. Sorry."

"No, it's a prom thing. The boys give the girls a flower to wear. Not on your head, Lou," he adds.

"I think it's too late now," I say, struggling to untangle it from my plaits.

"Maybe move it to the side?" Dad says, frowning at my head. "It looks like a tiny hat."

When did everyone become a prom expert?

We're all clustered in the hallway when Gabe catches sight of something outside and opens the door again. There is a looooong black car pulling up in front of our house. We all stare at the driver, who gets out and walks towards us with a bunch of flowers.

"Courtesy of *Stylie* magazine," he says, handing them to Lav, who looks flushed with excitement and, for the first time, like she's actually enjoying this. Mum and Dad get out their phones and start taking photos.

Roman puts his hand on Lav's waist and gestures her towards her waiting car, like a real-life Prince Charming. If I was her, I would forgive him every pouting duck face selfie and every oblivious moment. He is the perfect boyfriend. He dips towards her cheek to kiss her and whisper something meant only for her. But we're crammed tightly in the hallway so we all hear it too.

"Aren't you glad I entered you in the competition now?"

38

Mum and Dad stop taking photos and we all stare at Roman. Our horrified faces say it all and the dashing smile slides off his face.

"What?"

"What...?"

"WHAT?"

The poor driver loiters on the driveway, sensing something is terribly wrong. I think the clue is the way Lav is walloping Roman around the head with her huge bunch of flowers. Dad finally wrestles them off her.

"Lav, careful! Bet these weren't cheap!"

"I entered us both!" Roman is protesting. "I wanted us to do it together. I didn't get in but that's OK. I was still proud of you."

"Well, that's bloody big of you!" Lav says, shoving him away from her. He steps backwards onto Mum, who yelps.

"Sorry!"

"Lav! Stop shoving, there's no room. And YOU –" Mum turns Roman around to face her – "what were you *thinking*? Never do things like this, not behind her back, not without her permission. Do you understand?"

"Yeah, mate. Not on," agrees Dad, who isn't quite as articulate in an argument. "Seriously out of order!"

"I know it's been a bit rough," says Roman. "But it's worked out well, right? You're going to win – I've been working on getting you votes for weeks."

"Stop doing things behind my back!" Lav is near tears now. "I thought I could trust you."

"It's FOR you, though. For your own good."

"I am not six. And you are not my parents. You don't know what's for my own good," says Lav, sticking a finger under each eye so she doesn't smudge her mascara.

"Well, look," says Ro, losing his temper, "I'm sorry, obviously, but let's not fight about it. Let's just go to the ceremony and have a good time. You'll win, come home twenty-five thousand pounds richer and you can thank me later."

Sometimes I could slap Roman.

Lav sniffs, blinks hard to stop her tears and smooths down her dress. "Mum? Will you come to the awards ceremony with me, please?"

Mum gives Ro a small guilty glance but I can tell she's thrilled. "I'd love to, sweetheart. 'Scuse me, Ro."

Roman has to stand aside to let Mum pick her way past him. She and Lavender march down the driveway arm in arm.

"Unlucky, mate." The driver gives Roman a sympathetic look then nips around Mum and Lav to open the car doors for them. The car starts up again with a tiny, expensive-sounding purr and swings out of our road.

"No!" Ro calls after them. "Laaaav! Please?"

It's chilly in the hallway, so Gabe shuts the door and we're left standing slightly aimlessly.

"Well," Dad says, "I would tell you off but I think my wife and daughter covered it all."

"Yes, Mr Brown," says Roman. He looks gutted. He's never called my dad anything but Mark. This is the most meek I've ever seen him.

Now, I am not the cleverest person in the world. I'm rarely the cleverest person in the room. But at that moment, I have two undeniably excellent ideas. They're so good I feel a little dizzy.

I nudge Ro with my shoulder. "Want to come to prom instead?"

He shrugs. "Is there still space?"

"I can sneak you in. On one condition," I tell him.

★   ★   ★

Ten minutes later, I'm sitting on the toilet.

"Lou! We gotta go soon!" Dad is calling up the stairs.

I'm texting at furious speeds. To Hannah first.

You ready for prom?

Yes! Finally sorted all the boring organization
stuff and you know what...?

Something to ask you.

... I don't NEED a date to prom! I'm an independent
woman. This is just stupid peer pressure.

Oh.

What?

I was wondering if you wanted to go with Roman?

GABE'S BROTHER?

Yeah?

She sends me a string of smiley faces with sunglasses.

I take that as a yes. The evening may not have gone how Ro planned but, hey, it's his own fault and it's nice for Han. She's at Dermot's already, she says, to help out in the kitchen, but she'll come find her "date" when prom begins.

Then I text Pete, choosing my words carefully.

YOU KNEW.

That's all I say. He rarely replies to my texts, but I know he will this time.

What?

About Ro entering Lav in the competition.

He entered both of them!

Doesn't matter. It was still wrong, and you knew.

How did you know I knew?

I didn't. I guessed and you just confirmed it.

I crack my knuckles. I am an utter genius sometimes. Old eighty-six per cent strikes again.

Pete starts typing. Stops. Starts again.

I'm sorry.

That's OK. You know how you can make it right.

?

We're onstage at 9.30.

"LOUISE!!" Dad yells again. "If I run late, all my timings will be out of sync and I will be furious!"

"Coming!" I run downstairs and find the front door standing open and everyone already outside, clambering into the car with great care. The boys are anxious not to crease their suits. "Mine's velvet!" Ro tells me as I try to squeeze in next to him. "Mine's velvet too!" I retort. "*And* it's vintage."

Who *am* I this evening?

Dad drives so slowly I can feel Ro fidgeting impatiently next to me. He keeps checking his phone. I bet Lav's ignoring him and I'm not surprised. As our car sweeps up Dermot's big driveway, Gabe and Roman point out the misshapen gnomes and laugh at them.

Now it's darker, I can see lights dotted on the lawn, illuminating each gnome's face. It's brilliantly weird. In contrast, I can see Uncle Don loitering in a dark suit by the front door, looking like he could kill you with one hand and never take his eyes off the telly.

"For once," Dad says, "I'm pleased your mother's family are a bunch of reprobates."

"Hey!" I say. "Uncle Vinnie got you your job—"

"*Ahem-hem-hem!*" Dad coughs meaningfully and gives me a stare in the rear-view mirror. His secret identity. Sozzles, Bruce Wayne.

We park around the back, and as we're heading towards the house, we see Mr Peters getting out of a taxi. He eyes up some of my even beefier relatives patrolling the garden. "I feel silly offering myself as security now..." he says to us and Uncle Vinnie overhears.

"No, no," he reassures him. "You know their names. While we sit on their heads, you can yell at them."

Mr Peters laughs because he thinks Vinnie's joking.

"How's, uh … business?" Uncle Vinnie asks Dad, quietly.

"Ticking along nicely," murmurs Dad, looking around, shiftily. Great, now they're both at it. This sounds so dodgy, I bet my teacher thinks Dad's a drug dealer.

Dermot flings open the front door, resplendent in a three-piece tweed suit and a cape down to his ankles. "I made it myself!" he says, unnecessarily. He looks like a cross between a Scottish lord *and* lady and the effect is fabulous. He gives us all a twirl. We *ooh*.

"Come into the kitchen!" he announces, looking mischievous. I leave Gabe, Dad and Ro and follow him.

There's steam billowing out of the kitchen door, making me a little nervous. Five grim-faced women are wrestling vast pots and pans off the kitchen worktops. Aggy rushes in with an armful of tea towels. "More here for you, ladies!" she says. "Can I get you anything else? Is the hot water still coming through?"

"You're grand," one of the women tells her. "Sit, have a rest."

"No! This is totally unacceptable!"

I'd know that voice anywhere. Dermot looks at me and presses his lips together to stop himself laughing. Camilla's voice is coming from the pantry. Why is she in the little room where Aggy and Dermot keep the beans?

All the women look up at the sound of this, and one of them points a ladle threateningly towards the noise.

"I don't want to hear ANOTHER WORD about this. Got me, Melia?"

The pantry door bangs open and Melia, Nicole, Hannah and Cammie enter the kitchen. They're wearing black shirts, black trousers and scowls. I guess the woman holding the ladle is Melia's mum. I wouldn't get on the wrong side of her.

"You have barely enough money for this food," she says, straining to lift another pot of sauce onto the hob. "Thanks, Aggy. And you definitely don't have enough money for waitresses. So, you have to serve the food."

Cammie and Nicole look surly. Melia looks embarrassed and Hannah looks like she'll do anything to make Melia's mum less cross.

"Can I help?" I say from the doorway. Melia's mum swings towards me. "Are you on the Prom Committee?" she asks.

"No, ma'am," I say.

"Then have a lovely prom." She flashes me a charming smile. "And get out of my kitchen!"

We scuttle out of the kitchen, which apparently doesn't belong to Aggy or Dermot this evening. I feel bad for laughing but I do anyway.

"She sprung it on them half an hour ago," Dermot tells me. "Probably knowing that if Cammie got wind of it, she wouldn't turn up."

"How long are they waitressing for?"

"First two hours, then they're allowed back into their party outfits," Dermot says. "Nicole's raging. She's in Chanel apparently."

"Really?" I say, smoothing my jumpsuit self-consciously.

"It's just a black dress," sniffs Dermot. "Doesn't even have pockets."

We have another half an hour to kill and everyone has that pre-party feeling. Even Mr Peters seems nervous. We distract ourselves by tidying up the fairy lights threaded through Aggy's banisters.

Roman pokes his head in the kitchen to say hi to his "date", and I give him the flower that Dermot gave me. He gives Han the full charm offensive, tucking the flower into her hair, and I bet she doesn't care at all that she's handing round canapés.

Gabriel and I are put to work too, hanging people's coats up in the cloakroom. Some people get very demanding. Do I look like someone from *Downton Abbey*, chum? They'd better not try it on Cammie-the-waitress or they'll get a canapé shoved up their nose.

A girl called India is especially snooty, handing over her coat with precise instructions. "Don't put it near any other coats," she snaps at me. "It's vintage, and the pile can't be brushed the wrong way."

I obediently take it into the cloakroom and rub it all over in every direction I can. Gabriel comes and helps me. It looks like it's been in a cat fight by the time we're done. Most of the guests are lovely, though, and you get to see everyone arrive when you're in the cloakroom. Loads of girls admire my jumpsuit and the flicky eyeliner Lavender did on my eyes. I'm getting flushed with compliments and hard work, I'm glowing bright red by the time everyone's in.

I can hear some people laughing at the gnomes as they crunch up the driveway, then they step into the hallway and – it's like they're watching a firework display. When they see the polished chandelier and the twinkling fairy lights winding up the stairs, they *have* to gasp. I feel very proud of Dad and all his project management. I take it back – it *is* cool.

"Lou!" He clicks his fingers at me. "Look lively! Take these coats."

Less proud of him now, more irritable.

Karl Ashton chucks his coat at me without a backward look.

"Karl!" I wave a little numbered ticket at him. "You need your... Never mind."

I hope he doesn't act up tonight and bully Dermot in his own home – that would be horrible. Just in case, I wipe my nose on his coat.

After forty minutes there are no more people arriving. I guess *No latecomers* and *Admittance not guaranteed*, though rude, does make people punctual. So now we're free of cloakroom duties, Gabe and I can run upstairs to join everyone.

"What do you want to do first?" Gabe asks. "Food, drink, find people, cut some shapes?"

"Honestly?" I say. "I would love to sit in a corner by myself and feel sick for the next forty-five minutes until stage time. Is that OK? I will join you afterwards. Unless it was so bad I have to run home."

"Don't be silly," he says. "You'll be amazing!"

I stare deeply into his eyes. He's lying. He's never seen Perf Class, and everything I've told him about it does NOT sound amazing. But I appreciate the effort.

He sits me in a quiet corner, as requested, and backs away, waving goodbye and giving me encouraging thumbs-ups.

I check my phone: still nothing from Pete. I thought he'd be here by now ... if he was going to come. I can see Dermot mingling and twirling his cape around for people to admire. Poor Dermot. Imagine if he gets to taste popularity then is humiliated onstage and falls right back to the bottom of the social heap, all in the space of an hour.

For now, everyone seems to be behaving. My bulky uncles looming in various doorways probably helps with that. Plus, Mr Peters has stationed himself next to a big bowl of fruit punch and he keeps tasting little sips of it, determined that it won't be spiked on *his* watch.

Cammie stalks past so fast that no one has a chance of grabbing any food off her tray. She's basically taking mushroom canapés for a speedwalk. I see Sasha cornering her and demanding food and I admire her courage.

I check my watch. Half an hour till we're due onstage. Still no Pete.

WORRY DIARY

✱ Five minutes to stage time. Still no Pete.

I'm standing in Dermot's smallest living room (the third one? Fourth, maybe. Anyway, it's called Backstage tonight) in a circle with Uliol, Patrice, Eli and Dermot. No Pete.

I'm disappointed but I don't blame him, we're about to humiliate ourselves in front of 200 school colleagues, and when Pete went to our school, he was Ro's cool, older friend. Who wants to trash that reputation for fifteen minutes of pratting about onstage? Not him, clearly.

Uliol is making some of the least helpful comments imaginable. "Stay loose," he tells us, "be in the moment, feel your funny and don't be afraid to experiment."

When I was in charge of a team last year, I used to say things like "Keep your arms tight, remember the routines we practised, for God's sake, don't drown" and then I'd blow my whistle at them. If you gave Uliol a whistle, he'd examine it and ask how it made you *feel*.

I keep loosening the belt on my jumpsuit before I realize it isn't too tight, my stomach is just tense with nerves. I peek out of the door at the prom. Cammie, Melia and Nicole are still circulating at top speed with trays of food and faces of thunder. They don't seem to realize that if they stopped and offered people food, they'd get rid of it quicker and would be able to join the party.

I look around for Hannah and spot her chatting with Gabe and Roman. I'm so happy they're getting on. The boys are steadily eating their way through all the food on Hannah's tray, which is clearly a good motivation for them to keep talking to her. And she's delighted to have Prince Charming as her prom date, so it's a win–win for everyone.

I stare at Gabe, willing him to turn and give me an encouraging look. But he's caught up in the noise and the fun of prom. I feel lonely backstage worrying, while everyone else is having fun. As I'm staring out, I see a gang of gangly guys in their forties, dressed in black, being led towards us by Mr Peters, who keeps staring at their faces with a weird fascination. *Be cool, Mr P! I haven't seen anyone with three septum piercings before either, but you don't see me staring up a stranger's nose.*

They reach "backstage", and I step back to let them in.

"Hey, I'm Jase from Plastic Jesus," says a tall guy with a huge head of dyed white hair.

"Oh yeah, Hannah's cousin!" I say.

"Well, that's why we're doing it for fifty quid," says a guy holding a pair of bongoes, looking sour.

"Come on, man. It's for charity," Jase says to him.

"Err, no—" I begin but Jase treads firmly on my toe. *Shut up.*

"Yes!" I say. "Charity!"

Look at me, thinking on my feet, creating fake scenarios, I hope Uliol's proud. But when I look over, he's not even noticed the band's arrival and is busy balancing on his head.

"Can you be in charge?" Mr Peters interrupts. "I've left the punch bowl unattended and I know Marianne M. was hovering nearby. Her handbag was making glugging noises." He hurries back out.

"Don't worry," Jase assures me. "We have several songs about the evil of drink."

"Brilliant," I say. "So long as people can dance to them?"

"Oh, yeah. We've played a lot of religious festivals. What time are we on?"

"About nine forty-five," I say. "After the improvised comedy."

Plastic Jesus all pull a face like, *Eeew.* I know. It's a terrible idea. I can hear whoops and yelling in the main room. Prom is getting rowdy. We're going to be torn apart. I swallow the thought and show Plastic Jesus where they can relax and have some snacks.

"Is that OK?" I ask, unsure how to cater for a rock band. "Um, do you want beer or something hot to eat, or...?"

"No, this is great," Jase tells me. "If we eat too much, we get sleepy onstage."

I never knew that. Good thing I haven't eaten yet, though there's no chance of me feeling sleepy now. I'm practically vibrating with nerves.

I leave Plastic Jesus to it, because I've got something I need to do urgently.

I need to sit in a corner of the room and stare out of the window. I don't want to go out onstage in front of everyone I know from school. I just want to run away and hide.

I clutch my Worry Diary tightly. I'm glad I brought it, it feels like a gloomy security blanket. I run my fingers over the cake on the front. Oh, I realize, feeling all the bumps and sprinkles, it's not a cake, it's a *doughnut*.

I frown at it then start laughing.

Doughnut worry!

Do Not Worry.

I'm such an idiot! That joke was staring me in the face for weeks!

"Lou?" Uliol is looking at me across the room. Even he looks a little green, and I can barely hear him over the riotous noise of prom. "It's time." I tuck my diary away under a sofa. *Doughnut worry!* the cover tells me, breezily. *Stupid book – you've no idea.*

I give one last wistful look out of the window and see something moving. *I hope it's not gatecrashers or intruders,* I think, before I recognize that familiar lanky shape sprinting across the front lawn, hurdling lights and kicking over Aggy's gnomes. Pete! He came! I AM a manipulative genius, Lady 86% FTW!

"Hang on." I turn to Uliol, Dermot, Patrice and Eli. "We've got one more performer on the way."

Uliol claps his hands and bounces on his toes and we're still doing that together like a pair of mad rabbits when Pete finally hurtles through the backstage door.

40

We are (I sneak a glance at my watch) two minutes into our performance and already Uliol's nerves are jangling. I told him it wasn't children. I told him it wouldn't be "lovely". But he wouldn't listen – and now here we are. I can see Mr Peters and Ms Peel leaning against a doorway, their brows creased as if in pain. Ms Peel catches me looking at her and hastily slaps an encouraging smile on her face.

"So. Let's try again. I want you to shout out a location." Uliol holds up a finger, practically quivering with rage. "NOT a toilet, not a sexual health clinic, not inside an animal's backside."

There's a long, bored silence. Fine by me – this is all eating up our fifteen minutes. The second my watch hits half past nine, I am getting offstage. Uncle Don can't take the silence any more and yells out a location: "Essex!"

"NO!" Uliol explodes with rage. I feel sympathy for my uncle. I made that mistake too. "SMALLER!" Uliol shouts.

Uncle Don shrugs and goes back to staring out of the window, clearly feeling he *tried* to help, and now Uliol's on his own.

"A cupboard?" a kid at the front says, looking concerned for Uliol's mental health.

"NO, NO, NO!"

Several tentative hands go up from the audience. "A – a post office?"

"Fine!" Uliol is calming down. "Excellent. A post office." Patrice, Pete, Dermot and I nod obediently. Uliol turns to the audience. "And what are we doing in the post office?"

Sasha looks bored. "Posting letters, obviously."

"NOOO!" I swear you could hear Uliol several streets away. "Something else! The location and the activity need to be different or else it's not fun!"

"This is fun?" Karl looks genuinely baffled and, for the first time ever, I agree with him.

"Karl!" Ms Peel barks from the doorway but it's clear her heart isn't in it.

I catch sight of Gabriel in the crowd and make pleading eyes at him. He frowns back, questioningly. *Say something,* I mouth.

"Modelling!" he shouts from the crowd. Which is a terrible suggestion but, whatever, I'll take it.

"Fantastic!" Uliol is his bright-eyed enthusiastic self again and he skips across the stage to let us begin our scene. Pete sashays into the "post office" and queues, lounging and pouting like a model. Several boys wolf-whistle but he doesn't react. He's such a pro and I feel a new burst of gratitude that he's here.

Dermot follows Pete, with a manly glance at his watch and a thoughtful stare into the middle distance like a catalogue model. Rule of three – no pressure, Lou, but the third one has to be the funniest! I put my hands up into paws and strut onto stage, kicking my hind legs and joining the queue like a poodle at Crufts. There's a big laugh from the prom, like 200 people properly belly-laugh, and the sound is amazing. I'm actually shaking with relief.

Patrice gets into position as the post office worker and we start to play out a scene. The boys refuse to lift their parcels up to the counter in case their arms get muscly, and I'm just a dog, so I bark and pee on things. (PRETEND to pee on things.) I've really chosen the easy role here but it's the one that gets all the laughs.

We keep going until Pete gets a massive laugh from a daringly rude joke about getting his bits waxed and I'm sure Mr Peters is relieved when Pete slaps the floor as a sign that we're done. Everyone applauds and I start to breathe more easily. This might be OK! This might actually ... be ... good?

Dermot's looking enthusiastic, but then we know he's immune to shame. Pete's looking happy, though, and I take him as a more reliable barometer. I have a quick look at my watch. We meant to do two scenarios but Uliol spent a surprisingly long time berating the room, so now there's only two minutes left. Shall we go now? Leave on a high?

I glance backstage. Plastic Jesus are waiting with their instruments, ready to come on. Just as Jase puts his foot onstage, Eli pulls a piece of paper out of his pocket. That's all the signal I need.

"This is a spoken-word—"

"Thank you, everyone, and goodnight!" I shout. "Please welcome Plastic Jesus! The singer is Hannah's cousin!"

Not the smoothest intro but it'll have to do. Pete and I grab Eli's elbows and persuade him offstage. Plastic Jesus shove past us and immediately launch into a blistering cover of Taylor Swift's "Shake It Off". I guess they *have* done proms before.

They electrify the whole room. Perf Class bundles backstage, where we all have a shaky laugh, compare how sweaty we are (very), agree that was a bit hairy but that we got away with it and say, *Sorry, Eli, did you want to do your poem? So sorry, we didn't realize.*

When we rejoin the party, everyone is dancing. I go looking for Hannah and find she's changed into a red dress that's so tight she can only dance by pogoing. I pogo next to her, the pair of us bouncing high, bodies straight.

"You were amazing!!" she squeals.

"I was OK," I concede. "But more importantly, it's over!"

We dance some more. I'm so happy that's done. I think I might even have enjoyed it?

"They're not what I expected!" I yell at her over a Kanye mash-up. I thought Plastic Jesus would be a lot more … Bible Metal.

"Yeah," she marvels. "They say this is their prom set."

"Oh God!" Mr Peters dashes past me as an oil painting almost gets knocked off the wall. "Dave, put Sasha down! Off your shoulders, right now!" I spin round to watch everyone help Sasha down onto a sofa, in a tangle of arms and legs. I see Dan and Brendon dancing near by. Dan has a prom flower in his buttonhole, Brendon has one behind his ear.

"Well done, Lou!" says Dad, bouncing up to us, a little flushed. "You were great and I thought you'd be rubbish! You're so funny! I called Mum to tell her and she couldn't believe it wasn't a disaster!"

He gives me a big rib-cracking hug while I pick through

the insults to find the compliments.

"Also –" Dad points at some couples entwined around each other in various corners of the room – "so glad we nailed the bedroom doors shut."

I wonder where Gabe is, so I pogo as high as I can to look over the room. This is where being crazy tall has its benefits. I spot him leaning over Roman, who is crouched in a corner like he's being sick. I hurry over to them.

Ro is squatting down and Gabe is taking off his jacket to fling over his brother's head.

Dad is hot on my heels as I approach them. "Boys," he says, unusually serious, "what's going on?"

Gabe and Ro both swivel round to shush him. Ro is holding his phone to his ear.

"Don't shush me at my own prom!" says Dad, outraged. Is it me, or is he starting to sound like Cammie?

Gabe hunkers down next to Ro and puts his ear by the phone. Dad, Mr Peters and I stare down at them for a long minute, then Gabe and Ro explode with energy at the same time, leaping into the air.

"Third!!" they shout, hugging each other and waving the phone at me. I snatch it out of Ro's hand.

"Lavender?" I can barely hear her over the sound of Plastic Jesus. I try to stick my head out of the window but Dad locked them all shut because teens are morons who don't understand gravity, apparently.

I'm struggling to hear her, but finally, I get the few very simple words she's yelling at me.

She came third. And she won five thousand pounds.

It's not twenty-five thousand but I'll take it! I tell Dad and his yelling delight confirms that yes, five thousand pounds in the teapot could make a world of difference.

Now, I think it was at this point – while Dad was hugging Mr Peters and I was explaining to him over Dad's shoulder how brilliant five thousand pounds is and how much we hate Evil Grandma – that someone spiked the punch and events began to unravel a little.

I had two cups of punch because my mouth was still so dry from being onstage, and I remember feeling woozy as I watched Melia's family load up their catering van, give Cammie a final piece of advice about her attitude problem, and take off down the driveway. It's a shame I wasn't all there for that bit as I would've really enjoyed it.

Everyone was so hot from dancing to Plastic Jesus that they were all knocking back the punch, and my uncles soon had to "escort" several people outside to "calm down". (Basically, sit in the rain until they sobered up.)

I went to the toilet, suddenly so tired, and rested my face on the toilet roll holder for a teeny tiny nap. I *thought* it lasted about twenty minutes, but when I tidy up my smudged make-up and head back out to prom, it's a lot emptier. I'm surprised by how quickly it's come to an end. I ease my cowboy boots off and pad downstairs.

Karl slopes downstairs ahead of me. "Oi." He turns back. "Where's my coat?"

"Where's your ticket?"

"I don't know."

"No ticket, no coat, sorry."

"Louise!" a familiar voice shouts. "Help him."

"Mum! What are you doing here?"

Mum's in the hallway, kissing Dad hello. "We wanted to come and celebrate Lav's win with you lot."

"Plus, the celebrities were rubbish." Lav is lying on a chaise longue, exhausted. "I didn't recognize anyone. Nice nibbles, though."

"That's because you don't *know* any celebrities!" I spot Roman rubbing her feet, still paying penance, I see. "Describe everyone you saw and I'll tell you if they were famous."

"No, Roman." She pats him on the head. "That won't be fun for me. Will you pull my fake eyelashes off?"

I go into the cloakroom. There is one lone coat hanging on the coat rack. Karl is such a numpty. I'm not sorry I wiped my nose on that. I bring it back to him and he says thank you. Well, it sounds more *Finally.*

The last few prom guests are getting in cars on the driveway. I can see a couple of parents exclaiming in horror that their kids are soaking wet. But better wet than too drunk to stand, I can see Uncle Vinnie explaining to them. I can hear someone complaining about it being too early as they're marched to their waiting parents, but ... "Always leave them wanting more," Jase winks at me as he and Plastic Jesus carry their instruments out to their van.

"By the way –" he turns back – "you guys are really funny."

"THANKS!" I gasp. *Be cool, Lou.* "That means a lot coming from a fellow performer such as yourself!"

Louise. That is no one's idea of cool. And now you must stop talking as you've proved you cannot be trusted with words and human interaction.

I wave Plastic Jesus goodbye, feeling warm in my stomach. I think it's pride and spiked punch, but it feels good.

I sit down heavily on the stairs. From there I can see Gabe and Dermot stretched out on sofas, sound asleep with their jackets as duvets. Roman keeps rubbing Lav's feet – he's got a lot of grovelling to do, despite the five thousand pounds. I can't see Hannah; she must've gone home. My eyelids are drooping, and Dad ruffles my hair as he walks back upstairs to root out any final guests. "Probably trying to steal..." I hear him grumble as he passes.

Uncle Vinnie and Mr Peters are drinking the spiked punch and laughing at how strong it is. Aggy is bringing around a plate of leftover food but I haven't got the energy to chew. I watch her put down the tray and join Mum, who has a bin bag and is roaming the house, stuffing rubbish into it. I suddenly remember my Worry Diary. I should go get it from the backstage area, make sure they don't throw it away, but I'm so warm and sleepy.

I sag against the wall, which is surprisingly comfortable when you're tired enough. I'm not sleeping, I'm just resting my eyes. Just resting them ... for a minute.

41

The Diary of Monty: Dancer, Muse, Bee.

It's the morning of the Cup Final and I have had a restless night's sleep. I nibble some honey for breakfast and confide in my friend Clive. "I have full faith in the team," I tell him. "I just want to make sure they give their very best. In a way I feel like that's down to me, to be the inspiration they deserve. You know what I mean, Clive?"

"I'm not Clive," he says. "I'm Isabella."

Gadzooks, it can be hard sharing a hive with 85,000 bees when you're bad with names.

"*Gadzooks?* Would Monty really say that?"

"Stop reading over my shoulder." Mum shoos me away. "And yes, he would. He has an old-fashioned vocabulary because he learned to read and write from museum leaflets and is a little insecure about it. So he uses needlessly formal language to compensate. Bees don't go to school. It's called a back story."

"I'm sorry I even asked." I mean that sincerely. She carries on writing, with the rapid *tap tap tap* that feels so familiar. It's nice to hear it in the house again, even if she does keep stopping to snicker at her own wit.

I leave her to it and go to the kitchen for a bowl of cereal. It's a weird job, being your husband's ghostwriter, but when Monty became so popular he started getting requests to write articles for websites and magazines, Dad baulked at the thought of it. "I express myself best through two media: dance and spreadsheets." So Mum stepped in, with her beautiful vocabulary and years of creative writing, and Monty the bee has become a minor celebrity! (Dad wouldn't say minor.)

It's not hugely well paid but it's fun, much like Dad's mascot job. So we still have money problems, but they're no longer the wake-up-sweaty-with-fear-in-the-middle-of-the-night sort, now they're just the sort where Mum and Dad pretend to open bills like bomb-disposal experts, crawling towards them on the mat and opening the envelopes with dramatically trembling fingers.

But the threat of living with Evil Grandma has been lifted, and we're all grateful for that. I reach for my cereal, it's my favourite brand. When Mum started getting regular writing work, we were each allowed a treat. Lavender petitioned for more heating and hot water, and I wanted to see the back of that horrible emu. Dad said he was proud his daughters had such low standards for happiness.

Lav rushes past me with a bathroom towel in her hand and panicked look on her face. She rummages silently in the cupboard under the sink for stain remover and starts scrubbing hair dye out of the towel. She puts her phone on the side and I see a text from Roman pop up, something about using salt on stains. He means well, even Mum agreed that – once she'd sat him down for a good long talk about trust and privacy and respect.

"It's nice for once that Janet's kids are the idiots," Dad smirks, oblivious to our feelings. My phone buzzes.

Bloop.

I still get an excited feeling in my stomach whenever Gabe gets in touch, even if he is just saying Bloop and sending me some vegetable and civic building emojis.

Want to come and clear a haunted house?

Haunted??

Well, it could be. Certainly old and creepy.

With Dermot and Aggy?

Obvs. Bring Hannah.

I pull my coat on as I text Hannah. She replies instantly. Since I lost Hannah to the Prom Committee and got her back again, I appreciate her a LOT more. I've been taking care to balance my time evenly between her and Gabe, which is definitely easier now that they get on.

"I'm running out of things to complain to Hari about," she said one day. "We chatted about films for most of my last session. Have you got anything you'd like me to ask him? Any anxieties, worries…?"

I think for a while.

"How to deal with big, difficult hair?"

"Sozzles. He's bald as an egg."

I try to picture the lists in my Worry Diary. I know there were loads in there but the diary got chucked out with the rest of the prom rubbish and I can't remember all the small things now.

"Never mind, then."

MY ~~WORRY~~ THANK YOU DIARY

* Agent Hellie Ogden (consistently amazing – sleeps with one eye open)
* Editor Emma Lidbury (so many kind ways of saying "that is not a good idea")
* Frances Taffinder (brave survivor of one of the longest, most boring title brainstorms ever)
* Illustrator Agathe Sorlet (making Lou feel prettier than a velvet jumpsuit)
* Chloé Tartinville (designed this kick-ass cover and then introduced us to Agathe)
* Anna Robinette (made every chapter heading beautiful and gnomey (gnomesque?))
* Mum and Dad (another year of great parenting, I'm a credit to you)
* Margot the cat (zero help in writing this book – quite the opposite)

* Diarmuid (cleans around me while I stare at my laptop for 20 hours a day, so I named the smelly kid after him)
* Holly Smale (always cheering me on, cheekbones you could hang a coat on)
* Kirsty Gordon and Rebecca Folland (pulling my ass outta bankruptcy and answering my bewildering array of questions – there's SO MUCH I don't understand!)
* Rebecca Carter (keeping me out of trouble while Hellie was away)
* The Coven

Nat Luurtsema was a stand-up comedian for eight years until she got tired of talking about herself and having sandwiches for every meal. So she started making films. Her first short film was nominated for a BAFTA, and now she writes and directs comedy films. This is Nat's third book, the sequel to *Girl Out of Water*. Nat's teenage years were an over-dramatic turmoil of tears, spots and eating disorders so she likes to write happier ones for other people. She is also writing a series of picture books about dinosaurs, and they are being turned into adventure theme parks around the UK. Nat played Tallulah Bankhead in the film *Florence Foster Jenkins*. One day she will concentrate on doing just one job, but not yet.

Enjoyed Lou out of Luck?

We'd love to hear your thoughts.

🐦 #LououtofLuck
@WalkerBooksUK
@WalkerBooksYA

📷 @WalkerBooksYA

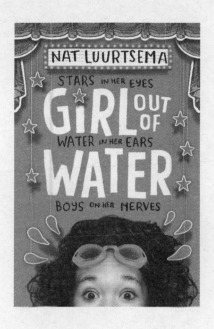

I am **LOU BROWN**:

SOCIAL OUTCAST,

PRECOCIOUS FAILURE,

5'11" and *STILL GROWING*.

I was on the FAST TRACK

to OLYMPIC SUPER-STARDOM.

Now I'm TRAINING boys

too *COOL* to talk to me.

In a sport I've just MADE UP.

In a FISH TANK.

My LIFE has GONE WEIRD very Quickly.

#HELP

The **vlog** where **me** and **my best friend Lauren** give hilarious advice about the things that really matter: **cats**, parents, **make-up** and **boys**.

Not even Erin Breeler, Queen of Instagram, is going to stop us **vlogging**. But is a cat who likes standing on my head enough to make us an **online sensation**?

Praise for Rae Earl:

"Hilarious" *Telegraph*

"Brilliantly funny" *Den of Geek*

"Will charm us all" *Guardian*

more than one way to be A Girl

DYAN SHELDON

"Face it, ZiZi.

You'd be lost without your make-up and your girly clothes."

"And you think 'feminine' is a dirty word. You're the one who's never going to change, Loretta."

"You want to bet?"

When Loretta and her best friend ZiZi make a life-changing bet, one thing's for sure: **the summer is about to be turned upside down.**

He's young. He's hot. He's also evil.
He's ... the librarian.

EVIL
LIBRARIAN

"Smart and funny,
with just the right touch of evil."
Stephenie Meyer

MICHELLE KNUDSEN

DATE DUE	BORROWER
SEP 0 9 2014	Cynthia Rothschild
OCT 3 1 2014	Annie Gibson

Cynthia's best friend, Annie,
has fallen head-over-heels for the
new, very good-looking librarian.
But something doesn't seem right to
Cynthia. Maybe it's the weird feeling
she gets around him, or the strange look
in his (literally) mesmerizing eyes.

Before long, Cynthia begins to
suspect that Mr Gabriel is,
in fact ... a demon.